ONE BOOK
IN THE GRAVE

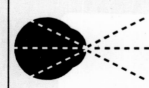

A BIBLIOPHILE MYSTERY

ONE BOOK
IN THE GRAVE

KATE CARLISLE

WHEELER PUBLISHING
A part of Gale, Cengage Learning

GALE
CENGAGE Learning·

Detroit • New York • San Francisco • New Haven, Conn • Waterville, Maine • London

GALE
CENGAGE Learning

LIBRARY OF CONGRESS CATALOGING-IN-PUBLICATION DATA

Carlisle, Kate, 1951–
    One book in the grave : a bibliophile mystery / by Kate Carlisle. — Large print ed.
        p. cm. — (Wheeler Publishing large print cozy mystery)
    ISBN 978-1-4104-4938-2 (pbk.) — ISBN 1-4104-4938-6 (pbk.) 1. Books—Conservation and restoration—Fiction. 2. Rare books—Fiction. 3. Murder—Investigation—Fiction. 4. Large type books. I. Title.
PS3603.A7527O54 2012
813'.6—dc23   2012019517

Published in 2012 by arrangement with NAL Signet, a member of Penguin Group (USA) Inc.

Printed in the United States of America
   1 2 3 4 5   16 15 14 13 12
FD244

This book is dedicated to my favorite Beast, my brother, Daniel Patrick Beaver, and to his beautiful and very clever wife, Deborah, and their amazingly perfect children, Campbell and Callan.
I love you all!

ACKNOWLEDGMENTS

As always, I'm indebted to so many people for their help in getting this book written. My grateful thanks go to:

My brilliant editor, Ellen Edwards, whose support, encouragement, and guidance are invaluable to me.

My wonderful agent, Christina Hogrebe, for her wit, enthusiasm, and good counsel.

Obsidian senior editor Sandy Harding, and everyone at NAL and Penguin, who work so hard to make book magic happen.

Illustrator Dan Craig, whose artistic talent makes my beautiful book covers the envy of all the others on the bookshelf.

Bookbinder Rhiannon Albers at the San Francisco Center for the Book, who shared the story of Dard Hunter and suggested that a mystery about a papermaker might be interesting.

Book artist Wendy Poma, for making it look so easy.

My fabulous sis-in-law, Jane Beaver, who drove to the ends of the earth and walked for miles in the rain with me, just to find the perfect spot for a Marin County goat farm.

My inner circle, my lovely and generous writer friends, who keep me sane, sort of. Thanks and love to Maureen Child, Susan Mallery, Christine Rimmer, Theresa Southwick, Jennifer Lyon, Hannah Dennison, Laura Bradford, Daryl Gerber, and the notorious Romance Bandits.

The many bookbinders, librarians, booksellers, and readers who have taken Brooklyn into their hearts. I can't thank you enough.

Finally, to Don, my bartender and partner in crime. Thanks, lovey. You make it all worthwhile.

CHAPTER 1

Hello. My name is Brooklyn Wainwright and I am a book addict.

It was Friday morning and I was on my way to the Covington Library to sniff out my personal version of crack cocaine: books. Old, rare, and beautiful.

I didn't need a twelve-step program; I just needed more bookbinding work to keep me off the streets. That was why I'd driven over to Pacific Heights to see my good friend Ian McCullough, head curator of the Covington Library in San Francisco. He'd called earlier to let me know he had a job for me.

I found a lucky parking spot less than half a block away. *Lucky* was the perfect way to describe how I was feeling that day. As I walked up the broad concrete steps of the imposing Italianate mansion, I took a moment to appreciate this beautiful building, its setting at the highest point of my favorite city, and this glorious early-fall day.

A few months ago, after coming within striking distance of yet another callous criminal bent on killing me and a few close friends, I had made a vow to be grateful for every wonderful thing in my life. My family; my friends; my gorgeous, exciting lover; the career I enjoyed so much; my books; pizza — I was grateful for them all. Life was good.

So now I stopped to breathe the crisp, clear air; smile at the colorful sight of newly planted pansies lining the sidewalks; and savor the stunning view of San Francisco Bay in the distance.

The moment passed and I strolled up the last few steps. Pushing open the heavy iron doors, I walked through the elegant foyer of the Covington, with its broad checkerboard marble floor, coffered ceiling, and sweeping staircases. Those stairs led to the second and third floors, where dozens of rooms held priceless artwork and countless collections of the greatest books ever written. In almost every alcove and nook, a visitor would find a comfortable chair with a good light for reading. It was the most welcoming place for a book lover I'd ever known and I loved it as much now as I did the first time I went there, when I was eight years old.

I bypassed the main exhibit hall and headed straight for Ian's office, down the wide corridor that led to the inner sanctum. I was eager to get hold of the book he was so excited about, and envisioned myself rushing home, tearing it apart, and putting it back together again. With utmost love and care, of course.

Yes, life was good indeed.

That thought was snuffed out as a sudden, cold sense of dread permeated the very air around me. I shuddered in dismay. In any perfect apple, a worm might be found.

"What the hell do you think you're doing here?"

Shudders rippled through me at the shrill voice of Minka LaBoeuf, my archenemy.

My stomach bubbled and roiled in revulsion and I instantly regretted the Spanish omelet I'd eaten for breakfast. I turned to face her and was sorry I had. Chartreuse-and-fuchsia-striped leggings appeared to have been sprayed onto Minka's ample lower body. As God was my witness, the leggings were topped by a matching tube top (a tube top!) and a pixie band (a pixie band!) in her hair. She looked like a demented barber pole.

I couldn't make this stuff up.

"I was invited to come here today," I said, shielding my eyes from the glare. "I know you can't say the same, so you should leave.

Be sure to let the door hit your ass on the way out."

Baring her teeth, she snarled and said, "You're such a bitch!"

I smiled with concern. "Really? Is that the best you've got? Pitiful."

She moved in close — so close that I could smell her new perfume, Eau de Goat — and hissed at me. "If you don't stop trying to take away my jobs, I'll make sure you never work in this town again."

Never work in this town again? Had she really said that? Of course she had. Minka was the queen of the tattered cliché.

"Threats, Minka?" I backed away from her, knowing she had an unruly left hook. "Ian won't like hearing that you threatened me."

She sniffed imperiously. "Ian is a jerk."

"I'll be sure to tell him you said so."

"You're a jerk, too."

Feeling disappointed, I shook my head. "Have you been sick or something? Your comebacks are so lame, it's pathetic." I didn't stick around to hear her answer, but turned and hurried off. I didn't look back, either — possibly a tactical error where Minka was concerned, since she was the master of the sneak attack. But honestly, I couldn't take another violent shock to my nervous system.

"You'll be sorry!" she shrieked.

I rubbed my arms against the chill but kept moving. Minka had the kind of aura that stirred up all the frigid, stagnant chi that existed in any space. Or maybe auras and chi had nothing to do with it. I just knew she scared the hell out of me. Once I turned the corner and was out of her sight, I breathed easier. It was warmer now. The spell was broken.

I knew that sounded a little wacky, but I'd been stalked and harassed and, yes, punched in the face by Minka LaBoeuf. I wasn't about to question the possibility that she could cast spells with those evil eyes of hers.

Strolling briskly down the wide hall, I entered the suite of business offices and greeted Wylie, Ian's current assistant.

"He's waiting for you, Ms. Wainwright. Go right in."

"Thanks, Wylie."

I knocked, then opened Ian's door.

"Hey, you," Ian said, jumping up from his chair and rushing to greet me with a hug. "I'm glad you're here. I've been itching to get your opinion on what to do about this book."

Shaking off the last of my Minka-induced negativity, I smiled and hugged him back.

13

"I can't wait to see it."

"I'll warn you beforehand that the outside of the book is less than impressive. Well, actually, it's in horrible shape, but I know you can make it shine. The inside is exquisite." He led the way across the room to his lovingly restored Chippendale conference table. We sat, and I watched him slowly unwrap several layers of white tissue paper to reveal a rather nondescript book.

The book was big, probably twelve inches tall by nine inches wide, but it was less than one inch thick. The leather cover was green, or it had been at one time; now it was faded to a dull gray. The front cover was badly frayed along the inner edges and outer hinge, where it would probably break apart at the least jarring movement.

And it was disturbingly familiar. I frowned and chewed my lip as I reached for it.

"I know it's ugly," Ian reiterated, misreading my reaction. "But the paper is still in excellent condition, and just wait until you see the illustrations."

"Okay." I picked it up cautiously, not only because it was old and falling apart, but because I was afraid of what I would find when I opened it. I stared at the spine. *Beauty and the Beast,* it read, though the letters had lost most of their gilding.

I opened the book, bypassed the flyleaf, and turned to the front illustration across from the title page. It was colorful and sweet and classically Victorian. A tea party for two. Beauty wore a regal red cape and her golden blond hair flowed in waves down her back. She sat at a table, pouring tea for the Beast, who was depicted as a huge brown bear. His appearance was hairy and scary, yet he seemed dignified and well mannered. The tea set was blue. I could've described it blindfolded.

I paged back to the inside flyleaf and stared at the inscription written there. My throat tightened and the pressure building in my chest began to ache.

"It's very rare," Ian said in a rush. "First edition. Look at the interior pages. They're fantastic. I just need you to fashion a new cover and do some cleanup, and we'll have a masterpiece to display in the children's gallery."

I ran my fingers over the dried ink and reread the sentimental inscription. The scrawled penmanship had a beauty all its own.

"Earth to Brooklyn," he snapped. "What's going on? Can you do the work or not?"

I shook myself out of my melancholy and glanced up at Ian. "I'm not sure I can."

"What do you mean, you're not sure? You could do this restoration in your sleep."

"Oh, yeah, I can do the work." I turned the book over to see if the damage extended to the back joint, but it was still smooth and unfrayed. "But . . . I don't think I can do the work."

He scowled, shoved his chair back from the table, and stood over me. "You're speaking in riddles. What's wrong with the damn book?"

"Nothing's wrong with the book," I said, and met his gaze directly. "Except that it was stolen."

"No, it wasn't." He stared at my expression, then shook his head vigorously. "No way. What the hell are you talking about? I bought it from Joseph Taylor, the most reputable bookseller in the city. It was a clean deal."

"I believe you." Joe Taylor was an old acquaintance of mine. My mentor, Abraham, had known him forever, and over the years we'd done a lot of bookbinding work for him.

I touched the crisp, deckled edges of the paper and fought to stay calm. "But I'd like to find out who sold it to Joe, because I know they weren't the rightful owner."

Frustrated, Ian scratched his head, causing his hair to spike wildly. "What aren't you telling me, Brooklyn? How do you know this book was stolen? Who did it belong to?"

Awash in memories, I didn't realize until too late that I had tears in my eyes. I brushed them away with a fierce swipe of my hand and faced him. "Me, Ian. Once upon a time, this book belonged to me."

CHAPTER 2

"You?" Ian shook his head in confusion. "So what happened? You sold it to someone?"

"No." Reluctantly, I pushed the book away and stood. "No, I gave it away."

"Well, then there's no problem."

I laughed, but the sound was empty. "Believe me — there's a problem."

"I was afraid you'd say that," he muttered, and began to pace back and forth between the conference table and his massive antique mahogany desk.

Confused and unsure what to do, I leaned my hip against the table and glanced around the office, trying to distract myself by admiring Ian's latest artwork. He still had the Diebenkorn painting of a woman drinking coffee prominently displayed behind his desk, but there were three miniature Rembrandt engravings on the wall closest to the door that I didn't remember seeing before.

As always when I visited Ian, I thought

how nice it would be to borrow from the vast Covington collection to furnish one's office. And if the artwork didn't impress a visitor, one could always enjoy the incomparable view of the Golden Gate Bridge seen through the big picture window by the conference table. I turned and stared out at the wide expanse of the bay and tried to appreciate the amazing vista.

"You want to tell me what happened?" Ian asked from close behind me.

I sighed and slowly turned around. "It's a long story. Are you ready to hear it?"

He folded his arms across his chest. "I suppose I'll have to."

I smiled. "Did Austin ever introduce you to Max Adams?"

"Max? Sure. Didn't he die a few years ago?"

"It was almost three years ago," I said. But thanks to the reappearance of *Beauty and the Beast,* I was reliving the day as if it were yesterday.

I'd had a crush on Max Adams from the first day I'd laid eyes on him when I was ten years old. Max's family had followed Avatar Robson Benedict — otherwise known as Guru Bob — to the Sonoma commune he'd established, just as my family had a few years earlier. So we all grew up together in Dharma. Max was my oldest brother Austin's best friend until they each went away to different colleges.

While at Stanford, Austin met Ian and brought him home for Thanksgiving dinner. That was how Ian and I met, way back when. I was long over Max by then and started dating Ian, who made me laugh and shared my love of books and art and Monty Python movies. Our relationship got serious for a minute or so when Ian proposed marriage, but it didn't take long for us to realize we weren't meant for each other. Happily, we'd remained close friends and book-world colleagues.

Ian had recently proven correct my decision to end our engagement by coming out of the closet. But that was a whole other story.

I walked around the table and over to the window. "You know about Guru Bob and how he first got Abraham to hire me as an apprentice, right?"

"Of course. You were just a kid, right?" Ian said.

"Right. So back then, it was —"

"Wait a minute," Ian interjected. "Do I need to hear the entire history of the world or can you skip to the good parts?"

"I promise I'll keep it as short as I can.

So, anyway, Guru Bob did the same thing for Max, asking Abraham to mentor him."

"I thought Max worked with paper."

"He did." I gave Ian the abbreviated history. Max had been helping out Abraham Karastovsky at the same time I was working as his official apprentice. My little heart would go pitter-patter whenever Max came into the studio. I would dream of him and me bookbinding our way to our very own happily-ever-after.

Sadly, though, Max didn't care much for bookbinding; he was always more interested in the paper itself than in the binding procedures. So instead of helping with binding books, he began to experiment with all sorts of different papermaking techniques.

"It was all good, because Max's talent with paper fit right in with Guru Bob's master plan for Dharma," I said. "Guru Bob wanted to revive as many of the ancient guild crafts as possible, thinking that our finely crafted products would provide income for the fellowship to stay afloat into the future."

Ian laughed. "And planting a few thousand grapevines didn't hurt, either."

"No kidding." Guru Bob had hedged his bets early on by suggesting that his followers plant grapes across the commune property, adding more acreage over the years. Our vineyards and renowned winery had made the members wealthy beyond even Guru Bob's expectations. But it was still nice to walk into the boutique shops along Dharma's Shakespeare Lane and see our members' artwork and beautifully handmade crafts on display.

"Meanwhile, Guru Bob had seen the level of artistry in Max's work and suggested that he go to art school."

So he did. And in the small world of papermaking, Max became a rock star, complete with groupies and an entourage. It didn't hurt that he was tall and dark and ruggedly built, or that he brought his own brash, avant-garde style to the quiet art of making paper, thus catching the attention of everyone in the book arts universe. Some compared him to his hero, Dard Hunter, the legendary papermaker and printer, though Max insisted he could never be that good.

Max ended up teaching at the prestigious Sonoma Institute of the Arts, just a few miles south of Dharma. His acolytes enrolled by the dozens to study at the feet of the master. He gave lectures all over the country and hordes of groupies followed him from city to city, from lecture to art exhibit to papermaking demonstration.

"It was unbelievable," I said, still a bit awestruck after all these years. "I went to some of his lectures and saw the fanatical adoration for myself. The truly amazing part was that Max seemed unfazed by the attention."

"That's all really fascinating, Brooklyn," Ian said dryly, "but where does this copy of *Beauty and the Beast* come in?"

"I'm getting there," I groused, even though I could've regaled him with another hour's worth of ancient history. "So the year before he died, Max met and fell in love with a woman, a young schoolteacher, Emily Branigan."

"Ah, a woman," Ian said, nodding astutely. "That always spells trouble."

"Very funny," I said, backhanding him in the arm.

He chuckled. "Knew you'd like that one. So, what happened?"

"Max had recently broken up with this really bizarre woman who also taught at the institute." I had to think for a few seconds, then frowned. "Angelica — that was her name." I'd heard Max call her Angel once, but she was the furthest thing from an angel I'd ever met.

"Max's friends couldn't stand Angelica,

23

so when he finally broke up with her, then met and fell in love with Emily, we were all overjoyed. They threw a party in Dharma to announce their engagement, and I needed to bring a gift. I'd had this copy of *Beauty and the Beast* for years, and I thought it would make a perfect gift."

"For an engagement party?"

"I know." I smiled ruefully as I sat back down at the conference table. "But it was the perfect gift for Max. You remember how big and brawny he was. He reminded me of that bear in the frontispiece."

Ian picked up the book and opened it to the engraved illustration of Beauty serving tea to the Beast. "Okay, whatever. That's sweet, I guess. But, seriously, you gave them a fairy-tale book for their engagement?"

"Come on," I insisted. "We're all book people. That's what we do."

"I'm teasing you," he said with a grin. "Sort of. It's sweet, as I said."

I sighed deeply. "I cornered Max alone and gave him the book. I told him I would be glad to rebind it as a more appropriate engagement gift for Emily, but he wanted it kept exactly as it was."

"Why?"

"He said he was a scruffy old beast and

the book would always remind Emily of him."

"I don't recall him being particularly scruffy," Ian said, his eyes narrowed in thought.

"He wasn't, but he was a big guy — remember? Whenever he came back from a camping trip, his beard was so bushy, the first thing he would do was shave it off. Otherwise, his mother wouldn't let him in the house." I smiled at the memory. "Anyway, he loved the book and didn't want any changes made. Emily was so sweet and petite and proper, she was the ideal Beauty to his Beast."

"Sounds like a man in love," Ian said.

"He had a great laugh," I said softly, then turned to the flyleaf and tapped the inscription. "I watched Max write this to her."

Ian picked up the book and read the words aloud. *"To my beloved Beauty from her devoted Beast."* It was signed and dated, as well.

Ian looked at me sideways. "That little scribbling probably decreased the book's value by thirty percent."

"Would you shut up? You're so cynical." I sighed. "Emily loved the book. She kept it clutched in her hands all during the party. Then a month or so later, Max was killed in a car crash."

Ian cringed. "I remember that part. It was tragic."

"It was," I said. "At his funeral, I offered again to restore the book for Emily, but she wanted it to remain the way it was in memory of Max."

"So that was it, then?"

"Sadly, no. A few weeks after Max's death, Emily called to tell me her house had been broken into and someone had stolen the book. She could barely speak, she was so upset. And that's the last time we ever spoke."

"I'm really sorry, Brooklyn," Ian said. He sat down and pulled his chair close so he could wrap his arm around my shoulders. He gave me a little squeeze and said, "I guess seeing the book again is bringing up a lot of old memories for you."

"Yeah, it is." I pulled a tissue from my bag and blew my nose.

He sat back and gazed at the book for another long moment, then waved his hand in frustration. "Damn it, Brooklyn, do you know how much money I paid for this book?"

I smacked his shoulder. "You couldn't pretend to be sensitive to my pain for another minute or so?"

"Sorry, kiddo. But what about my pain?"

I knew he was kidding, trying to coax me out of my funk, so I tried to smile. "I'm just glad the book has resurfaced."

It was his turn to sigh. "I guess you'll contact Emily now."

"I will." I folded my hands on the table. "Look, she might not even want it back. She could be married with a kid by now and not even give a hoot about the book or Max."

"It's possible," he said, his tone skeptical.

"Tell you what," I said. "Once I find her and let her know the book's been recovered, I'll ask her to consider donating it to the Covington."

Buoyed by the possibility, he nodded. "I would appreciate that. Thanks."

"I just wish I knew where to start. I must have an old phone number for her, but she might've moved away by now."

"Google her," he said. "Or check Facebook."

"Yeah. Or maybe I'll just call Information."

"You're so old school sometimes."

I smiled as I covered the book in its tissue wrap and slid it into my bag.

"Be careful with that," he said, watching my moves. "If I told you what I paid for it . . ." He shook his head in misery.

"So tell me."

With a look of disgust, he said, "Twelve thousand. And I considered that an awesome deal until you came along and popped my beautiful balloon."

"You're insured," I pointed out. "It's a write-off."

"You're a cold woman, Brooklyn Wainwright."

It felt good to laugh.

"As soon as you leave," he said as he walked me to the door, "I'm going to call Joe and have a little talk with him about conducting better due diligence on his clients."

"I'll be glad to tell him for you," I said, "because I'm driving over to see him right now."

"You are?"

"Yeah. I want to find out who sold the book to him." I figured that even if Joe didn't get the seller's real name, he would at least be able to give me a description of whoever had sold the book to him.

Ian had a weird look on his face. "I just remembered something Joe told me. He said the seller had urged him to call the Covington Library to see if we wanted the book, and that's why he came to me first."

"Maybe they heard you were starting the children's gallery." I frowned. "But why wouldn't the seller just call you himself?"

"I don't know." Ian pursed his lips in thought. "Is it because I'm so intimidating?"

I chuckled, then let go and laughed out loud. "Yeah, right. Not."

Affronted, he glared at me. "I am."

"Mm-hmm," I said, reaching for the door handle.

He shrugged. "To everyone but you, apparently."

"You just keep on believing that, sweetie," I said, and stretched up to kiss him on the cheek. "Talk to you soon."

Back in my car, I took a chance and called Information in Sonoma County for Emily's phone number. The mobile operator gave me the number of an Emily Branigan in the Santa Rosa area. I don't know why I'd thought it would be so difficult to track her down. It hadn't even been three years. She might be teaching at the same grammar school.

I punched in the number and got her voice mail. At least, it sounded like Emily's sweet, birdlike voice, and it gave me a chill to hear her familiar tones. I didn't say why I was calling; I just left my name and number and asked her to call me back.

Pulling away from the curb, I drove down Pacific, skirting the Presidio until I could zigzag over to Arguello and head for the Richmond District. A number of used bookstores were miraculously still thriving in a five-block stretch of Clement Street. I drove past Joseph Taylor Fine Books and parked a half block away.

When I got to the door of Joe's bookstore, I saw a sign hanging in the window of the door.

BE BACK SOON — GODOT

It caught me by surprise and I had to read it twice before I started to laugh.

I must've just missed him, I thought, glancing up and down the sidewalk. He couldn't have gone far, maybe just down the street for a sandwich.

Then it occurred to me that he might keep that sign up all the time, just for laughs. So I twisted the doorknob and the door opened easily.

"Joe?" I called as I stepped inside. There was no answer, but maybe he was back in the stockroom. I knew he wouldn't mind if I ventured inside.

The first thing I did when the door shut behind me was close my eyes and inhale the lovely, musty scent of aged leather and vellum. I hated that so many rare-book stores were disappearing faster than the northern spotted owl, so whenever I got the chance to walk inside one of the few stores left in the city, my senses jumped up and did a happy dance.

Glancing around, I remembered what it was that I loved about Joe's store and Joe himself. His place appealed to two divergent types of book hounds, and the space had been divided to appease them both. The front half of the store was jammed with old cloth-bound books and pulpy paperbacks crammed into the tall, bursting shelves that ran floor to ceiling across the width of the room. Tacked to every shelf were book reviews and recommendations. Perched on the floor of each narrow aisle were step stools that allowed customers to reach the highest shelves.

But for the discerning collector in search of true treasures, one could bypass the untidy shelves and follow the arrows and signs that read ANTIQUARIAN ROOM. They pointed the way through a narrow, arched doorway and into another world.

It was like entering the innermost cave. Joe's rare-book room was filled wall to wall with beautifully polished wood display cabinets with glass fronts, each holding a selection of priceless books and ephemera. In the center of the room, under an ornate chandelier, were three waist-high glass cases resting on pedestals. In these were Joe's most valuable antiquarian books. A number of Oriental rugs overlapped one another, so the entire floor was covered. The chandelier cast a warm glow over the room.

In the largest cabinet was a whimsical display of all fourteen books in the L. Frank Baum Oz collection. They were all first editions, all in excellent condition. Who knew there were so many adventures to be had in the Land of Oz?

Each of the Baum covers was bright and colorful, with an odd Oz character featured on the cloth binding. The price tag for the collection was hefty: one hundred fifty thousand dollars. All I could think was, *Wow.*

Displayed in one of the center cases was a well-preserved copy of *The Little Prince,* signed by the author, Saint-Exupéry. A description of the book and its condition was typed on a small card along with the price: twenty thousand.

That seemed a little steep for a book that was still available on the market, but maybe the author rarely signed his work. I moved past two wingback chairs that Joe had provided for his customers to sit and enjoy or study a particular book, engraving, or ephemera. I thought about sitting and waiting for him in here, but there was too much cool stuff to see.

I hurried to the next display case on the other side of the chair. It held a stunning antique Russian bible with a thick cover fashioned out of a sheet of hammered and engraved silver attached by rivets to thick wood boards. I moved closer to examine the foreign symbols carved in the silver — and stumbled over something. I grabbed onto the edge of the sturdy display case to steady myself and looked down to see what had caused me to trip. It was a man's shoe.

A man's shoe?

I looked closer. It was still being worn by the man lying on the floor behind the chair.

"What the . . ." Pure terror coursed through me, sending chills and shivers out to every part of my body. I was shaking too much to think straight. I gulped in a breath and forced myself to stay calm instead of running screaming out into the street like I wanted to. It wasn't easy.

"This is not happening again," I whispered aloud, needing to hear the sound of a human voice, even my own.

Stomach spinning, mind racing, I grabbed

the arms of the chair and yanked it forward. It was so heavy, it barely moved two inches, but that was enough to allow me space to peek around the side. Enough space to make out the inert form of Joseph Taylor lying on the faded Persian carpet, his throat slit. He was dead.

CHAPTER 3

I stared into the sightless eyes of the dead man lying on the floor. My shoulders were still shaking, but now my knees were wobbling, too. Spots and spirals flooded my eyesight.

"Oh, no." I backed away from the body, away from the chair.

"Oh, God." Poor Joe. He was a sweet man. He didn't deserve this.

And neither did I.

Yes, I felt really, really bad for Joe, but why was it always *me* who discovered the dead body? I was getting a complex. What was going on with me? Not that it was all about me, but, seriously, this was insane.

My heart started beating so hard I could hear it in my ears, and those dots in my vision got bigger.

"No, no, no. Don't you dare faint," I muttered as I backed farther away from the body. "Don't you dare. I mean it."

I repeated the words again, louder this time, because I couldn't hear myself think over my own moans. The thing is, I've been known to faint at the merest sight of blood.

"Not now, not now, not now." I repeated it over and over again in between sucking in great globs of air. I couldn't faint just yet. Nobody would catch me.

I'd seen so many dead bodies by now that you'd think I'd be a little more blasé about it, but no. My head was dizzy and my ears were ringing. I kept talking to myself and taking deep breaths, and that seemed to help a little.

I heard a creak and let out a tiny shriek. Was the killer still in the store? There were all sorts of nooks and crannies in this place. Was he hiding somewhere? Waiting for me? Or was my mind playing tricks?

I tiptoed quickly across the room to the two largest display cases, took a deep breath, and squeezed into the space between them. I stood there barely breathing, listening, for what felt like an hour, but was probably less than a minute. I hated hiding. It made me feel like a complete idiot, but at least I was a living, breathing idiot.

A door slammed and I yelped again.

"Okay, that was a real noise." And it came from inside Joe's store.

Before I could think too much about it, I slunk out from between the cabinets and took off running in the direction I thought the slammed door might be. Back in the front area, I skirted the room and ended up in Joe's small, grimy office near the back of the building. The screen door leading to the alley was still swinging and I headed right for it. Then stopped.

A killer had just run out that door. Was I really going to chase after him? Anything was better than hiding in fear, although my inner scaredy-cat was willing to argue the point.

"You can't go out there," Scaredy-cat whined. But I could. I had to see who was running away. If I could identify Joe's killer, even from behind, that would be a good thing.

I nudged the screen door open an inch or two and leaned my head out for a peek.

It was a back alley in the San Francisco style, which meant it wasn't an alley at all, but another street. A very narrow, tidy, one-lane street, with a tattoo parlor, a postcard shop, and a bar on the side opposite Joe's. There were potted ficus trees on either side of the door to the postcard shop. It was all very neat and pretty. Not a Dumpster in sight. No killer, either.

I looked both ways, but saw no one running away. I figured it had taken me twenty or thirty seconds to get here from my hiding place in the antiquarian room. That was probably how long it would take to race to the end of the alley and disappear out on the cross street.

My sigh of relief was audible as I stepped outside into the cool, shadowy space. The day had turned cloudy, and I shivered as I glanced around. There was only one escape route; the alley dead-ended a few yards north of Joe's store. I turned south and jogged to the nearest side street, six doors down. There was no one running in either direction there, so I gave up and walked back to Joe's to call the police.

On the side of the building was a street sign that read JIM PLACE. So this alley had a name. That, too, was typical for San Francisco, and I wondered which Jim they were talking about, since many of the city's alleys were named for famous people, like Damon Runyon and Isadora Duncan.

I looked up and saw second- and third-floor apartments above the storefronts on both sides of Jim Place. Was it too much to hope that someone inside one of the shops or apartments saw whoever ran out of Joe's bookstore?

Hurrying back inside Joe's office, I locked the alley door and turned the dead bolt. That was when I realized I'd made a strategic error by leaving my purse with my cell phone on the wingback chair next to poor old Joe's body.

"Damn." I stopped and gave myself a serious pep talk. Yes, there was a dead body, but I could go back in there. I took twenty or thirty deep breaths and darted back around to the antiquarian room. I made a beeline for my purse, grabbed it, and turned to scurry away. But my conscience nagged at me and I found I couldn't leave the room without paying some respect to Joe.

Sucking in another breath and letting it out, I whipped around and forced myself to gaze at Joe's inert form on the Persian carpet. I had the worst urge to apologize, as if the very act of my showing up here had somehow caused his death.

Gadzooks, as my dad would say. This wasn't all about me; I knew that. I didn't have the power of life or death over anyone, but it was a plain, hard fact that the body count among my circle of acquaintances was growing monthly and I seemed to be the common denominator. I lived in fear that my friends and family would begin to shun me for their own good.

I found my cell phone and called the police. The dispatcher told me to hang around until the police arrived and I assured her I would. I had no intention of leaving Joe alone.

Now that I knew the police would arrive soon, I took the opportunity to observe the scene more objectively — without looking at Joe too closely. I tried to piece together his last minutes. He'd probably been in this room, putting away a book or straightening one of the displays. Or maybe the killer had lured him into the room, pretending to be a customer. Maybe they had a few words, discussed a book or two. Maybe Joe offered him a seat in that very chair. They walked over toward the Russian bible, Joe turned, and the killer attacked.

Did the killer push him back? Was that why Joe was almost hidden by the heavy chair? I forced myself, holding my stomach as it pitched and rolled, to look at his body.

I had issues with the blood that continued to seep out of Joe into the lovely, faded Oriental rug. The fact that it was still seeping out meant that Joe had been dead only a short while. If I'd arrived a few minutes earlier, I might have saved him.

"And you might be dead now, too," I told myself sternly, putting an end to that line of thinking.

I tilted my head as something caught my eye. There was an object in the carpet reflecting the light from the chandelier. I took a step closer to the body, then reconsidered. I didn't want to disturb the crime scene more than I already had, and I certainly didn't want to step in any blood. But my curiosity got the best of me. I grabbed hold of the back of the chair. Using its weight as leverage to keep from stepping too close to the body, I got a better look at the glimmering object.

It was a knife. A bloody knife, oddly shaped, with a short wood handle and a four-inch, squared-off steel blade. I recognized it as a type of shearing knife used by bookbinders and papermakers. It was sturdy and inexpensive and sharp. I knew because I had several of my own that were almost identical to this one.

"Oh, crap," I whispered, and there went my stomach again as I contemplated the worst. It couldn't be my knife, could it? This was a nightmare! I leaned over the chair as far as I could to study the knife. But it took almost a minute of squinting and peering before I was able to determine that it wasn't one of mine.

"Of course it's not mine," I mumbled.

Why would it be? Just because someone had once stolen some of my bookbinding tools to use as murder weapons didn't mean that my knife was the one used to kill Joe. I was just being paranoid. But come on. Who could blame me?

I had the strongest urge to grab the knife and throw it away, but it was too late. The police would be here any minute, and let's face it: anywhere I hid it, they would find it, along with my fingerprints.

It made me sick to think someone in the book arts world had killed Joe. But with that knife as the weapon, who else could've done it? Joe probably knew a hundred different bookbinders in the city and probably a few papermakers, too. It was a small community and a fairly peaceful one, or so I'd always thought. And Joe was one of the most mild-mannered men I'd ever known. Why would anyone kill him?

A more important question — to me, at least — was, Did the killing have something to do with *me?*

I stepped back and had to blink once or twice to clear my vision. As I did so, the colors and patterns of the rugs grew more vivid, the intricate inlaid wood designs of the cabinets more complex. The lights from the chandelier twinkled more brightly. It was as if the moment was being imprinted on my mind.

Some experts — like my mother — say that at traumatic times like this one, the smallest details are marked in your memory and you can recall every facet of the scene for years to come. That must've been what was happening to me now. Or maybe I was getting a migraine headache. Either that or I was going crazy.

"You're not crazy," I told myself, "but this situation is."

Glancing around the room again, I noted that nothing seemed to have been disturbed — except for Joe. And once again, one incredibly selfish thought whirled through my brain: *Why me?*

How had I become the Angel of Death? Was it karmic? Some kind of payback for living a really bad former life? That life must have been a beaut.

Maybe I would talk to Guru Bob about this alarming proclivity for finding dead bodies. Would he have a theory or would he laugh at me? He was a pretty powerful guy when it came to knowing things that were ordinarily unknowable.

Where are the police? I checked my phone for the fourth time. Then, since I had it out anyway, I called Derek Stone.

I'd met Derek a few months ago when I was accused and later absolved of the murder of Abraham Karastovsky, my bookbinding mentor. Derek was tall, dark, handsome, and dangerous. He carried a gun and was willing to use it, and despite the fact that I'd grown up in the peace, love, and flower-power world of the commune, I had found Derek and his gun reassuring on more than one occasion.

Derek and I had become friends during Abraham's murder investigation, and since then, we'd become even closer. Our feelings for each other seemed to grow stronger every day. He was a former intelligence officer with Britain's MI6 and now owned Stone Security, a company that provided armed security to people and objects — rare books, artwork, buildings, and anything else that required safekeeping — all over the world.

Derek had recently announced that he was opening a branch of Stone Security in San Francisco. I was shocked, and even more surprised to find out he'd done it to be closer to me. While his office staff searched the city for a suitable home for him, I invited him to stay at my place. So he moved in with me and he didn't seem to be putting a whole lot of energy into moving out. I was okay with that. I liked having him around.

"Brooklyn, darling," he said after answering on the first ring. "What a nice surprise."

"You won't believe what just happened," I said, stalking out of the antiquarian room and into the stacks out front.

"What is it?" he said, his voice edged with concern. "You sound as if you might've found another dead body."

"That's your first guess?" I said, my voice a little higher-pitched than I would've preferred. "That's what I sound like? Because that's exactly what happened. Do I have some kind of weird bull's-eye on my back or something?"

"Of course not," he soothed. "But I must confess, I've taken to fretting about the very same thing lately."

"It's only because you're hanging around with me." The fact that Derek ever "fretted" about anything was almost amusing. I walked up one aisle and down the next, rolling my shoulders and stretching my neck to shake off the tension. "Anyway, poor Joe Taylor is dead, murdered. I found him. And the fact is, things like this are happening to me with alarming regularity. Don't you think?"

"I do indeed," he said soberly. "But let's

talk about that later. Tell me, who is Joe? And where are you? I'm coming to meet you right now."

I leaned against the last shelf of books. "I appreciate the offer, but you don't have to do that. I'm sorry for snapping. I'll be fine. It just gets a little old, that's all."

"Yes, of course it does. Can you tell me what happened?"

I sighed. "Joe Taylor is a bookstore owner I've known for a long time. He sold Ian a book that I needed some information about, so I drove over to see him and found him dead. It must've only happened a minute or two before I got here. His throat was cut."

"So there's blood," Derek murmured, then added briskly, "What's the address?"

I gave up pretending I didn't need his help. "Thank you," I whispered. Derek knew my aversion to blood and was willing to come and hold my hand. I was touched. "I know you're busy. Maybe you shouldn't —"

"It's Friday and I'm the boss," he said. "Besides, I'm never too busy for you, darling. Now give me Joe's address."

CHAPTER 4

Derek arrived ten minutes after the first police officers showed up. He walked right into the shop and pulled me close, and I just about melted in his arms. The man oozed dark sensuality and charm, but that wasn't the only reason I was happy to see him. I'm not a wimp about this stuff; I'd faced the police alone plenty of times and I was used to it by now. But Derek and I, we were a team. Especially when it came to dealing with dead bodies.

Maybe that made us sound a bit suspicious, but with Derek's intelligence background and his current work in security, he definitely came in handy around a crime scene. That was how we first met, after all. Me kneeling over Abraham with my hands covered in blood. Derek, the first to accuse me of murder. It was a match made in heaven. Call me a romantic fool, but when it came to finding a body dripping blood on an Oriental rug, there was no one else I'd rather have on my team than Derek Stone.

"The police officers are cordoning off the back room," I said, pointing in that direction. "That's Joe's antiquarian room, where he died. They told me to wait out here."

"Have they called Homicide?"

"I don't know, but I went ahead and called Inspector Lee." I shrugged. "I've got her on speed dial."

"That's handy."

"Isn't it? I had to leave a message." I told Derek exactly what had happened from the moment I walked into Ian's office at the Covington and saw the *Beauty and the Beast* to my arrival at Joe's bookstore, where I found the body. I explained about the papermaker's knife and concluded by confessing what I did when I heard the killer run out the back door.

That was when Derek pulled me back into his arms and held me tightly. "You scare the hell out of me, you know," he muttered against my hair.

"You've mentioned that before," I said, then admitted, "It was disconcerting." I was still shaken by the reality of what might have happened if I'd managed to catch up to the killer. "I tried to be careful. But I'm not looking forward to telling the whole story to

Inspector Lee. I'm sure I've left fingerprints on everything."

I could just imagine what my favorite Homicide cop would say when she found out I'd stumbled over another dead body. This wasn't going to be pretty.

"Joe was a sweet old man," I whispered. "Who would want to hurt him?"

"He might've overheard something he wasn't supposed to hear," Derek suggested. "Or perhaps he angered a business associate."

"Maybe."

"It could be as simple as a robbery gone wrong."

"Except for that knife," I said. "It's definitely a papermaker's knife."

"You would know best," he said. "I can see it hurts to think someone in your community might be responsible, but I believe it's a good thing you saw that knife. Now we know what we're up against."

"Do we?" But I knew what he was saying. Now that we were aware that the killer could be someone I knew, Derek and I might be able to sort out who knew what and when they knew it.

I rubbed my forehead where a headache was forming. "I had the strongest urge to grab the knife and throw it away, Derek. I hate to see this happening all over again."

"It could be an unfortunate coincidence. You might not know the people involved."

"I suppose," I said skeptically.

"Or it could be a setup."

"I've considered that, too, obviously."

He smoothed my hair back from my face. "Brooklyn, darling, this isn't about you."

"Mind if I hold you to that?"

"You can hold me to anything you'd like," he murmured, and kissed my neck.

I stared into his smoldering blue eyes and felt sparks ignite inside me. It continued to amaze me that Derek seemed to have the same reaction to me as I had to him. I hugged him a little tighter, then reluctantly pulled away. There was something wrong about snuggling within a few feet of a dead body.

On the other hand, there was a dead body just a few feet away, so what better time to seek comfort? I rested my head against his chest and he wrapped his arm around my shoulder. We stayed like that for a few minutes while the muted voices of the two officers in the other room wafted toward us. I couldn't hear what they were saying and didn't really want to. I just wished Derek and I could walk out the door and go home.

But no such luck. The front door swung

open and SFPD Detective Inspector Janice Lee walked inside. "Well, well, if it isn't my favorite dead-body magnet."

I cringed. She didn't mince words. But at least I was her favorite.

"Commander Stone," she said, greeting Derek in a more respectful tone. He had been, after all, a member of law enforcement.

"Hello, Inspector," Derek said pleasantly, as I buried my face in the lapel of his thousand-dollar suit. I wasn't shy; I just didn't think it would be wise to flash her the dirty look I had on my face in response to her smart-ass comment.

After a few more seconds, I calmed my features, turned, and smiled tightly. "Hi, Inspector. Long time, no see."

"Not long enough, Wainwright," she said, smirking, then sobered up and glanced around the front room of Joe's shop. Janice Lee was a first-generation Chinese American woman who took care of her mom, dressed way too fashionably for a cop, and had the most beautiful hair I'd ever seen. Lately, she was always sucking on a mint, probably to keep from smoking, a habit she'd given up only a few months ago. She was about my age, tall, thin, smart, and snarky, and I liked her a lot. We could've been great friends if only I weren't such a dead-body magnet, as she'd pointed out.

"Figures we'd be surrounded by books," she muttered, peering around at the bookshelves. "So where's the body?"

"Right through there," I said, gesturing toward the antiquarian room.

She pulled her notepad out of the pocket of her gorgeous black Burberry trench coat. I was the furthest thing from a fashion maven, but I knew it was Burberry because I could see the coat's signature plaid lining when she moved. Forgive my weakness at a moment like this, but I was having trench coat envy.

"Stick around, Brooklyn," she said. "I'm looking forward to hearing all the gory details on this one." Then she strolled off down the narrow center aisle to check out the crime scene.

By late afternoon, I'd given Inspector Lee and her partner, Inspector Nathan Jaglom, every ounce of information I could think of, right down to which art-supply stores I'd purchased my own inexpensive, square-bladed shearing knives at. Several uniformed officers had left to canvass the neighborhood for possible witnesses, and the medical examiner had taken Joe's body away.

After Inspector Lee told us she'd be in touch, Derek walked me to my car. Good thing, too, because I had a flat tire.

"Damn it. This day just gets better and better." I stomped over to the driver's side and squatted next to the tire. It wasn't just flat; it looked like it had been slashed by something sharp. Had I run over something on the way to Joe's?

"Don't touch anything," Derek said abruptly, and yanked me back up. That was when I noticed the object sticking out of the tread. It looked like the handle of a small knife.

"You've got to be kidding," I said, thoroughly disgusted and, yeah, frightened.

"Somebody's not kidding," Derek muttered, grabbing my arm and pulling me out of the street, onto the sidewalk. He called Inspector Lee immediately. He caught her just as she was driving away from Joe's, and she said she'd meet us in less than a minute.

It took Derek exactly thirty seconds to rush over and take pictures of the knife and my tire with his phone. He finished and was standing next to me on the sidewalk by the time Lee dashed up.

"This is getting stupid," she said.

"Tell me about it." I rubbed my arms to

keep the scaredy-cat chills from overwhelming me.

"You okay?"

"No, I'm taking this all very personally," I said.

"I kinda don't blame you," she said. With her phone in her hand, she also took pictures of my tire and the knife. Then she slipped one rubber glove onto her left hand and eased the knife out of the tire. She walked over and showed it to me, turning it so I could see it from different angles. "Look familiar?"

It was an expensive Japanese paper knife with a beautifully tooled handle. I recognized it because I owned one like it; I'd bought it a few years ago for almost two hundred dollars. The entire knife was about nine inches long, with a fat, curved blade that looked razor-sharp.

I moved closer and studied the Japanese figures that had been carved along the length of the handle. At the pommel, or butt end of the handle, three ornate letters were also carved into the hardwood surface. The knife was old enough that the design was worn smooth, but I knew the letters spelled out *MAX*.

"Max?" I whispered as goose bumps formed on my skin. "Max Adams?"

"Who'd you say?" Inspector Lee demanded.

Alarmed, I shook my head. "Nothing. Nobody. It's not possible. He's been dead for years. This knife could belong to anyone."

"Don't screw around with me, Brooklyn," she said, her eyes narrowing.

"I'm not," I cried. "The only person I know by that name died almost three years ago."

She gave me a withering look as she dangled the knife in front of me. "Uh-huh. And what're the odds of another Max owning a knife so much like the one your dead friend owned? Or are you saying this is some kind of sign from the grave?"

I glanced wide-eyed at Derek, whose concern for me showed in his expression. Turning back to Lee, I said, "I didn't say that. Maybe someone stole the knife from Max's family or they sold it somewhere. But other than those possibilities, I don't have a clue how it got here."

"I think you do, Brooklyn," she said quietly. "You know these book people; you're part of that world. And I'm thinking you've got a pretty good idea of who might've killed Joseph Taylor."

"I don't," I insisted. "I swear it."

"You can swear all you want, but this connects you to the murder," she said quietly as she dropped the knife into a plastic Ziploc bag. "You know that, right? Whether you like it or not, you're in this up to your eyeballs. Again."

"I don't like it one bit," I muttered, glowering at her.

Derek stepped forward. "This is a busy neighborhood. Somebody must've seen the person who did it."

"Good thinking," I said, flashing him a grateful look. "They would've had to have jabbed the tire a bunch of times to shred it so badly. Somebody must've noticed."

"Possibly." Lee pulled out her cell phone and dialed the police dispatcher. After requesting patrol assistance, she hung up. To us, she said, "We'll do some canvassing, but I wouldn't hold my breath waiting for someone to come forward."

In less than a minute, we heard a siren.

"Can we go now?" I asked.

"Sure, you can go," she said with an evil grin. "But not in your car. It's just been turned into a crime scene."

CHAPTER 5

Reluctantly, I left my trusty hybrid in the hands of the San Francisco Police Department and Inspector Lee, who promised I could have it back by Tuesday. Then, to cajole me out of my depressed, dead-body-magnet mood, Derek drove straight to my favorite steak house. We were ushered to a comfortable, dark green booth in the corner with a view of the bustling room.

I was hoping a bottle of wine would magically appear on the linen-covered table.

Chalk it up to ennui or just plain exhaustion, but for the first time in my life, I allowed a man to order dinner for me. Derek knew all my favorite foods, namely, red meat, red wine, and chocolate soufflé. We both began with a lettuce wedge doused in blue cheese dressing, and I felt myself rebounding as the meal progressed. The comfort food, the dark green booths, the wood-paneled walls, the waiters in white shirts with their long black aprons tied neatly at the waist — all of it gave the room a warm, clubby feel that pampered and soothed my spirit.

Some women might've chosen a pedicure or a massage to perk them up, but for me, it's all about food. The steak house provided the miracle cure I needed. The fact that Derek had known exactly what would work to snap me out of my doldrums was just one more feather added to his cap. Seriously, what woman wouldn't love a boy friend who acted all James Bond, looked all Hugh Jackman, and knew me well enough to ply me with my favorite foods?

We got to bed early that night, since we'd planned to leave the next morning to spend a few days in Dharma. Tomorrow was the grand opening of my sister Savannah's new restaurant, Arugula, on Shakespeare Lane.

Dharma had grown to become quite the wine-country tourist spot, and the Lane, as it was called, was currently the hottest destination in the area. Everyone in my family was geared up to make Savannah's opening a great success.

But Joe's death and his connection to Emily and Max's *Beauty and the Beast* had caused me to rethink some of my weekend plans. I felt as though I'd lost Max all over again. The knives I'd found at the crime scene and in my tire had spooked me badly. I wanted to spend some time commiserating with my family and others in Dharma who had known Max all those years ago. I was also hoping to talk to Guru Bob about the whole dead-body-magnet phenomenon. With any luck, he would have some good advice for me.

Derek and I were on the road at eight o'clock the next morning. It was a disturbingly early start, especially after having shared a bottle of wine the night before. I was happy Derek was driving, because I figured I could work in a quick nap on the way, but we started talking and I realized I'd much rather be wide-awake to enjoy his company than sleep for a few extra minutes.

As we drove over the Golden Gate Bridge and into Marin County, Derek reached across and patted my leg. "Darling, why don't you give your mother a call and ask her to arrange a meeting for you and Robson? Then you won't have to worry about trying to track him down all day."

"Good idea," I said, and searched in my bag for my phone. "Why didn't I think of that?"

"Because your mind's been occupied by bigger and darker problems."

"True." I gazed at him, unsure whether to be relieved or worried that he could read me so well. I decided to go with feeling ridiculously pleased. "Thank you."

He reached across the console and squeezed my hand, holding on to it while I spoke with my mother. Mom insisted that she was thrilled to play my appointments secretary for the day and assured me that everything would be taken care of. She signed off by saying, "Peace out, Punkin'," and I hung up feeling lighter already.

An hour later, we left the highway and drove into Dharma. Derek slowed down as we cruised Shakespeare Lane, so I could get a good look at Savannah's restaurant space.

A wide picture window revealed a light, wood-paneled room with a good number of tables covered in white linen. The tables were already set with sparkling crystal and flatware, and I imagined every table was spoken for. A small bar in the back corner was fully stocked and six barstools stood in front of it.

There was no actual signage out front, just a pretty painted picture of a thick bunch of green arugula tied with a pink ribbon. It was whimsical and colorful, just like my sister. I knew she was already at work in the kitchen, knew she would be nervous all day, knew that a number of well-known restaurant critics were driving up from San Francisco to experience the opening-night menu. But I also knew without a doubt that Arugula would be wildly successful and that Savannah Wainwright, my bald-headed, slightly wacky sister, was on her way to becoming the next celebrity chef of the Bay Area.

At the end of the Lane, Derek turned right and drove up Vivaldi Way toward my parents' home. Over the years, a number of commune members had built homes in the hills overlooking Dharma, and as we climbed, we passed Abraham's Spanish colonial on the right where his daughter, Annie, now lived. The Westcott family lived in the Tudor-style home tucked into the hillside on the left side of the road. Around the next turn, Carl Brundidge, the lawyer for most of the commune members, owned the sleek contemporary on the right.

Despite being in a commune, we all had our own individual styles and our houses demonstrated that.

A minute later, we pulled up in front of my parents' spacious ranch-style home. Before the car had rolled to a stop, Mom and Dad came running out to greet us. They were holding hands, and seeing them together eased more of the tension around my heart.

The weather was warm enough that Mom had pulled her hair back into a ponytail, and she wore a tie-dyed tank top, cargo shorts, and utility boots. Mom had great legs and her arms were toned from the exercise she got picking apples and grapes all year long.

"Looks like Mom's been out in the orchards this morning," I said to Derek. "You know what that means?"

He shut off the engine and glanced at me. "What?"

"She might be making her crazy-delicious apple crisp while we're here."

"Apple crisp?" His eyes were instantly alert. "Don't toy with me, Brooklyn."

I laughed as I climbed out of the car. Mom's crazy-delicious apple crisp with its awesome, spiked caramel sauce was worth the hour-long drive from the city to Sonoma.

I hugged my dad, surprised to see him all dressed up in Dockers and a clean, pressed, denim work shirt. His loafers were shiny, too, and he was wearing one of the Jerry Garcia ties I'd given him for Christmas. For Dad, this was formal wear. The man rarely wore anything but faded jeans and a T-shirt, since he spent most of his days out in the vineyards or in the barrel room, tasting and experimenting with the wines.

I knew I was probably prejudiced, but I thought my parents were adorable. They never seemed to age, which probably should've annoyed me, since I was getting older all the time, but it didn't. It just made me happy to be here with them.

"I've invited Robson and some of the children over for lunch," Mom announced after she'd hugged us both and tried to wrestle my overnight bag from me. As we walked into the house, she turned to Derek and added, "And I've cooked up a few of your favorite dishes."

"You're a goddess, Rebecca," Derek said, and Mom giggled like a little girl. He was the only one besides Guru Bob who called her Rebecca.

I was hoping "some of the children" Mom had invited included my best friend, Robin, and my brother Austin. They were a couple now, living together in Austin's home in the hills above Dharma. I missed Robin living close by me in the city, but I was overjoyed that she and my brother had finally found each other. Of course, Robin had to almost *die* for Austin to wake up to the fact that he was in love with her and she was meant for him, but at least they were together now.

"Dad, why are you all dressed up?" I asked.

"I've got a board of directors meeting," he said with a pensive sigh.

Dad was on three boards of directors, so I asked, "For the winery?"

He nodded mournfully, and I laughed again. "It's a real bitch being so successful."

"Language, Brooklyn," Mom said mildly, rubbing my father's arm. "But you're right. Jimmy was much better off as a poor but rugged farmer. I miss those days."

I snorted. "Dad was never a poor farmer."

"True," she said, winking. "But he's always been rugged."

Dad wiggled his eyebrows at her. "I'll wear my overalls later."

"Ooh, boy. Here we go," I said, covering my ears as I rushed ahead into the house.

Once inside, I couldn't make eye contact with Derek. The thing was, we'd never spent the night at my parents' house together. Mom and Dad were old hippies, so I didn't think there would be an issue about the sleeping arrangements, but you just never knew with parents.

"I've put you and Derek in your old bedroom," Mom said briskly, leading the

64

way down the hall.

I finally looked at Derek and rolled my eyes. The man was big, bad, and dangerous, and I couldn't picture him sleeping in the old bedroom I'd shared with my sister China. We'd slept in narrow twin beds with a third rollaway bed squeezed against one wall to accommodate Robin for her lengthy sleepovers. It was like a small dormitory in there. Was Mom really expecting Derek and me to sleep in twin beds?

Ah, well, I guess I could give her some credit for letting us stay in the same room together. But I wouldn't blame Derek if he decided to bow out and check into the new boutique hotel down on Shakespeare Lane. I had suggested the hotel when we'd made our plans to come for the weekend, but Derek had insisted he was perfectly content to stay with my parents.

Mom opened the door to my room and stepped aside to let us pass. "What do you think?"

"Whoa," I said, taking it all in.

The twin beds had been replaced by an elegant, dark wood sleigh bed covered in a thick brown and gold duvet. Piled on top were all sorts of decorative pillows of every shape and size, in colors that ran the gamut from light pearl to sparkly gold to rich brown.

The walls were painted a stylish shade of dark cocoa with pale beige trim and cool, light linen curtains. There was a stately new chest of drawers along one wall and a small mahogany desk and chair on the other.

"You've outdone yourself, Mom," I said softly. "This is beautiful."

She clapped her hands. "I think so, too. I got a little help from Robin."

"She's got great taste."

"Yes, much better than mine." She tugged at the curtains, and I realized she was nervous. "I asked her not to make it too girly, because I know that's not your style."

"It's perfect, Mom," I assured her.

"Thank you for going to so much trouble for us," Derek said. He took my bag from me and placed it on the new wooden luggage rack under the window.

"Thanks, Mom," I whispered, and hugged her.

"You're welcome, sweetie," she said, straightening a pillow before heading for the door. "I've asked Robin to redo your father's and my bedroom, too."

"That's a great idea," I said.

"It's been more than twenty years since we bought anything new, so I'm excited," she said. "But I'm glad Robin's doing it. I was afraid if I did it on my own, we'd end up with bordello red walls and white wicker furniture or something."

"Interesting design choices."

She laughed, then checked her wristwatch. "I'll let you kids get settled. Robson should be here in half an hour; then lunch is at noon."

CHAPTER 6

"Something is troubling you, gracious," Guru Bob said.

To the leader of the Dharma commune, *everyone* was *gracious*. But I still liked to think that the other kids and I who had been raised in Dharma were extraspecial to him. He was my parents' spiritual leader, but to me he was simply a true friend and a terrific listener.

"Yes, Robson," I confessed. I always called him Robson to his face. Guru Bob was a fun nickname we kids had always used, but it was too irreverent to call him that in person.

We were alone on the terrace of my parents' home, overlooking Mom's apple orchard on one side and rolling hills of grapevines on the other. The sky was brilliant blue and the air was so crisp and clear, it almost hurt to breathe. It was turning out to be a warm day but I still felt a touch of the morning chill. Or maybe it was just my state of mind.

Guru Bob sipped the tea my mother had brought him and assured me he was in no hurry, so I took a few moments to gather my thoughts. It was good to know that no matter what I told him, he would be kind. I trusted him and loved him as I would a cherished uncle.

It was hard to explain Guru Bob to outsiders. On paper, he probably came across as a charlatan, a deceitful crackpot whose charm and clever wiles were responsible for brainwashing several hundred followers twenty-five years ago. Why else would all those intelligent people sell everything and move from the city out to the Sonoma boondocks to establish the Fellowship for Spiritual Enlightenment and Higher Artistic Consciousness?

That picture couldn't have been further from the truth.

I guessed he was in his mid-fifties, but he seemed younger. He was tall and lanky, a gentle, spiritual man, although I wouldn't call him religious. My parents believed him to be a highly evolved conscious being. All I knew was that Guru Bob was smarter and kinder and more aware of . . . well, everything than anyone I knew.

I'd also seen him coldly draw a line in the sand when he was betrayed by someone he'd considered a friend. I never wanted to see that look on his face again.

Sitting here in the sun, I suddenly remembered that a few months back, during Abraham's murder investigation, Derek had followed me to Dharma and heard Guru Bob speak at Abraham's memorial service. I was still regarding Derek as an adversary then, but, nevertheless, I was nervous about his reaction to Guru Bob. When Derek called him powerful, in a most respectful tone, I was delighted. Thinking back on it now, I realized that that might've been the moment my attitude warmed toward Derek.

"Gracious, what is upsetting you?"

I cleared my throat and made eye contact with him. "I found another dead body yesterday. I'm afraid there's something negative growing inside me that's causing me to attract death. Murder, I mean. And murderers. I keep finding these victims of murder, and I'm afraid I am going to scare off my friends. I know it sounds stupid, but it's getting bad and I'm getting paranoid. What if people think they might get killed if they stay friends with me?"

He smiled. "My dear, have you not considered the possibility that the dead seek you out? In each of the instances of which you speak, even when the victim was not your friend, you have been compassionate, as well as passionate, in leading the charge for justice. Do you not think the universe recognizes this?"

"Wait a sec," I protested, then winced for being less than polite with him. "Sorry, Robson. But I mean, seriously, you think the universe is putting these bodies in my path so that I'll bring them justice?"

"I do."

"That's just bizarre. Sorry." Oops, there I was, being rude again. "The police are pretty good at this, you know."

"Ah, but in many of these situations, it is my understanding that you have led them to several clues they might not have otherwise uncovered." He took a sip of his tea and gave me one of his genial smiles.

Another quirk of Guru Bob's was that he never used contractions. Sometimes I couldn't help but imitate him, but I tried to avoid it. Guru Bob sounded fine talking that way, but I sounded deranged.

I pursed my lips in frustration as I tried to make sense of his words. In a flash, I remembered an old Agatha Christie story in which Miss Marple received a request that came from beyond the grave. A man she'd known who had recently died had sent her a card asking her to investigate the suspicious death of his son's fiancée, for which his son had been imprisoned.

"*Nemesis,*" Guru Bob murmured.

I blinked. "What? What did you say?"

"*Nemesis.*" He smiled. "An Agatha Christie novel. Do you know it?"

"Of course I know it," I cried, waving my hands. Then I sat back and frowned at him. "Why did you say that? I mean, sorry, but that was weird." I took a calming breath and let it out. "Anyway, yes, I know the story of *Nemesis.* I was just now thinking about it."

"Ah, well." He smiled innocently. "That is a coincidence. Is it not?"

Still frowning, I stared at him, watching him for signs of more trickery, but he just continued to gaze at me with a gentle smile. Okay, this was a staring contest I couldn't win, so I changed the subject. "Robson, do you remember Max Adams?"

His smile faded. "Yes, of course, gracious. Why do you ask?"

I gave him the shortened version of what had happened yesterday with the *Beauty and the Beast* and Joseph Taylor's death and my flat tire and the papermaker's knives with Max's initials carved into the handles.

He seemed to grow more and more uneasy

72

as I spoke, but who wouldn't after hearing the news of Joe's murder? And the mention of Max's knives must have disturbed him, too.

"Stop." He held up his hand and interrupted me in midsentence. "Please, gracious. Wait a moment."

I was kind of shocked. I'd never seen him do that before. "Okay."

He stood, agitated and distracted now. Very un–Guru Bob–like. "I must go inside and call Gabriel."

Gabriel? Why did he have to call Gabriel? Did somebody need saving? Or shooting? I'd first met the dashing, mysterious Gabriel when he saved my life in a noodle restaurant on Fillmore Street. I still wasn't sure whether he was a hero or a thief or both, but he was a good friend.

Guru Bob continued. "I will need to speak with Derek, as well. Please do not go anywhere, gracious. It is important that we discuss this matter further."

"Um, sure."

He dashed off. I couldn't remember the last time I'd seen him move so fast.

"You are all sworn to secrecy," Guru Bob said sternly forty-five minutes later, when we'd regrouped in Mom's living room. "Is that clear?"

"Yes, of course," Derek said, sitting comfortably on the sofa beside me.

"You're upset, Robson," Mom said. "What happened?"

He closed his eyes and drew in a breath. After a moment, serenity returned to his features. "I apologize for my brusqueness. Brooklyn gave me some distressing news a few minutes ago and I am afraid I reacted badly."

"I'm so sorry!" I said, clamping my hands over my mouth. "I didn't mean to."

"No, gracious. It is not your fault. You will understand my reaction in a moment."

The front door slammed and Dad came rushing into the room. "I got here as soon as I could. What's going on?"

Guru Bob held up his hand, and Dad calmed immediately. Mom poured another cup of tea and handed it to Dad. He sat in one of the upholstered corner chairs, still catching his breath.

This was getting odder by the minute. Derek took hold of my hand in apparent agreement.

"Rebecca, James," Guru Bob said, speaking to my parents. "You remember Max Adams and the circumstances surrounding his death."

74

"Oh yes. Poor Max," Mom whispered. "I wish you'd known him." Her eyes softened as she gazed across at Derek, then over at Gabriel, who stood leaning against the mantel over the fireplace, looking fit and handsome in a black leather jacket and well-worn jeans. He'd been injured badly a month ago and had been recuperating in Dharma while he weighed his options and planned his next move.

Frankly, I'd been worried about Gabriel for a while now. What would he do next? Where would he go from here? I didn't have time to think about that right now, but I would ask him later.

"Max grew up in Dharma," Mom explained. "He was great friends with Austin and the other kids, and after high school he went on to become a talented artist and papermaker. Eventually he met a lovely woman and they got engaged. A month after their engagement party, he was killed in a car accident."

"I'm sorry," Derek said to Mom. "It must've been difficult for you all."

"It was," Mom said, sitting on the arm of Dad's chair.

"Yes, it was, indeed," Guru Bob said, "but now Brooklyn has introduced a new wrinkle to the saga." He was standing now, and began strolling slowly around the room as he related an abbreviated version of the story I'd told him a few minutes earlier.

"Oh, Brooklyn, sweetie," Mom said. "I'm so sorry about Mr. Taylor. I wish we could've been there for you."

"Thanks, Mom."

Dad shook his head. "Honey, you should've called us."

"Thanks, Dad. Derek was close by, so he came over." Staring at our joined hands, I murmured to no one in particular, "There was a lot of blood."

Derek squeezed my hand.

Gabriel had been watching us, but now he folded his arms across his chest and lifted his chin toward Guru Bob. "What's this all about, Robson? Has someone else died?"

"No." Guru Bob looked around the room, meeting each person's gaze in order. "But I have kept something from you for far too long. The time has come to reveal the truth."

This really was beginning to feel like an Agatha Christie novel. But Robson's eyes were grave as he turned them on me, and I gripped Derek's hand a little tighter.

"Max Adams is very much alive."

CHAPTER 7

"What?" I might have shrieked the word, but nobody would have blamed me right at that moment. "That's impossible! Max has been dead for three years."

"No, gracious, he has not," Guru Bob demurred.

"You're wrong." I jumped up from the couch and looked around the room in desperation.

"Robson's never wrong, sweetie," Mom said, but she was just as shocked as I was.

I stared at her for a moment. "Okay, maybe not. But this can't be true."

"I don't understand," Mom said. "Are you sure, Robson?"

"You said he's never wrong," I protested.

She blinked. "I know, but we all went to his funeral. There must be a mistake. Robson?"

"There is no mistake, Rebecca," Guru Bob said, kindly ignoring my outburst. "I saw Max with my own eyes the day after his death was declared. I arranged for his safe departure. Believe me, he is very much alive and living in a safe place under an assumed name."

Now I knew what people meant when they said it felt like the floor had opened up beneath them. Max? *Alive?* Why didn't he tell me? Why did he let all of us think he was dead? I *sobbed* through his funeral! I'd missed him for so long after that. I still missed him.

"Where is he?" I asked.

Guru Bob glanced around the room. He seemed unsure of himself. And that was just one more oddity in a day filled with them. Guru Bob had never been unsure of anything as long as I'd known him.

I happened to catch Dad giving a minuscule nod to Guru Bob.

"Wait!" I said, wondering whether my eyes could possibly bulge out of my head more than they already had. "Dad? You knew about this?"

"Jimmy?" Mom whispered, betrayal clear in her hushed tone.

"But . . . why?" I stammered. "How?"

"Yes, why, Robson?" Mom demanded, turning her back on my father, who winced as if in preparation for what would no doubt be an unpleasant evening later. "It's not as if Max were some sort of master spy or something."

"Becky —" Dad started.

Mom whipped around. "Don't you 'Becky' me, mister. How could you keep something like this from me? I loved that boy. His family was devastated. How could you —"

"His life was being threatened," Guru Bob said flatly. "When the people after him began to direct their threats toward his family and his fiancée, Emily, Max made the decision to stage his own death to protect them all."

"But that . . . that's crazy," I muttered lamely. "Where were the police?"

"It was an unusual situation," Dad said. "The police weren't helpful."

"So you stepped in and helped him get away," Derek surmised, his gaze directed at Guru Bob. "With Jim's help?"

"To one of your safe houses?" Gabriel said.

My mouth gaped open. "Wait a minute." *Safe houses?* I felt as if I'd wandered into an alternate reality, where Guru Bob was a spymaster and my own father was capable of keeping state secrets. "Safe houses?"

"What?" Mom screeched the word, and

Dad covered his ears. "You have safe *houses?* Plural? As in, *more than one safe house?* Why? And, Jimmy, you knew? What else aren't you telling me?"

Guru Bob flashed Gabriel a fulminating look, but Gabriel seemed unfazed that he'd just busted the secret wide-open. Then again, he didn't have my mother throwing daggers at him or me yelling at him. Not yet, anyway.

Robson turned to my father. "James, you mentioned a new Phelps Viognier you wanted to try."

"Damn straight!" Dad said joyfully, and bounced up from his chair in sheer relief. "Must be time for a little wine tasting."

"Jimmy." Mom's voice held a tone of warning, but Dad ignored her and rushed off to the kitchen.

He was back a few seconds later with a chilled bottle and a corkscrew. "You're going to love this baby. It's got a creamy mouthfeel with hints of apricot and mint that'll go down like silk and ease your troubled mind."

I raised my hand weakly. "Yes, please."

Derek laughed. "I'll try a sip or two, Jim."

"James Francis Wainwright, I asked you a question," Mom said, her normally smooth forehead lined in distress.

I cringed at that. Mom used our full names only when she was about to ground us for eternity. I'm not sure how that translated for one's spouse, but I knew Dad was in deep trouble.

"What's that, sweetie?" Dad said as the cork popped out of the bottle. He glanced around, feigning confusion, then said, "Oh, hey. We'll need some glasses."

"I'll get them," I said quickly, earning a suspicious look from Mom, who threw her hands up in disgust.

"Thanks, Brooksie," Dad said, cheerily ignoring Mom's wrathful vibe.

I raced into the dining room and pulled six wineglasses out of the cabinet. I would've used any excuse to get out from between Mom's eyes shooting flames at Dad.

As I walked back into the living room, I caught Mom waggling her finger at Dad. She was strutting now and her head was moving back and forth on her neck like a bobblehead doll. "Jimmy, you got some 'splainin' to do."

Derek laughed, and Gabriel, who hadn't said much up until now, grinned with delight. "God, I love you people."

It took the whole bottle of Viognier to ease our troubled minds enough to calm down and listen to Guru Bob's explanation. In the past three years, he had purchased *five* safe houses, all under different names in remote areas of northern California. Max's had been the first.

"For two months after he 'died,' " he explained, "Max camped on the Columbia River up in Oregon. Once the Marin house was purchased, he moved there."

Mom had calmed down considerably, but she still scowled at her longtime spiritual teacher and friend. "So you just go out and buy houses and new identities for people?"

Dad and Guru Bob exchanged glances. Finally, Guru Bob said, "I provide . . . sanctuary."

"Oh." Mom thought about that for a few seconds; then her shoulders relaxed. "All right. That makes sense. Thank you, Robson."

He nodded solemnly, as if that settled everything.

"Wait. It makes sense? Really?" I was almost more confused than before. And not that I would mention it in front of Mom, but did Dad have something to do with those safe houses? I'd seen that look he gave Guru Bob.

"Yes, sweetie," Mom said. "Sanctuary is a good thing." She looked around at the faces in the room and smiled. "Now, who's ready for lunch?"

Huh?

Don't get me wrong, I'm always up for lunch. But where did my mom go? Her expression had transmogrified into the Sunny-Bunny smiley face she made whenever she didn't want to discuss an uncomfortable topic.

Maybe she was lying low, figuring she could get more answers by grilling Dad later. Or maybe the idea of Guru Bob providing sanctuary for those in need was honestly something she could get behind. Sanctuary was, after all, considered a noble cause by some. But I had a feeling there was more to the story than that.

And there was still the little matter of Max being *not* dead. And the fact that Guru Bob and my dad had been lying about it for three freaking years.

However, everyone but me seemed relieved to drop the subject for now. And with the lure of food, I was cajoled into relaxing for a while, too. We all stood and helped bring the various casserole dishes and platters of food outside to the sunny terrace. As usual, Mom had prepared enough food for a small army, and we ate at the patio table under their big, colorful umbrella.

"Who wants dessert?" she asked when everyone had eaten their fill. "It's apple crisp."

Derek held his stomach. "I'm stuffed to the gills, but I can't resist."

"Me, too," Dad said, and sat back in his chair, clearly suffused with a sense of contentment.

Gabriel helped Mom bring out the dessert, and, sure enough, she'd made her amazing apple crisp with caramel sauce. She served it with ice cream on the side. After we were finished, we all looked ready to nod off.

Once the dishes were cleared, we went into the kitchen and Robson announced he was leaving. Mom gave him a hug and he patted her back. "If it makes you feel better, Rebecca, I plan to sell the homes soon."

"Sell them? Why?"

Dad snorted. "They won't be safe houses now that everyone knows about them."

That was when Mom flashed her scary, wild-eyed rodent glare at him. No one in the family — heck, no one in the *county* — crossed her when she glared at you like that.

Guru Bob glanced at Derek, then over at Gabriel. "I would like someone to drive out to see Max and warn him of these latest developments."

"I'll go," Derek said immediately.

"I'm on it," Gabriel said at the exact same time.

Robson smiled. "Thank you both. That is what I hoped you would say."

"Can't you just give him a call?" Mom said, proving to me that she was still on top of her game.

"He will not answer the telephone," Robson explained. "It is a precaution we set up in the beginning."

Now, that was just plain bizarre. Guru Bob sensed my distress and touched my arm. "All will be explained soon, gracious."

"I hope so," I said, and looked at Derek. "I'm going, too."

"No," Gabriel and Derek said at the same time, then looked at each other. Gabriel grinned, but Derek was smart enough to refrain.

"You two don't even know Max," I said reasonably. "I do. He'll talk to me. So I'm going with you."

Derek glowered at me.

"She's got a point." Gabriel sat at the kitchen table and stretched his legs out in front of him. "Now, I hate to bring this up, because I realize this guy is Dharma's favorite son. But I hope you're all prepared to deal with the possibility that he might've killed that bookseller."

"Oh no, dear," Mom said straight away.

I shook my head. "He didn't. It's not an issue."

Gabriel cast a sideways glance at me. "His tools were found at the crime scene."

"Doesn't matter."

"Okay." He held up both hands. "Just saying."

"I understand what you're getting at," I said, nodding. "But you don't know Max. He would never hurt anyone."

"You haven't seen him in years."

"It's barely been three years, and people don't change that much."

"People change when they have to," Gabriel said, his tone matter-of-fact. "Would the Max you knew a few years back have lied to you? Would he have let you think he'd been dead all this time? Would he let you all mourn him?"

Well, he had me there. I chewed at my bottom lip, caught my mom's eye, and realized we were both thinking along the same lines. It was so out of character for the Max we knew. But murder? There was no way Max was responsible.

"This whole thing's got to be some kind of setup or something."

"How do you figure?" Gabriel asked as he

tapped his fingers on the table.

"Well." I took a last sip of wine to give myself time to think. "Someone wanted to divert suspicion away from themselves. Or wanted to specifically blame Max for Joe's murder. I just can't figure out why yet."

"It's possible." Gabriel shrugged. "That means that whoever killed the bookseller must know Max Adams pretty well."

"That's right," I said, and wondered why I hadn't thought of that already. I suppose a vague feeling had been circling around my consciousness, but it hadn't caught hold. The fact was, I hadn't been thinking very clearly since I found Joe's body. "So maybe the killer wants to draw Max out into the open."

Derek leaned against the butcher-block table by the stove, his eyes narrowed in thought. "If the act of killing Joseph Taylor was meant to draw out Max, then the killer must know he's alive."

I shivered and pulled my sweater tight around me. That hadn't occurred to me, either. But now that it had, I was scared to death for Max. "Which means the killer could already know where Max lives."

Gabriel said, "He may be in big trouble out there."

Derek had seen my reaction and pointed

his finger at me. "And that's why you ought to stay right here with your parents while we go collect him."

"Nice try, but you won't get rid of me that easily."

"I don't want to get rid of you, darling," he said softly. "I want to protect you."

"Aw, that's sweet," Mom said.

"Yes, it is." I smiled at him. "Thank you, Derek. But the fact is, you need me there with you." I pushed myself away from the sink. "So let's go."

"Whoa, hold on. Nobody's going anywhere today," Mom said. "Tonight is Savannah's grand opening and I expect you all to be there."

"But Max might need us," I insisted.

"He's been on his own all this time. He can wait one more day." She flashed a piercing look at Guru Bob. "And if I know Robson, he's probably got some sort of fail-safe number Max can call if he's in deep trouble. Probably goes to some untraceable cell phone somewhere. Am I right?"

Guru Bob said nothing but held up his hands in surrender, as if to admit he couldn't pull anything over on my mother. But he had, hadn't he? For years now.

"Mom, how do you expect us to enjoy ourselves tonight, knowing Max is stuck out there all alone?"

She patted my cheek. "Because, my darling girl, tonight is all about good food."

"But I'm already so stuffed from lunch."

"You'll be hungry by seven o'clock tonight."

She had a point. I didn't like skipping meals. It wasn't healthy, right? Yeah. So, okay, I would force myself to enjoy an evening with family and friends, eat a fabulous meal, get a good night's sleep, and rescue Max Adams in the morning. Once I was sure he was alive and in a safe place, I was so going to bop him over the head with something big and heavy.

Before Guru Bob left Mom and Dad's, he pulled Derek aside and handed him a slip of paper. Then he said good-bye, and we all walked outside with him.

As soon as he drove away, I turned to Derek. "What did he give you?"

He smiled as he smoothed a strand of hair away from my cheek. "Nothing escapes you, does it?"

"No, so just make it easy on yourself and tell me what he slipped you."

Chuckling, he pulled a small square of bond paper from his pocket and handed it to me. It was an address in Point Reyes Station, a small town in Marin County near Drakes Bay.

"Is this it?" I asked, gazing up at him. "Is this Max's address?"

"No." Derek took the note back. "Robson said we should go here first and they'll tell us where to find Max."

"Sounds like a scavenger hunt," I said, wrinkling my nose.

With a frown, he said, "Let's hope it's not that complicated."

"It's already complicated. We're going off to rescue a dead man."

"Good point."

CHAPTER 8

Later that afternoon, the irresistible aroma of warm baked bread filled the kitchen as Mom pulled the last loaf pan from the oven. She set it on a rack next to two other loaves, then whipped off her apron and turned to me. "The bread can cool while you and I go downstairs to perform a peace-and-safety ritual."

My eyes widened and I looked around for an escape. "Gosh, Mom, I should probably go help Dad with . . . something."

"No, young lady," she said, taking my hand and pulling me out of the kitchen. "You're coming with me."

My shoulders slumped as we walked down the hall to the basement stairs.

"I'm very worried about you going off to find Max," she said. "So humor me."

Fine. I could use a little peace and safety in my life. Downstairs, she lit a fat stick of white sage and whooshed it around. "Now, when you find Max, I want you to bring him here. We'll do sacred chanting and I'll treat him to a cleansing Bhakti yoga shala bliss."

"What in the world is that?"

"It's a little concoction I dreamed up all on my own. Last week in my Ayurveda stretch class, Yoganina Robayana declared it *delicious.*"

"Good to know."

"Now sit, and we'll meditate. Have you seen my new drum?" Mom sat on a fat, fluffy, Indian-print pillow; picked up a two-sided drum off the table; and began to beat its sides in a slow rhythm. "First we'll do the sacred chanting. Ohmmmmmmmmmmmm."

And she was off. I couldn't just walk out and leave her, so I folded my hands together in a yoga pose and prepared myself for the show.

"Ohmmmmmmmmmmmm." She closed her eyes and smiled beatifically as she tapped both sides of the drum double time. "Dig this vibration, sweetie."

"That's quite a groove you've got going."

She put down the drum, then waved her arms over her head in an undulating movement. "It's the dance of the divine."

"Awesome." I made a face.

"Are you making a face?"

I gulped. Could she see with her eyes closed? "Never. It wasn't me, Mom."

She smiled patiently. "Have a little brahmacharya, sweetie."

That meant "self-control." Self-control was one of the yamas, or ethical codes of conduct outlined in the Yoga Sutras of Patanjali. There were others: nonviolence, truthfulness, nonstealing, nonpossessiveness.

Her eyes rolled back in her head and I think she went into a trance as she began to sing, "Shri Rama Llama Jala Walla Ram Ram."

"Oy vey," I muttered.

"Sing with me! 'Shri Rama Llama Jala Walla Ram Ram / Shri Rama Llama Jala Walla Ram Ram / Shri Rama Llama Jala Walla Ram Ram.'"

"Mom," I said loudly, but she kept singing the same phrase over and over again. She picked up the drum again and beat her fingers and thumbs rapidly against the skin in rhythm with her song.

"Shri Rama Llama Jala Walla Ram Ram."

"That's beautiful, Mom," I yelled over the lyric, "but I've got to go upstairs and get ready. Thank you for taking care of my peace and safety."

"Wait," she cried. "There are forty more verses!"

"I'll be humming along," I said.

She sucked in another breath and kept singing, "Shri Rama Llama Jala Walla Ram Ram."

"Namaste. Love you, Mom," I shouted over the pulsating rhythm, then clapped my hands together and bowed to her before escaping up the stairs.

That night, despite my reluctance to enjoy life while Max might be in trouble, Derek and I joined Mom and Dad for an incredible dinner at Savannah's restaurant. My brother Austin and my pal Robin sat nearby at a cozy table for two. My sisters London and China and their husbands showed up for the occasion, too, along with half of Dharma. There were a few unfamiliar faces that might've belonged to those reviewers from San Francisco I'd heard about. I prayed their meals were excellent. For me, the service was impeccable and the food was phenomenal, and not just because my sister owned the joint.

I had moments of uneasiness during the meal whenever I remembered that Max was still alive. None of my sisters knew it and I couldn't tell them. Not yet, anyway. Since there was nothing I could do about it for a while, I tried to relax and enjoy the fun company and the incredible meal.

Savannah came out later to say hello, and the entire room burst into applause. She wore the traditional white chef's jacket over checked pants, but instead of the tall white toque on her head, she wore a red beret. It was adorably jaunty, but, yes, she still had a bald head. Somehow it worked for her.

I couldn't believe everything I'd eaten was vegetarian. I'd been scared to death that we'd be chewing alfalfa sprouts and raw lentils, but no. I'd ordered an endive, goat cheese, and pear salad with all kinds of yummy little goodies sprinkled on top, followed by an amazing entrée of handmade raviolis stuffed with butternut squash and wild mushrooms, all floating in a creamy herb butter sauce. The pinot noir our waiter recommended went perfectly with everything. And, hallelujah, there was chocolate mint soufflé served with a pot full of whipped cream for dessert.

By the time the check came, I was forced to admit that my loony, bald-headed sister had become a true artist with food, even if she refused to include red meat in her palette. At least she hadn't turned her back on chocolate.

■ ■ ■ ■

There were no freeways, no shortcuts, no easy way to make the long, circuitous drive west from Sonoma to Point Reyes Station in Marin County. There were only narrow two-lane roads that twisted and wound through rolling hills and mountain passes for more than fifty miles. But since it was a beautiful — if slightly treacherous — drive, and since I was being driven by Derek in his sleek Bentley Continental GT with Gabriel in the backseat — in other words, two of the most handsome men in the northern hemisphere — you wouldn't hear me complain about it.

After checking the map and his GPS, Derek decided to drive a few miles north up to Santa Rosa, where we would pick up Highway 101 going south. It might have seemed like we were going out of our way, but the highway was actually faster and we'd make up some time before we had to turn west on Petaluma Point Reyes Road. That's where we'd start to lose time on those winding mountain roads, but Derek assured us that the Bentley would handle the turns and switchbacks with class and ease.

"I'll let you know how that works out from

the backseat," Gabriel said amiably as he squeezed in his six-foot-plus frame. I had offered to sit in the back, but he insisted, so I moved my seat forward to accommodate his long legs, and we hit the road.

As Derek drove, I filled in some of the blanks in Max Adams's history. I told them about Emily and how much I'd liked her, and how much she'd loved the *Beauty and the Beast* book I'd given them.

I was glad I'd brought the book along with me on this trip so I could show it to Max — if we were able to find him, of course.

I was still having a hard time believing that Max was alive. And oh, my God, *Emily.* How could he have done this to her and to all of us? How had he managed to keep us in the dark for three long years? *Max, what were you thinking?*

I pulled out my cell phone to double-check my voice mail. But Emily hadn't returned my phone call. It had been two days already, and I had to wonder why I hadn't heard back from her. I knew I'd called the right number. Her voice hadn't changed at all.

Would the people who lived at the address Guru Bob gave us be willing to lead us to Max? Did I really want to see him? Yes, but I had questions. Too many, really. I needed to know how his tools could have shown up next to a dead man and buried in my tire. I knew he hadn't killed Joe. Max was too good a person to ever have killed anyone. But, then, the Max I knew would never have lied to his friends and family for three long years. Could he have turned into a cold-blooded killer?

Absolutely not. But I had to admit that I was getting a strange feeling about this whole adventure.

Derek touched my knee. "Stop worrying."

"How do you know I'm worrying?"

His mouth twisted in a sardonic grin as he applied a little more pressure to my knee. "Your leg is shaking enough to overturn the car. You always shake your leg when you're fretting over something."

"I do?" I slapped one hand to my knee to hold it still.

"Yes, love, you do. And another thing." He kept his eyes on the road but reached over and stroked my forehead with his fingers. "You get the tiniest, most adorable frown line right here, between your eyebrows."

"Damn, I thought the Botox would take care of that."

I appreciated the snicker I heard from Gabriel in the backseat.

Derek tweaked my cheek. "Don't even joke about that."

"There's nothing adorable about frown lines," I muttered.

"Everything's adorable on you, darling."

I smiled adorably at him, then laughed when Gabriel began swearing under his breath. I couldn't quite catch what he'd said, but was pretty sure I didn't want to know.

"There's nothing to worry about," Derek said easily, keeping both hands on the steering wheel now as the twists in the road became more unwieldy. "We'll find Max and bring him back to Dharma. Robson and Gabriel will make sure he's unharmed until the police find the murderer."

My leg was shaking again. I pressed my hand on my knee to make it stop, then shot Derek a look. Did I really have such obvious tells that he could know what I was thinking or feeling? Or was he just tuned in to me? I was tuned in to him, too, but I could no more tell what he was thinking than I could move that mountain on the other side of the pasture we'd just passed. It wasn't fair.

"I'm not really worried," I lied. "I'm more angry. And hurt. I was just thinking about Max and Emily and *Beauty and the Beast,* and, you know, everything that was happening back then."

"This situation has brought up a lot of old feelings for you," he said.

"True," I admitted, then realized that Ian had said the same thing to me. The men in my life were a little too observant sometimes. "But that's not what's bothering me." I turned in my seat so Gabriel could hear me, too. "I've been thinking that it wasn't Joe's murder that set everything into action to draw out Max."

"What do you think it was?" Gabriel said.

"It was me."

Derek took the curve too quickly and swerved, then swore ripely as he maneuvered the Bentley back into the lane.

"Are you okay?" I asked, clutching the dashboard.

He said nothing, just glared at me with his teeth clenched in . . . anger?

"What did I say?"

"It's okay, babe," Gabriel said, and patted my shoulder. "Our driver's got shaky nerves. Now, where did you get this idea that you're the catalyst in all this?"

I cast another uncertain glance at Derek, then related what Ian had told me on Friday. "The book's so-called owner suggested to Joe that he call the Covington to buy the book. Ian thought it was because the new children's wing was getting a lot of attention, but I think it's because they knew about Ian's connection to me, knew that he would call me in to restore the book. They also knew about my connection to Max and that as soon as I saw the book, I would recognize it and go looking for Joe."

"And find him dead," Gabriel concluded.

"Exactly."

I looked at Derek again. His jaw was clamped shut and it was pretty obvious why. Okay, so maybe I was able to tell his moods better than I had thought. And since it looked like he wanted to chew on the steering wheel, I decided to follow his lead, stop talking, and try to enjoy the scenery.

It was noon when we drove into the deceptively sleepy town of Point Reyes Station. The center of town consisted of one main street that stretched for three short blocks. The town had a faded sixties vibe with an eclectic blend of upscale cafés, building-supply stores, bakeries, cheese shops, art galleries, a funky old auto-repair garage, and a fresh fruit stand. On one corner was the Old Western Saloon, a Victorian-era bar that was a little seedy but had clean bathrooms, a classic rock jukebox, and a friendly bartender who took only cash.

It was hard to believe that this town was the driving force in the multimillion-dollar organic and artisanal food industry that served the San Francisco Bay area and beyond. The cafés and restaurants in and around Point Reyes Station were like nirvana to food fanatics, who drove from all over northern California to sample the local artisanal cheeses, vegetables, baby lettuces, free-range chicken, grass-fed beef, pâtés, fruits and preserves, and oysters.

Derek drove around the corner and parked the car in front of the Cowgirl Creamery store.

I smiled tentatively. "Maybe we can get something to snack on here."

"You can snack all you want," he muttered. "I need a drink."

He settled for a local beer on tap at the saloon. Gabriel had one, too. I ordered ginger ale. Gabriel took one long sip, then looked at me and Derek. He checked his pocket for change, winked at me, then walked over to the jukebox.

"Here's the thing," I said to Derek once we were alone. "I know you don't like that I might be a target."

"Don't like it? I bloody well hate it."

"I hate it, too. But for some reason, it's happening again. So let's not make it worse by being angry with each other."

He slid an astonished look at me. "Do you think I'm angry with you?"

I looked at him evenly. "Do you think I'm dumb?"

He stared at his glass and absently smoothed away the condensation with his thumb, then finally met my gaze. "No."

"Thanks," I said, not feeling it.

"Come here," he said, and pulled me into his protective embrace. I went gladly, needing to feel his hard chest pressing against me, marveling at how complete I felt in his arms.

Say what? What was I thinking? That I wasn't *complete* a moment ago? Ridiculous. I shoved that pathetic thought right out of my head. I was a complete person, damn it.

"I can feel your mind working even when you're silent," he murmured, chuckling.

"I can't seem to shut it down once I get going."

He leaned back and made eye contact with me. "You're right; I was angry. It was a knee-jerk reaction and I'm sorry."

"It's okay." I gave him a quick, hard hug;

then I stepped away and took a sip of my drink.

"No, it's not." He drank his beer, staring out the wide picture window at the front of the bar. "But I promise I wasn't angry at you."

As Bob Seger's whiskey-smooth voice wafted out from the jukebox, singing about secrets shared and mountains moved, Derek turned and looked at me for a long moment. "You know I'm in love with you. And I think you're the smartest, most courageous person I know. So, yes, I'm angry at the thought that you might become some idiot's target again."

My eyes stung with tears at his words. "I'm . . . I'm angry, too, Derek."

"I know." He trailed his fingers along my forehead, smoothed my hair back. "Darling, I work in dangerous situations all the time. I'm used to it. I know how to protect myself. But you . . . the thought of you . . ." He shook his head, exhaled heavily. "The thought that you could be hurt and I would be powerless to stop it? That scares me to death."

I slipped my arms around his waist and held him. The bar was beginning to fill with the noontime lunch crowd, but I didn't care. If people didn't like public displays of affection, they would have to get over it.

I pulled away finally and we both sipped our drinks in silence. After a minute, I faced him. "I need to rephrase what I said earlier. The *book* is the catalyst, not me. The book started everything. I'm just incidental."

"You could never be incidental, darling," he said, holding back a smile.

"Oh, stop it," I said, smacking his arm, then rubbing the spot I'd hit.

"All right. I think you're spot-on about the book being the catalyst." He nodded as though it had already occurred to him, which it probably had. "Unfortunately, whatever the killer had in mind, I believe we've played right into his hands."

My throat went dry and I glanced around the bar. "Do you think we were followed here?"

"No," he said firmly. "I was careful to watch the cars all the way over here."

"That was smart of you."

"Occupational hazard," he said, and drained the last of his beer.

"Must be. I never would've thought of it." I tapped my fingers on the edge of the bar. "I'm more convinced than ever that Max had nothing to do with any of it."

"You know him better than I," he said, "but one thing is certain: someone wants him out in the open."

"I hope we're doing the right thing," I said, then looked around for Gabriel. Right or wrong, we needed to get going.

As if he'd been watching for the right moment to return, Gabriel walked up just then. He plunked a ten-dollar bill on the bar and said, "Let's go find this guy."

We followed Sir Francis Drake Boulevard for almost fifteen miles. It was hardly a boulevard. *More like a two-lane country road,* I thought, as we wound our way up and down and around the rolling hills, through narrow, tree-shaded hollows and rich, open, green farmland, past pastures and ponds and farms so old they'd earned official state historic markers.

We were close to the ocean and I could smell it in the briny air. We drove higher into the hills, past cypress trees surreally misshapen by years of blustery winds blowing in from the rough northern California ocean.

"This is it," Derek said, and carefully turned off onto a dirt road, then wound around another hill and climbed higher, past another two farms. Scattered across the hillside were black-and-white cows chewing grass. A wire and wood-post fence separated the pasture land from the road.

"Are we there yet?" I muttered.

"There'd better be someone at home when we get there," Derek said.

"And they'd better know where Max is," Gabriel added.

Finally, Derek brought the car to a stop on the narrow verge. Up the hill on our left was a set of pitted stairs carved out of bedrock that led up another fifty yards to a two-story farmhouse.

"That's the place?" Gabriel asked.

"Yes," Derek said, opening his door, then glancing back. "This should only take a moment."

"Maybe so," Gabriel said, pushing the driver's seat forward, then stepping out of the car. "But you're not going alone."

"I'm coming, too," I said, unwilling to wait by myself.

"We'll cause too much attention if we all go," Derek insisted.

"Your English accent will cause more attention than anything else," I countered. "And then there's the Bentley you're driving."

Gabriel snorted. "She's got you there."

Derek shook his head. "I've lost control of the situation, haven't I?"

"Not sure you ever had it, pal," Gabriel

said helpfully.

"True." Derek shrugged. "Let's go, then."

We'd barely walked ten feet when the front door of the farmhouse opened. A tall, bearded man carrying a high-powered rifle stepped out on the porch and aimed the gun right at us. A dog stood at his side. It barked once and the man nudged him quiet with his knee.

"Oh, my God," I whispered.

Derek swore under his breath as he held his arms up.

"Ah, hell," Gabriel said, raising his arms high over his head. "That's never a good thing."

"Yes, it is," I said, my voice unsteady. "That's Max Adams."

CHAPTER 9

"Max," I shouted, and waved my arms in the air, as if he couldn't see me up close and personal in the crosshairs of his rifle. But would he remember me? I looked the same, basically, and I'd known him most of my life, so unless he'd developed amnesia, he couldn't have forgotten me.

Three years didn't seem like that long a time, but looking at Max now, it felt like ten years had passed. Except for the beard, I guess he looked the same, but on the inside, I imagined he must have changed a lot more than I had. For one thing, since faking his own death, he probably didn't go by the name Max anymore. And living out here, day after day, all alone for three long years, could've turned him a little paranoid.

Guru Bob had pulled another fast one by giving us directions that led straight to Max. It was alarming to be facing Max suddenly and without warning, but now that we were here, I was excited to talk to him. I just hoped he wouldn't start shooting. I had so many questions to ask him.

Starting, of course, with, Why did you lie to all of us for three years?

But there was more I wanted to know, too. Did he go outside his house much? Was he afraid to go into town because someone from his old life might see him? Did he wear a disguise? Besides the beard, I mean. It wasn't all that effective, since I had still recognized him.

What had happened to him three years ago that had been so awful that he'd staged his own death rather than face whoever had been tormenting him? Why hadn't the police helped? Had Max missed us as much as we had missed him?

Did he kill Joe Taylor?

"Max! It's Brooklyn." I shouted his name several more times, and after many long seconds he slowly lowered the rifle.

"Brooklyn?"

"Yes, it's me," I shouted, then shivered from the cold air. The marine layer had obliterated the blue skies and now it looked like it might rain.

"What the hell are you doing here? Who are those guys?"

"They're friends of mine. Guru Bob sent us."

"Robson knows you're here?"

"He gave us directions to find you." I took a cautious step closer. He wasn't pointing the rifle anymore, but he was still holding it, after all. "Can we please talk to you?"

He raked his fingers roughly through his hair and glared at us for another minute. He was probably wishing he could tell us all to go to hell, but hearing Robson's name put the kibosh on that. "All right. Yeah, okay." He waved us up the stairs, but he didn't put down the gun, and I guess I couldn't blame him.

I went first, climbing up the rocky, uneven steps. When I got close to the porch, I said, "This is Derek Stone and that's Gabriel." I turned to Derek and Gabriel and said needlessly, "This is Max Adams."

"Call me Jack," he said to the men, then looked at me and frowned. "What are you all doing here? What's going on?"

"It's a long story," I said, rubbing my arms and looking at the darkening sky. "Max — er, Jack, do you mind if we go inside? It's cold out here."

He clamped his lips together in a scowl, then exhaled heavily. "Yeah, I guess so. Come on."

As I stepped onto the porch, a gunshot blasted through the air.

Chips of wood went flying, and I screamed. Derek shoved me down on the wood planks and threw himself on top of me as a shield.

"Shit!" Max shouted, crouching in front of the door and grabbing the handle to open it. He shoved the dog inside and said, "Everyone get in the house."

"Go, go!" Gabriel yelled.

Derek yanked me up and pushed me toward the door. Max clutched my arm and propelled me inside. I careened into the sofa and felt manhandled and bruised in a few places, but I was safe. The dog, a big yellow Lab, licked my hand.

Gabriel scrambled up the steps, bolted inside, and slammed the door.

"Anyone hit?" Derek asked.

"No," Max said, checking the lock. He raced over to the picture window and whipped the curtains closed. "Damn it. You were followed here."

"We weren't," I said with conviction, but I was wrong, obviously.

I looked at Derek, who stared warily at Max. Gabriel was watching him, too. *What is going on?*

"We weren't followed," Derek said carefully. "But are you sure someone hasn't been here all along, watching your house?"

"You're kidding me, right?" He ran over to a side window, leaned his rifle against the corner wall, then used one finger to pull back the curtain an inch and stare outside. "I've been living here for years and nothing has ever happened. All of a sudden you three show up like the Mod Squad, and someone takes a shot at me. Pretty clear to me whose fault that is."

"How do you know that shot was meant for you?" Gabriel said sagely.

Max glowered at Gabriel, then turned his narrowing gaze on Derek. Abruptly he flicked his hand toward the door. "This wasn't a good idea. I want all of you to leave now."

"No," I said quickly. "Not yet. I need to talk to you. Besides, there's a killer outside, so we're not going anywhere for a while."

"Well, don't get comfortable," he said, "because you won't be here long."

I threw warning glances at Derek and Gabriel, then walked over to Max. "Could we stop arguing for a minute so I can tell you why we're here?"

He glared at me with the same dark look of suspicion he'd been wearing since we arrived. I stared back, silently willing him to remember better days when we were close friends.

From the corner of my eye, I noticed Derek and Gabriel had positioned themselves at opposite sides of the picture window and were taking turns peering outside. I'd forgotten about the shooter in the past ten seconds or so. Luckily, my companions hadn't. I pondered whether it might've been an errant hunter whose gun had gone off accidentally.

No, I didn't really believe that, either.

Max and I continued our staring contest until I noticed the lines bracketing his mouth soften a bit and the storm clouds in his eyes clear. And just like that, he was the carefree Max I knew from my youth. Outwardly, anyway. There had to be demons inside him. How could there not be after all this time alone?

"Fine, Brooklyn. Go ahead and say what you were going to say."

I smiled tentatively. "Can I have a hug first?"

He huffed. "Damn it, Brooklyn." Two seconds later, he grabbed me in a tight hug. The dog barked cheerfully. I laughed in surprise, then buried my face in his barrel chest and breathed in his scent. After a moment, I eased back.

"You look good, honey," he said, squeezing my arms affectionately.

"You do, too, Max. You look alive, and that's a good thing." I sniffled as misty tears fogged my eyes.

"Yeah, about that," he said, ill at ease.

"Yeah, about that," I echoed, then stepped back and punched him hard in the stomach.

The dog barked once.

"Ow!" Max rubbed his stomach. "What was that for?"

"Oh, please," I said, shaking and flexing my hand to get the blood flowing again. "That hurt me more than it hurt you. And you know what it was for. You've been lying to all of us for three years."

"It was important. Still is." The dog came over and nudged his leg. Max patted his back, then glared at me. "You know, I always wondered if my enemies would ever discover I was alive, but I never figured it would be my friends who would lead them straight to me."

Gabriel took a step forward. "You'll want to ratchet back on the accusations, Jack."

"Brooklyn didn't lead anyone to you," Derek retorted as he flanked me. "Your enemies know you're alive. It was a matter of time before they found you. You're lucky we found you first."

"Lucky?" He snorted. "How the hell would they know I'm alive if not for you?"

"Because it didn't begin here today," I said softly. The Lab came over and sat in front of me, staring and panting.

"What's your name?" I asked as I bent down to let him sniff my hand.

"It's Buckminster," Max said. "Bucky when he's good."

"Hello, Bucky," I said, patting his back as I observed Max.

But Max wouldn't make eye contact with me. Maybe he was starting to figure things out for himself. But then, obstinate to the end, he threw me another angry look. "Why are you here, Brooklyn?"

"Yeah, well, about that." Now it was my turn to look uncomfortable. Glancing around for the first time, I pointed at the couch and chairs arranged in front of the fireplace. "Can we sit down for a minute?"

"Before you get into it," Derek said, first meeting my gaze, then looking at Max, "do you have a back door?"

"Yeah," he said, jabbing his thumb toward a doorway. "Through the kitchen."

"Good. Gabriel and I will circle the area, and if the shooter's still out there, we'll trap him from behind."

"I'll go with you," Max said, grabbing his

rifle from the corner of the room where he'd left it.

Bucky immediately stood at attention.

"Somebody should stay here," Derek said, casting a quick look at me.

"It's my land," Max said.

Derek studied him. "Are you willing to return fire if it comes down to it?"

"Stone's in security," Gabriel said, as if that explained Derek's question.

"What do you do?" Max said, scowling at Gabriel.

Gabriel shrugged. "Little of this, little of that. Right now, I'm your best defense against whoever's out there shooting at you."

Max's jaw clenched as he glanced at me. I could see the turmoil in his expression. He was a big man and used to living on his own. But he didn't have the same kind of killer instinct Gabriel and Derek possessed, and I could tell he was beginning to realize that.

Reluctantly he nodded once, acquiescing to stay behind.

Derek moved into the kitchen with purpose, followed by Gabriel. I rushed after them. "Are you really going out there?" I whispered, feeling my throat dry up.

"Yes," Derek said. "If there's the slightest

chance someone followed us here, I want to make sure they don't follow us home."

"But there haven't been any more gun-shots," I said a little desperately. "Maybe he's already gone."

"That's what we'll need to determine," Gabriel said, and pulled a powerful-looking handgun out from behind his back.

"Oh, my God, what's that?" I asked stupidly. "That's a gun. What are you doing with that?"

He grinned. "Relax, babe."

I stared wildly at Derek. "He's got a gun."

"Yes, darling," he said, and pulled his own weapon out of a holster under his arm.

I felt my eyes cross. "You — you've had that with you all this time?"

"Just since we got out of the car," he said. "Don't worry, love. We'll be back in a few minutes."

"Don't worry? Are you insane?"

He chuckled, leaned over, and kissed me. Then he looked at Max. "You'll stay with her."

"Of course. We'll cook something."

I laughed a little hysterically. *They have to be kidding,* I decided.

Max opened the back door and pointed out a few details. "The fig orchard should provide enough cover until you get to the barn. Don't go inside unless you want to hear a deafening chorus of bleats from the goats."

"No, thanks," Derek muttered.

"It's wide-open on this side — no cover except for the oak tree." Max pointed the opposite way, then gazed up at the sky. "But it looks about to rain, so maybe he's already gone."

"We'll soon find out," Gabriel said, and zipped up his black leather jacket against the cold.

I watched them steal out of the house. Derek moved off toward the fig orchard while Gabriel hustled in the opposite direction, out into the open field.

Max shut the door. "Let's you and me make some pasta sauce."

"I thought you were kidding," I said, gripping the kitchen counter nervously as I stared out the window over the sink. "I can't cook while they're out there."

"You're not cooking. I am," he said. "You can talk to me. Tell me what the hell you're all doing on my farm."

"I thought it was Robson's farm." I sounded like a snotty little sister, which was probably how he'd always thought of me.

"Robson bought this place with my money," he explained as he pulled a frying pan off the pot rack over the stove. "I signed power of attorney over to him a few weeks before I left and asked him to buy a few more houses, just in case."

Just in case someone found you and you had to move quickly, I thought, but didn't say it. I slid onto one of the stools that was placed next to a beautifully finished, waist-high, dark-stained farmhouse table in the center of the kitchen. "So you had this all worked out before you died? I mean, before you left?"

"Yeah." He took a chef's apron off a hook near the door and wrapped it around himself. "I drew up a will making Robson the executor. I had him give some money to a few people and he kept the rest in trust."

"What in the world happened to make you think you had to go through this charade?"

"It's a long story, and I need to cook while I talk." He pulled mushrooms out of the refrigerator and onions out of a bag in the pantry closet, grabbed a head of garlic from a basket on the counter, then cut bits of herbs from several pots perched along the kitchen windowsill. I recognized thyme, oregano, parsley, and basil.

"I never knew you were such a cook."

"I never was until I moved here," he said as he briskly chopped the garlic cloves into tiny pieces. "No choice, really. It was learn to cook or starve."

He scraped all the garlic bits up with the knife and placed them in a small bowl. Then he handed me another knife and a small wood chopping board. "Can you mince the herbs together?"

"Sure."

He patted my shoulder. "And while you're at it, tell me why you came here."

"Oh yeah. Okay." *Although,* I reminded myself, *it's* Max *who has the most explaining to do.*

Walking back to the pantry, he pulled out two large jars of tomatoes and put them on the counter by the stove.

"Do you can those tomatoes yourself?"

"Yeah," he said, picking up his knife again. "They taste better that way. Now talk."

"Right." I pushed the stool away and stood to work at the center table. Suddenly a great bundle of fur brushed against my ankles and I almost screamed.

"Meow."

I looked down at the fat orange creature. "What's this?"

"It's a cat," Max said. "That's Clydesdale. Clyde, meet Brooklyn."

"Hello, Clyde," I said.

He blinked at me, wound his way in and

out of my legs, then curled into a ball under the table.

I had to concentrate on chopping herbs and not my fingers as I told him the story. "A few days ago, I got a call from Ian McCullough at the Covington Library. He had a book for me to restore for their new children's wing. I drove over there Friday morning to pick up the book and was surprised to see it was a copy of *Beauty and the Beast.*"

He stopped chopping and I noticed his grip on the knife was so tight, his hand was shaking. "Was it . . ." He shook his head and rolled his shoulders as if he were in a boxing ring, gearing up for a fight.

"Yes, it was the book I gave you and Emily."

"So. She sold it." He clamped his jaw shut, pressed his lips together. After a moment, he let out the breath he was holding and slowly continued his chopping.

Men. I rolled my eyes, then said, "No, Max, she didn't sell the book."

His chopping stopped again and he flashed a suspicious frown at me, but said nothing.

"It's true," I insisted. "Two weeks after you *died,* someone broke into Emily's house and stole the book. It's been missing for three years and it just resurfaced this week."

Kind of like you did, I thought, but didn't say it out loud.

"So . . . wait. I'm not following you. Explain how —"

"Just let me finish," I said, knowing his mind would drift off to Emily if I didn't get the story out fast. "I knew the book had been stolen from Emily years ago, so I had to break the news to Ian. He let me know who he bought it from, and I drove to that bookstore to talk to the owner, Joe Taylor. I wanted to find out who sold it to Joe — you know? Anyway, when I got there, I found Joe dead. His throat was cut."

That shook Max up. "Jeez, Brooklyn. I'm sorry."

I grimaced. "You will be when you hear what the murder weapon was."

"What do you mean?"

"Someone slit Joe's throat open with a special kind of knife. It's a papermaker's knife. Four-inch, square-headed blade, common as anything. I think I have three or four of them. You probably do, too."

His eyes narrowed. "Yeah. So?"

"So after I was questioned by the police, I went to my car and found my tire had been slashed."

"Sounds like you were having a bad day."

"You might say that. Anyway, whoever did

it left the weapon stuck in my tire. It was a Japanese paper knife, an expensive one. It had the letters M-A-X carved on the handle."

He frowned again and stared at the onions as though he might find enlightenment there. Then he looked up at me. "Say that again."

"I think you heard me."

"But how in the world . . . Wait." His eyes widened and he pointed the chopping knife at me. "You can't be thinking that I would ever . . . No. There's no way. First of all, I don't even know this bookseller guy. What'd you say his name was? Joe? And second, I haven't left this godforsaken mountain in three years. I had nothing to do with this. I don't know how —"

"I know you didn't do it, Max," I said as patiently as I could. "But someone's trying to make it look like you did. They had your tools. They had the book you gave Emily. They put the book out on the market to lure you out. They killed Joe to lure you out. And that means they must know you're alive."

"Ah, crap," he muttered, then followed the word up with an expletive stream that threatened to turn the air blue. Finally out of words, he let his brute strength take over and he plunged his knife into the chopping

124

block with all the force of a category-three hurricane. "Damn it, I know who —"

The kitchen door flew open and I screamed. Derek and Gabriel stomped into the house, looking wild, wet, windblown, and sexier than any two men had a right to be. Especially after scaring me half to death.

But seriously? If I took their picture right now, it would land on the cover of *People* magazine's Two Sexiest Men in the World Edition. Just saying.

"Thank God," I uttered, and wrapped my arms around Derek's neck. I could feel the cold and wet seeping into me, but I didn't care. I'd never been so happy to see him.

"Find anyone out there?" Max asked.

"No."

I grabbed Gabriel and hugged him, too. "I'm glad you're safe."

"No worries, babe." He grinned as he took a dish towel off the counter and wiped some of the rain from his face and neck.

"Let me get some more towels," Max muttered, and stalked out of the room.

"Did you tell him?" Derek asked quietly.

"Yes," I said, staring at the door Max had disappeared through. "And I think he was about to tell me who's responsible when you guys walked in."

Max came back into the kitchen a moment later and handed towels to Derek and Gabriel. "I'll make dinner for everyone; then you all need to leave. It's too dangerous for you here."

"You know who's doing this, Max," I said, grabbing hold of his arms. "Tell us who it is. We can help you."

He pushed my hands away. "You don't want to know. You've never dealt with anyone like them. They're relentless. If you leave tonight after dark, you might be able to slip out of town and go back to your lives. Just leave me alone. I can deal with it."

Gabriel chuckled as he walked out of the room.

Derek leaned his hip against the butcherblock island in the middle of the kitchen. "I can assure you, we're not leaving without you."

"I'm not going anywhere."

"I'm afraid you are," Derek said. "We'll get you back to Dharma and keep a security detail with you until the person you're hiding from is found and arrested. Otherwise, you'll have the police climbing all over this place within hours."

"You would turn me in?"

Derek shrugged.

Max considered this as he turned on the heat under the frying pan, poured in olive oil, then tossed in the minced garlic. Immediately it began to sizzle. Thirty seconds later, he added the piles of chopped onion and stirred, coating everything with oil. Finally, he looked up and said, "I can't go back."

"Someone's setting you up," Derek said brusquely. "Either you go back with us and try to clear your name or you'll be arrested for murder." Derek pulled out his phone and swiped the screen until he found a picture and showed it to Max. I figured it was the photo he took on Friday of the knife in my tire.

Reluctantly, Max stared at the phone screen for a minute, then handed it back. "It looks like one of the knives I owned, but I didn't slash your tire, Brooklyn. I left everything behind in my studio when I left. All my tools, my journals — everything."

"I know you didn't do it, Max."

"Yes, we know it wasn't you," Derek said. He sounded tired. Then in a heartbeat he sprang forward, gripping Max's arm and swinging him around to look him straight in the eyes. "But I won't allow Brooklyn to be terrorized by whoever's behind this. If you're not willing to tell us who you think killed Joe and planted this knife in Brooklyn's tire, I won't think twice about calling the police and telling them exactly where you are."

They stared at each other for another moment; then Max nodded. "Understood."

Derek stepped back, satisfied with Max's response.

Max straightened his apron, glanced around, then said, "There's a loaf of French bread in the pantry. Can someone butter it for garlic toast?"

"I'm on it," Derek said, as if nothing monumental had just transpired between them. But as he walked to the pantry closet, he passed behind me and suddenly I was in his arms. He held on to me tightly for almost a minute and kissed my neck, then let me go and continued on to the pantry.

"All rightie, then," I muttered, dazed but pleased.

Gabriel walked back into the kitchen. "Smells great in here."

I stopped chopping to stare at him. His dark hair was slicked back and still wet from the rain. He'd taken off his jacket, and the black T-shirt he wore defined every muscle in his chest, arms, and shoulders. Even his cheekbones were more defined. His eyes glittered more brightly as he looked at me and winked. How could he look even better than he did a few minutes ago? It was, like, otherworldly.

Is it rude to stare? I didn't care; I couldn't help myself. Just because I was madly in love with Derek didn't mean I couldn't appreciate some other guy's awesomeness.

And there is the answer, I realized with a start. The secret to Derek's appeal versus Gabriel's. Obviously this was a subject to which I'd dedicated long hours of thought, but hadn't reached an acceptable conclusion — until now.

No doubt about it, Derek defined the word *hunk.* He was solid. Tall, dark, handsome, protective, dangerous. Great body — did I mention that? But Derek's feet were planted firmly on the ground, and when he found something he wanted, he took hold of it with both hands and wouldn't let go. Apparently he wanted me, and I was thrilled to let him have his way.

Gabriel's appeal, on the other hand, was more ethereal, his energy more vibrant, his lean looks more elegant. He was dangerous, too, and there was no doubt in my mind that he'd killed before. But his danger to women? That classic bad-boy attitude. A love affair with Gabriel would be high drama, wild sex, and fast burnout.

Hmm.

Speaking of drama, it occurred to me that

ever since I'd met Derek, we'd been over-whelmed by high drama. Namely, murder. Victims. Suspects. I'd been involved in so many criminal investigations, I'd lost count. The fact was, I had never even seen a dead body until I met Derek. Had he brought the murder magnet Karma into my world? Or had he simply entered my world right when I needed him most?

I'd have to give that more thought.

"Dinner will be ready in thirty minutes," Max said as he filled a large pot with water for pasta. "Then we'll have a nice conversation about you all leaving."

"Not gonna happen," Gabriel said amiably, "but the dinner invitation is appreciated. That pasta sauce smells incredible."

"Thanks."

"The bread is ready to go in the broiler," Derek said. "Give me a three-minute warning and I'll turn on the heat."

"Perfect," Max said.

"Now, while I was outside," Derek said, switching subjects, "I dug the spent bullet from your veranda out front." He pulled a flattened bullet from his pants pocket, held it up to the light, then placed the chunk of mangled brass on the chopping-block surface.

Gabriel moved in, picked up the bullet,

and studied it. He pulled out a small pocket-knife and scraped at the edges.

"Hand loaded," he said, casting a meaningful glance at Derek.

"Yes," Derek said, nodding as though he'd already come to that conclusion. Nothing much got past him.

"Risky," Gabriel mused.

"What're you talking about?" I asked.

"Our shooter packs his own bullets," Gabriel explained.

Max stepped closer now, picked up the bullet, turned it over in his hand. "Oh yeah. Hand packed."

"How can you tell?" I asked.

With the tip of his knife, Gabriel pointed out minute grooves in the bullet's surface. "Shape of the bullet. The crimping pattern along the seal. Lot of ways to tell the difference."

"Right." I stared at it but still didn't have a clue. Maybe it was a secondary sex characteristic that allowed men to more easily recognize a hand-packed bullet. Like male pattern baldness, this was something I would never have the joy of experiencing.

"Why would anyone hand pack a bullet?" I asked. "It can't be any cheaper, can it? Are they zealots? Control freaks? I don't get it."

"It does have something to do with control, darling," Derek said. "An experienced gun enthusiast will load his own cartridges, increasing or decreasing the amount of powder in order to add to his accuracy or to customize the performance of a particular shotgun or rifle. In the long run, for serious gun owners, it can be cost effective."

"Good to know," I said, astonished by his knowledge of such matters. I smiled at all three men. "Okay, 'nuf said about guns. Are we absolutely sure there's no one out there?"

Gabriel shot me a look. "If he'd still been out there, we would've found him."

Derek met my gaze and nodded reassuringly. "Yes, he's gone, love."

"Or *she's* gone," Max muttered, his tone edgy with anger.

What?

Oblivious, Max continued stirring the sauce until he finally turned around and flinched at the sight of three pairs of curious eyes staring back at him.

CHAPTER 10

"You think it's a woman?" Derek said in surprise.

"Possibly." Max kept stirring. "Could someone grab two bay leaves from the jar in the pantry and throw them in here?"

I looked around and my two companions stared back at me with blank faces. *Okay, fine.* I raced to the pantry, then returned and slid two leaves into the tomato sauce. "Come on, Max. Tell us who you think is behind this."

"It makes sense that it's a woman," Gabriel said with a nod.

I frowned at him. "Why?"

"All the drama, the clues, the various scenarios. If a man wanted Max dead, he would've just shot him. But this person — this woman, I'm guessing — wants him exposed. She's letting go of clues inch by inch. It's theatrical. Messy. Not straightforward. In other words, female."

"So you're saying women are sneakier than men?"

He grinned. "No, I'm saying women are more clever, more complicated. Men are basic. Easy. *Un*complicated."

"Stupid?" I suggested with a smile.

He chuckled. "Sometimes."

"I'm kidding, sort of," I said. "I see your point about women, but I happen to know a lot of complicated men. Three of them are here in this room."

Gabriel glanced around and shrugged. "Maybe so, but I still think it's safe to say that none of us would go to this much trouble to kill a man. Personally, I would take out a gun and shoot him in the head."

I winced. "That's sweet."

"No, that's simple." Gabriel glanced around the room. "Am I right?"

"Fairly accurate, I'd say," Derek said.

"I agree with what you're saying," Max said, "but I'm also hedging my bets. There's a guy in my past who could have come up with all the clues and scenarios you're talking about. He thrived on that crap."

Derek's expression was guarded as he asked, "Is this the man who caused you to stage your own death?"

Max's jaw clenched and he seemed to debate whether to answer Derek's question.

He didn't have to. It was obvious to all of us that the answer was yes.

"Yes," he said at last.

I wasn't surprised, but it saddened me that someone in Max's past had hated him enough to destroy his life. It also bothered me that as close as I'd been to Max back then, I still didn't have a clue who he was talking about.

"There are two people, actually," Max said, his voice tinged with bitterness. "A man and a woman. Both of them are capable of straightforward, gun-to-the-head murder, but they also have the kind of warped personalities that would get off on playing the kind of games you've been talking about."

"They sound charming," I said.

Max gave me a look. "They would've stopped at nothing to destroy me, even if it meant going after my family, my friends, my loved ones."

"I have to wonder why the police didn't do more to help."

"The police were useless," he insisted. "They didn't believe me because my enemies were pillars of society and I was . . . well, I wasn't a pillar of anything."

I took hold of his arm. "You were a respected artist. A teacher. You gave lectures and classes all over the country."

"Yeah, that and five dollars will get you a grande latte." He went back to stirring his sauce.

"Who were these people, Max?" I asked. "I swear you can trust us. We're here for you."

"Brooklyn's right," Derek said. "It's time you let us know who you're afraid of. We can help."

Max wrapped his arm around my shoulder and squeezed me for comfort. I gazed up at him and said, "Not all police are like the ones you dealt with. We've been working with a pair of San Francisco detectives who won't give a damn how powerful your enemies are. If the people you're talking about killed Joe, these two detectives will take them down."

Gabriel leaned his hip against the counter by the sink. "I'm not a great lover of cops, but I still don't get why they wouldn't help you. Was there something else going on back then?"

"Yeah." Max went back to his saucepan and studiously avoided making eye contact with me. "I was kind of into drugs back then."

"But wasn't everyone?" Gabriel said. "Why would they single you out?"

Max clenched his teeth. "I'd gotten busted a few years earlier. One of the local cops decided to hold a grudge."

"You were into drugs, Max?" I couldn't keep the shock out of my voice.

Max turned and rolled his eyes at me. "Yes, Brooklyn. And so was everyone else. Except you, Miss Goody Two-shoes."

"That's not fair," I said. "I wasn't like that." *Was I?*

Derek gazed at me from across the center table. "You never did drugs, Brooklyn?"

"No. I never wanted to." I frowned and tried to explain away my deep, dark secret. "You've met my parents. Who needs drugs with them around?"

Gabriel smirked. "There's definitely a natural high going on in that house."

"I know, right?" I smiled but still felt a little defensive, so I folded my arms across my chest. "Look, despite my parents' wackiness, they were always happy. They raised us to enjoy life. I think we all do that pretty well now. I mean, clearly I'm not perfect — far from it. But I just never felt the need to get high."

Max grabbed plates from the cupboard. "Some of us weren't that lucky."

"On the other hand," I added quickly, "my family makes wine and I do love to drink it.

So I guess you could call that my drug of choice."

"You're a wild woman, Brooklyn Wainwright," Gabriel said, grinning at me.

"Yeah, right," I said, scoffing.

Derek smiled at me and winked. Okay, he was wild enough for both of us.

The cat came walking up to me so I stooped to pet its soft fur. I could hear him purring as he rubbed against me. "I think Clyde likes me."

"Pasta's ready," Max said, and drained the contents of the pot into a colander. "Three-minute warning."

Derek turned on the broiler, then squatted down to check the level of the flame. Standing, he turned to Max and said, "To get back to the original question, who do you think is behind all this?"

Max poured the drained pasta into the large pan with the sauce and tossed everything together. "I would be willing to swear it's one of two people, or it might be both of them working together. My old boss, Solomon, and an ex-girlfriend, Angelica Johansen."

"Oh, my God. I know them," I said. "Are you sure?"

"Does Solomon have a last name?" Gabriel asked, already typing something into his smart phone.

"Probably, but he never used it. Just went by Solomon. I think he tried to get his name changed legally but the court wouldn't go for it. I don't think anyone knew his last name."

"Huh. Like someone else I know," I said, casting a long look at Gabriel, who'd never revealed his last name to me. Even his business card simply read GABRIEL.

Derek checked on the toasting bread, then turned to me. "What did you know of these people, Brooklyn?"

I finished setting napkins and flatware around the kitchen table as I told them of the brief time I worked with Solomon and Angelica.

It was at least ten years ago, when I was twenty-one or twenty-two. I was an over-achiever so I'd already gotten my master's in art, and Max knew I was thinking of becoming a teacher. He was a rising star at the Sonoma Institute of the Arts and he recommended me for a summer job teaching a bookbinding class. It was a great opportunity for me and I was thrilled. But first I had to meet his boss, Solomon, the head of the department.

"I liked Solomon a lot at first," I said as I took the bowls Max filled and put them at each place setting. "He came across as funny and charming. I watched him teach, too, and he was charismatic, very attractive, and really artistic. But over the weeks I saw that he could also be demanding and mercurial. I tried to stay out of his way as much as possible, but he threw these Friday-night parties and expected the entire staff to attend, so I had to deal with him on those occasions. It was uncomfortable."

"Did that bastard hit on you?" Max demanded.

Gabriel opened a bottle of red wine, and Derek brought out the bread, golden brown and fragrant. He tossed all the slices into the bread basket Max had provided. I smiled at him as we sat down to eat. Everything looked and smelled heavenly. I had to take a bite before I could do anything else.

"This is fabulous," I said. Seemed like I hadn't eaten in hours and that just wasn't right. The sauce was tangy, rich, and chunky, and it made me and my taste buds stand up and cheer.

"Anyway, yes, he did hit on me. Frankly, he hit on every woman," I admitted finally. "But I just played dumb. It wasn't hard to do since I was such a newbie. I got out of more than a few awkward situations by acting like I simply didn't know what in the world these guys were talking about." I batted my eyelashes to demonstrate.

"He was an arrogant jerk," Max said.

I stared at him. "I just now realized why everyone was always leaving the party to go to the bathroom. That's where the drugs were, right?"

"Good guess."

"Just like every other party in the known universe," Gabriel said, then added, "This pasta is fantastic."

"Thanks," Max said, then peered at me. "You really were a youngster back then."

"Young and ridiculously naive."

"Darling, thinking back, can you imagine Solomon killing someone?" Derek asked.

I thought about it as I scooped up another bite of pasta, then shook my head. "He was creepy, but not in a murderous way. Not back then, anyway."

"Tell us about the woman," Derek said, pouring a bit more wine into my glass. Ah, cabernet.

Max swallowed a bite of pasta, then said, "Angelica was a renowned letterpress artist and teacher. Her résumé was awesome."

"Her résumé," I said, choking back a laugh. "Is that what they're calling it these days?"

"Very funny," he said, making a face.

I turned to Derek. "She was nutso."

Max chuckled. "Well, now I might agree. But back then, I just thought she was a little intense."

"You say *tomato*." I put my fork down. "Come on, Max. She never let you out of her sight. Her possessiveness was weird. Verging on psycho, really. She was especially vigilant whenever I was around."

"I don't remember that."

"Because she didn't show you that side of her. But I caught the vibe right away." I popped a warm chunk of bread into my mouth and savored the flavor. "You know I always looked up to you, Max. We were friends. I hate to say it, but Angie seemed jealous of our history together."

Gabriel leaned forward. "Did you spend much time with her?"

"God, no," I said quickly. "Whenever I came around, she would make up an excuse to leave, always dragging Max off with her. The few times I spoke with her alone, she mostly issued veiled threats."

"I'm sorry to say, I can believe that," Max said.

"She threatened you?" Derek looked aghast. "You can't be serious."

"It was usually vague," I said, "but basically she warned me not to hang around

Max and their friends, or she'd make me sorry I was ever born." I took a sip of wine. "Now that we're talking about it, I remember being scared to death of her. I was afraid she would slip something into my drink someday, so I stopped going to the department parties."

"I'm sorry," Max said, then slid into a thoughtful silence.

"It's not your fault," I said after a minute.

"Yeah, it is."

We all ate quietly for a while, each of us absorbed in our own little worlds.

"This pasta is incredible," I said, trying to coax Max back to the conversation.

"Thanks," he said, tearing off a slice of toast. "It's funny now to hear your side of things, Brooklyn. You're right: Angie was too possessive. I knew it all along. But she was gorgeous, wildly talented, and larger-than-life, so I put up with it. I thought she made me look good. And, I'll admit, I enjoyed the wild side of her."

"Men," I muttered, not for the first time.

"A man will put up with a lot of grief for a beautiful woman," Gabriel murmured, swirling his wine.

"She was a gorgeous disaster," Max admitted. "And it didn't hurt that Solomon was jealous of my relationship with her."

"No, that wouldn't hurt," Derek said, flashing me a quick grin. "Men can be ridiculous sometimes."

"I can see now that I was a complete idiot," Max said cheerfully. "As Brooklyn would probably concur."

"Well, I would now," I said, and everyone laughed. "But back then, Max was like a celebrity. He had a huge following in the book arts world. His techniques for making paper were considered revolutionary and groundbreaking."

"Okay, now you're getting carried away," Max drawled.

"No, really," I said, looking at Derek and Gabriel. "He had groupies."

"They were my students," Max protested.

I laughed. "No, they were your fans. Solomon absolutely should have been jealous of you. You were years younger, taller, and better-looking than him. He was your boss, so I guess he could have fired you, but he couldn't afford to lose you. I'm sure a decent percentage of people enrolled in classes at the institute because of you."

"Thank you for the positive PR, Brooklyn, but Solomon was mainly jealous of my relationship with Angelica, not my work. After we'd been together awhile, Angie confessed that she and Solomon had dated briefly in the past, before I came to work there. She often mentioned that he wanted her back. But for some reason, she was in love with me."

"Do you think she was seeing Solomon on the side?" I asked.

"Ah, a love triangle," Derek mused. "Murder would be a natural outcome."

I couldn't help but smile when he talked like that. Clyde the cat wound his fuzzy body around my ankles, then planted his entire body on my feet.

"We were hardly in a love triangle," Max demurred. "Angie told me about her earlier fling with Solomon only to keep me on my toes. She insisted she didn't like him anymore, but tolerated him to keep the peace. At the time I thought she was sincere, but now who knows what the truth was?"

"The institute sounds like a hotbed of thrills and intrigue," Derek said dryly.

"Apparently, it was rife with drugs and promiscuity," I said, then laughed ruefully. "And I was completely in the dark."

Gabriel wound a small amount of pasta around his fork, then looked at Max. "So why do you think the shooter might be Angelica, if she professed to love you so much?"

We gobbled up pasta as Max collected his

thoughts.

"I'd been thinking of quitting my job because Solomon was making my life miserable," he said. "His rantings had increased and he was making the strangest departmental decisions. He'd become a petty dictator. One night after we'd been drinking for hours, Solomon suddenly threatened to kill me if I didn't stop seeing Angelica."

"That's bizarre." I stared at him, shocked.

"You have no idea," Max said. "Solomon fancied himself a warrior and he was well-known for collecting exotic weapons. He told me he knew of ways to kill me that wouldn't leave a trace. I took the threat seriously."

"How did I not know this?" I wasn't expecting an answer and didn't get one. But none of it was fair. "He was your boss. You should've reported him to the school."

"Your naïveté is charming," Max said dryly, then faced Derek. "Solomon practically ran the school. He was on the faculty board and they made the decisions concerning scheduling, hiring, firing, which teachers got which classes. All of that."

"So Solomon was starting to lose it," Derek prompted. "Where did Angelica fit in at this point?"

"She was becoming more jealous and irrational with every passing day. I finally accepted that our relationship had run its course and I broke up with her. She wasn't happy about it. She called and e-mailed constantly. Left messages for me everywhere."

"What kind of messages?" I asked.

Max took a bite and chewed slowly, thinking. "She wanted to get back together. But then I would run into Solomon on campus and he would gloat that he and Angelica were dating again. Then I'd get another phone call from Angie denying it. They were both making me nuts. A few months later, I quit my job."

"While I sympathize," Derek said finally, "I still wonder how this relates to you faking your own death."

Max smiled. He'd grown more relaxed as the meal went on. The few sips of wine he'd had must have helped. "About six months after I broke up with Angelica and quit the institute, I met a woman. We fell in love."

"Emily," I said.

"Yes." He sighed. "Emily was wonderful, adorable, kind. She loved children and animals and represented everything that was good in the world. I was crazy in love with her. We announced our engagement and planned a great party to celebrate. A week or two before the party, my cell phone rang. It was Angelica. She'd gotten back together with Solomon a while before this, so I wondered why she was calling."

"Yes, I wonder, too," I said, bemused as always by Angelica's logic.

"She warned me to leave town or go into hiding because Solomon had gone off the deep end and was threatening to kill me again."

"Were you still living in Sonoma?"

"Yes. I'd planned to move to San Francisco, but then I met Emily. She taught first grade at a school near Santa Rosa, just a few miles away, so I stayed in the area. Probably my biggest mistake."

"Get back to the phone call," Derek said, his voice professional, crisp. "What else did Angelica say about Solomon?"

Max shook his head. "She was frantic. She said Solomon was convinced that she and I were still sleeping together. I had a sneaking suspicion that she was the one who'd put that thought into his head. She was always playing games like that with me, testing to see how jealous I could get."

"What a witch," I muttered.

"Yeah, she was. She told me Solomon had threatened to come after Emily, too."

Derek leaned forward. "Did you suspect

she was trying to cause trouble between Emily and you?"

"Absolutely. That was my first thought," he said. "But that night, I parked across the street from Emily's and when I stepped into the street, a car gunned its motor and drove straight for me. I was grazed and thrown backward. I must've hit my head on the sidewalk, because I was unconscious for a little while. When I woke up, I called the police. I'd recognized the car. It belonged to Solomon."

"What did the cops do?"

"Nothing." Max gritted his teeth in disgust.

"Why not?" I asked, outraged.

"Because Solomon was an esteemed professor at the prestigious Art Institute and by then I'd quit the institute. As far as the cops were concerned, I was just another local artist who'd once been busted for smoking pot." He shrugged, though I could see it cost him. "There were no witnesses. Just my word against Solomon's, and guess who they believed?"

"Oh, that's great," I muttered, then explained, "The Sonoma County Sheriff's Department wasn't exactly known for its enlightened views a few years back. They have a new sheriff and things are much better now."

"Lot of good that did me," Max muttered, then shook himself out of his brief bout of self-pity. "So, anyway, I decided to write off the hit-and-run as one of Solomon's drunken rants and ignore it. But over the next five or six weeks, there were a number of disturbing incidents. The brake line in my car was cut, Emily's tires were slashed at school, and then one of her six-year-old students was kidnapped."

"He kidnapped one of her schoolkids?" I cried. "That's horrifying. Are you sure it was Solomon?"

"I know it was," Max said flatly. "The boy was returned unharmed after twenty-four hours. He told his parents and the police that a nice, tall man in a mask took him to a house in the mountains, gave him hamburgers, and let him watch all his favorite TV shows. His only complaints were that he was blindfolded during the drive and that all the lights were out in the house."

"So they kept the kid happy and in the dark." Gabriel shook his head in disgust.

"Did you suggest to the police that they investigate Solomon for the kidnapping?" Derek wondered.

"Yeah. And I was warned that I could be sued for slander for dragging a good man's name through the mud."

"What happened when your brake line was cut?" Gabriel asked.

"I was lucky," he said. "One of my neighbors was also my mechanic. He would check out my car whenever he had time, and he noticed it before I'd driven very far. But later, I was able to use the brake-line story to stage my death."

"But why was Solomon doing this?" I shook my fist, appalled at the injustice. "What was the big deal? Not that you were, but even if you had been screwing around with Angie, why would he go to these lengths? He needed to snap out of it and get a life. Damn fool."

Derek reached for my hand. "People have killed for less."

"True." I guess I was getting a little overwrought, but, really, that guy was a nut job.

"Solomon was obsessed," Max said, "and he was getting worse all the time. And every day or so, Angie would call and warn me again."

"I'll bet she was in on it," I grumbled.

Gabriel nodded. "She was getting off on the danger and the drama."

"One of the last straws," Max continued, "was when I got into my car one morning and heard ticking."

"You're kidding," I whispered.

"No. I tore out of there and called the police. They wouldn't even come and check my car. They just blew me off, pardon the pun. I was completely on my own."

I reached over and touched his arm. "Poor Max."

"What happened to your car?" Derek asked.

Max paused, then forced himself to answer. "The following morning, I went out to the car and found an envelope tucked under the windshield wiper. I opened it up and a card slipped out. It said *BOOM*."

"Oh, what a creep." I rubbed my arms. "That gives me chills."

"I was half insane by now," he admitted. "The police were certain I was a deranged troublemaker. I probably was. Deranged, anyway. I was desperate but helpless. I'd never felt like that before."

"I can imagine."

"Mostly, I was scared to death that something horrible would happen to Emily. The kidnapping had almost destroyed her."

"I'm so sorry, Max."

"It had been going on for about a month when Emily's mother, Laura, was attacked."

"Emily's mother was attacked?" I couldn't

take it all in. Who would carry out such a relentless campaign against another human being and his loved ones? And how had I not known about it while it was happening?

"Laura made the mistake of coming to visit my place the day Solomon tricked up my stairway with an electrical-wire device. She took a bad tumble and wound up in the hospital with multiple injuries, including electrocution."

"She could've been killed," Derek said.

"Yes. By the time the police arrived, Solomon had managed to whisk away the wire, but Laura told me what happened. She's not a flighty person. If she said she was tripped and electrocuted at the same time, I knew it was all true. I swear, Brooklyn, by then I was considering hiring a hit man to kill Solomon."

"I don't blame you," I said darkly.

"The only thing that made sense was to fake my own death. So I took Robson into my confidence and he helped me clean up my affairs, write up a will, and arrange my own death."

"Did my father help you, too?" I asked a little too sharply.

Max frowned, then admitted, "Yes, and I was damn grateful. After I told Robson the whole story, he called your father first thing.

He's the one who met me in Big Sur and helped rig my car to drive off the cliff. Then he drove me up to Oregon and we camped out in the Columbia Gorge for a few weeks until Robson completed the purchase of this house."

It was my turn to frown. "But I remember Dad attending your memorial service."

Grinning, Max said, "Your father would make a great spy. He drove back and forth from the campsite to Dharma at least three or four times, just to keep anyone from suspecting anything. And he and Robson spread the word around Dharma and Sonoma that my brakes had malfunctioned. I guess my paranoia was contagious, because they were both determined to cover my tracks completely."

"And so they did," I muttered. Guru Bob had found him a safe place to live and Max became Jack, a goat farmer in Point Reyes. And my father had known all along. How did I feel about that?

"Did Dad ever come visit you here?" I asked. "Had you thought about returning to real life at some point?"

Again, Max paused and frowned, uncomfortable with the questions.

That was when I lost it. Jumping up from the table, I said, "Max, were you going to live in hiding forever? Did you guys have an endgame strategy? What the hell were you going to do here for the next twenty years? Was anyone monitoring Solomon and Angelica for you? What about Emily?"

Max threw his napkin down and glared at me. "I did this for Emily! For her parents. For those little kids in her class, damn it! God, how much more damage was I willing to inflict on them? I needed to get out of their lives before anything else happened. I told you I was desperate, Brooklyn. Maybe I wasn't thinking straight, but I did what I thought was right at the time."

He pushed away from the table, grabbed his empty bowl and utensils, and put them in the sink.

"Okay, I'm sorry," I said, grabbing him from behind in a hug. "I just . . . God, I mourned you. I missed you. I'm sick about what they did to you. I wish you would have said something. We have solidarity in Dharma. We could have protected you. We could have helped."

He turned and returned my hug. "Robson helped. Your father helped. We talked about finding the right time for me to return. We came up with all sorts of excuses to explain why I'd been gone. I decided I would claim amnesia from the dive off the cliff. Your father was the one monitoring Solomon's activities to figure out when I could return, but nothing had changed so far."

"My father is quite the little spymaster," I muttered, realizing now that the three of them had to have been in contact over the past three years.

Derek stood and took his bowl to the sink. "Angelica must have suspected all this time that you weren't really dead, since she's the one who suggested you disappear."

"Yeah, she is," Max said warily as he carried the two pasta pots to the sink counter.

Derek turned. "But if she is indeed the one behind all this, why did she never do anything about it until recently? Why wait until now?"

"I have no idea."

I gathered up the napkins. "Do you think she stole the book from Emily?"

"It had to be her," Max said with certainty. He took the napkins from me, opened a side door to reveal a small laundry room, and tossed them into a basket on top of the washer. "She was so jealous of Emily. Every time Angie called, she'd make some snide remark or take a dig at Emily." He closed the laundry room door. "Look, I hope you all know I'm not being boastful when I talk about her jealousy and possessiveness. It was sick and twisted, nothing to be proud of."

"We know that, Max." I patted his shoulder, then began to clear the rest of the pasta bowls and the bread basket off the table. I stacked them in front of Derek, who had appointed himself chief dishwasher.

"Emily's book was stolen three years ago," Derek said as he rinsed out the bowls. "Why didn't Angelica do anything about it until this week?"

"Maybe Solomon is dead," Gabriel put forward. "And now she wants you back."

"But why would she kill Joe Taylor?" I asked. "That's what bothers me most. Only the sickest kind of mind would think that murder was the best way to attract attention."

"I think Solomon had to be the one who killed your friend Joe," Max said, scowling as he scraped the leftover sauce into two containers, then stacked them inside the freezer.

"Why do you think so?" Derek asked as he filled the pots with soap and hot water to soak.

Max thought for a few seconds, then shrugged. "He had such a sadistic streak, I can't put it past him."

"You may be right," Derek said. A minute

later, he tossed the dishcloth on the sink, and I watched him turn from domestic house guy to ruthless security expert. "Max, is there someone you can call on to watch your house and take care of the dog and cat?"

"And the goats," I added.

"Yes, the goats," Derek said dryly. "You see, we're not leaving here without you."

Max bared his teeth and puffed out his chest. He was a few inches taller than Derek and probably outweighed him by forty pounds. But Max had the soul of an artist, not a fighter, and after a few long moments of posturing, he seemed to recognize who the true alpha dog in this pack was.

"Fine," Max said, throwing in the towel. "I'll call my neighbor, Sam. I pay his sons to help me with the goats, and Sam has a key to the house. He'll take care of Bucky."

"That about covers it," Derek said. "What about the cat?"

Max picked up the furry beast. "Clyde's coming with me."

CHAPTER 11

Once Max resolved to leave, the first thing he did was call his nearest neighbors, who sent their teenage son, Nick, over to pick up Bucky. Since Nick also helped Max with the goats, he went to the barn and fed them while Max got his things together. Max was packed and ready by the time Nick came back inside. Nick promised Max he would come by every day to feed and check on the goats and pick any figs that ripened while Max was gone.

I saw Max slip Nick a hundred-dollar bill and watched the kid's eyes light up. Then Nick gathered up Bucky's doggy stuff and took off.

"Brooklyn, can you get Clyde into his carrier?" Max called from down the hall.

Derek laughed at the look of panic on my face. "You can do it, darling."

"Easy for you to say," I muttered, then dutifully searched the living room for

Clyde's carrier. I found the small, sturdy, duffel-type pet carrier in the front closet, then looked around for Clyde. "Here, kitty, kitty."

This was not going to be pretty. Clyde seemed to like me and I wanted to keep it that way, because it was such a rare experience. Cats didn't generally take to me, even though I really liked them. For example, my neighbors' cats, Pookie and Splinters, showed me nothing but contempt no matter how much I showered them with love, attention, and food. At best, they ignored me, and at worst, well, it hurt to think about it. Let's just say that their pictures could be found on Wikipedia under the category Cats Who Hate Me.

"Meow."

"Huh?" *Hey, what's this?* Clyde was rubbing his face against my ankle, purring loudly.

"Hello there, cutie," I whispered, then stooped down to stroke his furry coat. Would he scratch my eyes out if I picked him up? But he just looked up at me with something like adoration, and I wondered if maybe he'd been isolated on this farm too long. He really seemed to love me a lot. Was I delusional? But he bopped my ankle again and I wasn't going to argue with the facts.

This cat was into me.

"Here goes nothing." I picked him up and carried him over to the small carrier. He didn't protest or drive his claws into me, just jumped inside, all on his own. I snapped the top shut.

"Best cat ever," I said proudly.

"Excellent job, darling," Derek said. I could tell he was trying not to laugh.

"Clyde digs me."

He chuckled. "So do we all."

Max carried his own large duffel bag into the living room and left it by the front door. Walking into the kitchen, he opened another door and said, "Brooklyn, come with me for a minute."

I flashed a puzzled look at Derek, but followed Max through a door I hadn't noticed before. It led to a basement via a precariously steep stairway, so I took my time going down. Max stood in the center of the brightly lit but windowless room with his arms spread out. "What do you think?"

I glanced around. It took me a few long seconds to figure out what I was doing down here, but I finally recognized that this was his papermaking studio. Dozens of samples of his work were pinned to the walls. Every surface was covered with rough sheets of handmade paper in various colors and shapes. And they were all stunning works of art.

"Oh, my God, Max," I said, my voice hushed in awe. "These are incredible. I can't believe all this is hidden down here."

"I didn't want to take the chance of working upstairs. Sometimes the neighbors come over for dinner." He shrugged. "It was too risky."

I turned slowly in a circle, taking it all in. "And you've never sent anything out? To anyone?"

He sighed. "I couldn't."

"Now, that's a crime. What's this?" I approached a small, ancient letterpress machine in the corner. "No way. You're doing your own typesetting now?"

He shrugged. "I thought I might try to write a book."

"And using a computer is so passé."

Laughing, he said, "That's right. You might have noticed I've got some extra time on my hands. I thought I would teach myself letterpress."

I picked up the setting stick and studied the neatly set metal block letters. "So essentially you can now craft a book from start to finish."

"Gives me something to do," he said modestly.

I laughed and shook my head in wonder. Turning, I stared at one wall covered in different sheets of beautifully raw, rough paper strewn with plant material, tiny flowers, twigs, leaves. There was paper in shades of green more vivid than anything I'd ever seen in nature, shades of crimson so vibrant I had to wonder if he hadn't drawn his own blood to stain it red. But no. Not even blood could achieve such a startling hue.

"How did you get this color?" I asked, touching the fibers to make sure they were real.

"Beets," he said. "I grow them myself. Saves time and money and trips to the store."

I turned and looked at him. "You've gotten better. I didn't think it was possible, but all this is just more proof that you're a freaking genius."

"And you're still crazy," he said, chuckling. "Why don't you grab a few sheets and take them with us? Maybe you can bind them into an album or something."

My eyes goggled. "You mean it? Seriously? I would love to." Instantly, I reached for the pins in the walls and began to gather up all the sheets I could handle. "I probably shouldn't take too many."

He laughed. "Too late. You're a paper pig."

"Fine," I said, laughing with him. "As long as I get all this paper, I can live with that."

"Take all you want, Brooklyn. I know you'll treat my work with love."

"I will." My eyes burned and I walked over and hugged him. "It's so amazing to see you alive and . . . Oh. I need a minute."

He held me for a moment, rubbing my back. "I'm glad you came. And I'm sorry for hurting everyone, but I'm glad we're going to end this thing."

"Me, too."

"Thanks, Brooklyn," he whispered.

I sniffled. "We should get going."

"Yeah." He let me go. "Take some more paper. It's better off going with you than sitting here in this basement."

"Okay." I headed for another wall. "This is like Christmas. I feel like I'm taking Rembrandt paintings off the walls of the Louvre."

"Now you're being ridiculous," he said, then added, "They're more like Van Goghs."

"Oh, shut up, Vincent," I said, laughing. "I think I've taken more than enough."

"Not yet." He waved toward another wall. "Come on, they're all just going to rot down here."

To prove he was serious, he walked over to a table in the corner where more sheets of pale golden handmade paper, thick and rough with deckled edges, were stacked. "Let's take these, too." He held them up for me to see. "They would make some cool journals, wouldn't they?"

"God, yes." I could already picture the bindings I would make for them. "Do you want to pack up any of your equipment?"

"I don't think much of it'll fit in the Bentley," he said wryly.

"Well, not the big stuff," I said, glancing at an industrial-sized sink in the corner. "But you could take some screens and tools with you."

"I was planning to. I hate having nothing to do."

"And maybe you'd like to pack up some of your goat cheese to take along," I said, trying to be subtle.

He laughed again as he gathered his tools. "I made some a few days ago with dried cherries. Tastes incredible on sweet oat crackers."

"If you insist."

On the long, winding drive back home, the four of us huddled in the Bentley and argued and brainstormed. Gabriel and I sat in the back and let Max, the tallest, brawniest of the guys, sit in the front, since he never would have been able to squeeze into the back.

We debated the best way to keep Max safe without alerting the entire world to the fact that he was alive and well and hiding in Dharma. His enemies were already responsible for one death. We didn't want to add to the body count.

"I hate this," Max blurted. "I've been taking care of myself for years and now, all of a sudden, I'm sitting in a Bentley, for God's sake, letting you guys take over. It's not easy."

"I imagine not," Derek said. "But you'll get used to it."

Max, Gabriel, and Derek all argued about the situation, with me throwing in a comment now and again. I knew Max was more than a little demoralized by the situation, but we all told him to let that go.

I was concerned that since his enemies had already tracked him to Marin County, they would easily follow us back to Dharma. But Derek and Gabriel had run another circumference check of Max's property an hour before we left. They were fairly certain no one had followed us from Max's farm, but the Bentley was so conspicuous. Anyone could've seen us driving down the main street of Point Reyes Station on our way back to Sonoma County.

I once again brought up the unpromising possibility that the shooter had been simply a hunter with bad aim. But even I knew I was grasping at straws.

We changed topics, hashing out the big question still on all our minds: Why now? What had happened recently to cause Angelica — for want of a better suspect — to put the book on the market and do it in such a way that it would attract my attention and ultimately lure Max out into the open?

Again, we discussed the possibility that Solomon was dead. Gabriel made quick work of quashing that prospect by Googling him on his smart phone and searching for him on Facebook. Solomon had posted an updated class schedule on his Facebook page that very morning.

So yes, Solomon was alive.

Maybe it was Angelica who was dead. I was convinced that the only way this scenario worked was if, on her deathbed, she had confessed to Solomon that Max was still alive.

"Stranger things have happened," Gabriel murmured, and checked her out online. He also found her Facebook page and reported that she was still teaching at the Art Institute.

Since Gabriel and I were sitting together, he passed me his phone. As much as I hated staring at Angie's Facebook page with all the vanity photographs she'd posted of herself, I had to give thanks for social media and search engines. They made it so much easier for all of us to snoop around in other people's lives.

And speaking of snooping, I made a mental note to look up Emily's name on Facebook later, when Max wasn't around.

"Where are you planning to hide me?" Max asked, his tone self-mocking.

I leaned forward. "We're driving straight to my parents' house."

He whipped around. "I'm not putting your parents in danger. Any of those people driving behind us could be following us with guns."

He was right, darn it. I could see Derek's eyes in the rearview mirror, narrowing in thought at the likelihood of our being tailed. If he was alone in the car, he would probably be able to evade anyone following him by turning the car into a racing machine and outrunning them. But with a car full of people, he didn't have that option now.

"Would you be open to staying at one of

my brothers' houses for a few days?" I asked.

Max turned in his seat and I could see his mouth twisting as he pondered the idea. "Yeah, I guess so. Your brothers can both defend themselves."

"Yes, they can," Derek said.

But then I thought of my friend Robin, who was living with Austin, and my decision was made. "I'll call Jackson."

CHAPTER 12

It was after ten o'clock when we pulled into Jackson's driveway. His house was perfectly situated on the top of a hill with 360-degree views that would allow us to see the entire valley. I was certain Max would be safe here for as long as he stayed.

A while ago in the car, I'd reached Jackson on my cell phone and explained the situation. It was fine with him, since he wasn't going to be home for a few days.

"Where are you?" I'd asked.

He'd hesitated, then said, "Paris."

"Paris, Texas?" I wondered, half kidding.

"No."

"What are you doing in Paris, France?"

"You don't want to know."

My brother traveled a lot on business, but seeing as how his main business was the commune winery, I didn't see why he was trying to keep the trip a big secret.

Now as we all hurried toward the house

with Max's things, I caught up with Derek. "Do you think we should call Inspector Lee?"

"No," Max said from right behind me. "No police. Not yet."

"But, Max —"

"Sorry, but this is my life we're talking about."

I used my key to open up the house, and we walked in and piled Max's belongings near the staircase leading upstairs. I kept Clyde in his cat carrier for now, placing the sturdy bag on the Oriental rug near the hearth.

Max looked around, studied the wall of river rock that surrounded the fireplace, the dark green sofa and two leather chairs, the rough wood coffee table, the entertainment center opposite the fireplace. Then he turned to me. "Nice place."

I nodded. "I hope you'll be safe and happy here."

He brushed his hair back with both hands. "Look, Brooklyn. I don't care if these cops are your pals. The first thing they'll do is arrest me for murder, then ask questions later."

Derek glanced at me but said nothing. We both knew what Max said was true.

As Max crossed the room to check out

the sliding glass door, he said, "Just give me a few days before you call the cops. I need to find some answers first."

"We'll get answers," Derek assured him.

Max turned and stared out at the dark night sky. "I want to talk to Angelica."

I sputtered in protest.

Gabriel was more succinct as he walked in and dropped another duffel bag next to the couch. "Not a good idea."

Max whipped around. "Why not? She'll talk to me."

"Don't go anywhere near her," he warned. "Not unless you're ready to bring in the police. Let us do some investigating first."

"Damn it." He sat on the couch and rested his elbows on his knees. "I guess you're right, but I just feel useless. And I'm worried about Emily. I want to make sure she's safe before anything else happens."

"Then you definitely shouldn't talk to Angelica," I said firmly. I didn't have to add what I was thinking. From the looks on their faces, everyone knew. Emily had been a target before. If crazy Angie knew Max was back in the area, she might be inclined to eliminate her competition.

And once again, I was reminded that Emily still hadn't called me back. Was she simply out of town, or had something sinister happened to her? If I didn't hear from her by tomorrow, I vowed to call her back.

Now I took a moment to gaze around the room. I loved Jackson, but he was definitely my most elusive brother, so I hadn't been here in a while. I'd forgotten how beautiful this place was. One of the men in the commune had come up with the design, and Jackson and a few of the commune members had built the two-story, craftsman-style mountain lodge.

The main room was two stories tall, open and welcoming, with dark wood walls and floors, and one wall that was almost all glass. It overlooked the rocky canyon below and the rolling, vine-covered ridge on the opposite side. The house was surrounded on three sides by a balcony wide and strong enough to hold a hot tub, a barbecue grill, and plenty of patio furniture.

The staircase near the front door led up to three bedrooms and a small office that acted as a balcony overlooking the first-floor living room. I took a minute and jogged upstairs to find the most suitable room for Max. Besides the master bedroom, there was one room that held Jackson's weights and the other was used for a guest room. I checked that there were clean sheets on the bed, then called out Max's name. After I showed him the room, he stowed his duffel bag against the wall, and we walked downstairs to find Derek and Gabriel talking logistics.

"What's up?" Max asked.

"I'll be sleeping here on the couch tonight," Gabriel announced. "Just a precaution."

"You sure that's necessary?" Max said.

"Yes," Derek said, closing the door to any arguments.

"Fine," Max conceded. "So, what's the plan?"

"You hunker down here for a few days," Gabriel said. "Tomorrow morning, if it's not raining, I'll drive back to your farm. I want to find the exact spot where the shooter stood, see if he or she left anything there. He's been careful so far, but if he was in a hurry, he might've neglected to police the area and left a cartridge behind. There might be footprints. A gum wrapper. Who knows?"

Max nodded. "Sounds good."

"And since there's a slim chance that the bad guys will think you're still living there, I'll check to make sure your neighbors are safe."

"Thank you." Max clenched his fists.

"Damn it, I never even thought of that."

"It's okay, Max," I said. "You and I aren't wired to think in those terms, but these guys are."

He gazed sideways at Derek and Gabriel. "Then I guess it's a good thing they're on our side."

"Yeah, it is," I said, smiling.

But Max was still tense. "I told Sam to be careful, but I'd better call him in the morning and make sure he understands. I don't want his boys to go to my place alone."

"Good idea," Gabriel said, keeping his tone casual.

"I'm already tired of this," Max admitted.

"It'll be over soon," I assured him.

"I hope to hell you're right." He paced a few feet, then turned. "I want to see Emily."

"Not a good idea," Gabriel said. "Whoever's behind this might be watching her, too."

"All the more reason to check that she's safe."

I glanced at the men. "I left a phone message for her, but I haven't heard back."

"She could already be in danger," Max said.

I pulled my cell phone out of my bag to double-check my messages, then groaned. "My battery's dead. I can't tell if she called or not."

"Don't you have your charger with you?" Derek asked.

"No, I didn't pack it." Stupid move on my part, but I'd figured we'd be back home by now. My mistake.

"I'll drive back to the city in the morning and pick it up for you," Derek said.

"You will?"

"I know you want to stay here."

"You do?"

His lips twisted in a smile. Of course he knew. There was no way I would simply drop Max off at Jackson's and drive back to the city.

"Look. There's probably another reason why Emily hasn't called you back," Max said, shoving his hands in his pockets. "I've been gone three years. She's moved on by now. I never even gave her a ring. She doesn't even have the book to remember me by."

I stared at him in surprise. "Jeez, Max, it's not like she threw the book away. She was planning to keep it forever. She didn't even want me to restore it."

"Maybe not, but as far as she knows, I've been dead for three years. She might've sold it by now, anyway."

I slapped his arm lightly. "Dude, it was stolen. You need to have a little faith."

"I gave up on faith a long time ago, Brooklyn."

I stared heavenward. "Where's my violin?"

"Brooklyn," Derek said in a warning tone.

"Max knows I love him," I said to Derek, then smacked Max's arm again. "That's a love tap and my little way of telling you to lose the doom-and-gloom attitude. We've all had a long day, and your whimpering is starting to bug me."

He frowned back at me and we had a brief standoff. Finally he said, "I'm a soulful artist, Brooks. Doom and gloom is my stock-in-trade."

"Oh, please." I made a scoffing sound. "You make goat cheese."

He flinched, then choked out a laugh. "Come here." He grabbed me in a choke hold and gave my head a noogie.

"Stop it," I cried, laughing as I slapped at him like a little girl. "I'm too old for this."

He let me go and we both collapsed on the couch. We really were like brother and sister. It was amazing that we'd fallen back into the same old behavior patterns so quickly.

After a minute, I pushed myself off the couch. "I've got something to show you." I found my bag, pulled out *Beauty and the Beast,* and handed it to him.

Max unwrapped the tissue paper and stared at the book for a long time. Opening it, he ran his fingers over the dedication he'd written to Emily a little more than three years ago.

"I'm just going to say this once," I murmured, standing next to the couch. "You should've had more faith in her."

He looked up at me and smiled crookedly. "You said it once already, so that makes twice."

"Okay, smart-ass," I said, smiling. "That's the last time I'll say it."

He studied the book, his slow breaths in and out the only sounds he made. A minute later, the smile was gone as he gazed at me again. "I lost faith in everyone, Brooklyn. I was thirty-two years old, but in a lot of ways, I was still a kid and scared to death. I couldn't deal with the insanity, so I ran. Maybe that was a mistake, but I couldn't see any other way out. And I'd do the same thing again in a heartbeat to keep Emily safe."

"Oh, Max." I sat and wrapped him up in a bear hug, then used his shirt to wipe the sappy tears from my eyes.

Derek and I drove back to my parents' house later that night and managed to get a good night's sleep in my luxuriously decorated bedroom.

When I woke up the next morning, I had a plan fully formed in my mind. I knew how we could find the answers to our biggest questions from last night.

The plan was simple. The Art Institute was close to Dharma, barely eight miles away in nearby Sonoma. The students and professors all lived in the area. Some were in my own family. Why not enlist their help?

"It's not only simple and easy, it's also subtle," I announced, as Mom placed a platter of eggs, bacon, potatoes, and fruit in front of me. She'd insisted on waiting on all of us this morning. There was a smaller plate of toast, butter, and several different jams. Enough to feed a medium-sized country, as usual. "Are we expecting company?"

"Are we?" Mom said cryptically.

"Okay," I said, letting that go. People had been coming and going through our house since I was a little kid. "Anyway, I'll need you and China to help me."

Mom's ears perked up. "I can be subtle. What's the plan?"

Derek walked into the dining room just then and shot me a look of incredulity. No, Mom wasn't known for her subtlety and

Derek knew it, but I figured we could work on it. Derek's eyes narrowed on me. "What plan is she referring to?"

I took a good, long gander at Derek and had to smile. The man looked way too dapper for someone who had awakened in a strange house at the crack of seven o'clock in the morning. *How does he do it?* I wondered. He appeared ready to sit down at a baccarat table in Monaco and ante up two million dollars or so, then parachute over a cliff into shark-infested waters to rescue an errant nuclear device.

And he wasn't even wearing a tuxedo, just jeans with a thick, forest green flannel shirt. So it had to be the British vibe. He'd been born dapper. He'd probably worn dapper diapers. Now, that was a weird image.

I chuckled at the direction of my reverie, then realized he was still watching me as he poured his coffee. He took a sip, then shook his head. "What goes on in that mind of yours?"

His voice was still a bit gravelly, so maybe he did have a tiny chink in his all-too-perfect armor. Good to know.

"You don't want to know," I murmured, taking a bite of toast.

"You're probably right." He sat down next to me, caught my chin, and angled my face so he could kiss me soundly. "Good morning, love."

"Good morning," I whispered.

Mom walked back into the room and set another plate in front of Derek.

"You don't have to cook for us, Rebecca," he said.

"Don't be silly. I love cooking for you." She sat down across from us and sipped from a cup of tea. "Let's hear the plan."

"Yes, let's do hear all about it," Derek said with a touch of sarcasm.

Flipping him a supercilious look, I said, "The thing is, Dharma's a small town. Small-town people pay attention to things going on around them. They see things. They worry. They talk. This is the perfect place to ask questions."

He shook his head but said nothing, so I continued. "I figured I'd walk around town, talk to people. My sisters might know something. They both took classes at the institute. We'll noodle around, ask a few questions, and find out what's going on with Solomon and Angelica."

Derek leaned his elbow on the table — a very un-British thing to do — and stared at me.

"What?" I asked finally.

He rubbed his jaw in frustration. "You do

181

realize these are the sorts of conversation that scare the hell out of me?"

"But this isn't dangerous," I said, grabbing my mug and taking a long sip of coffee. "It's going to be easy. And we need to find out who was shooting at us yesterday."

"Somebody was shooting at you?" Mom cried.

I clamped my mouth shut. *Crap! I am a loose-lipped nincompoop!* Glancing sideways at Derek, I could see he agreed.

"Nobody, Mom," I said quickly. "It was a hunter who was in the wrong . . . um . . ."

"Oh, stop trying to lie," she said. "You've got to be the worst liar in the world."

"I get that a lot," I muttered.

"This is why I don't want you asking questions around town," Derek said. "It's dangerous, and now you've upset your mother."

"Darn tootin', I'm upset," Mom said. She pressed her hands together in a yoga mudra, closed her eyes, and began to breathe deeply.

"I'm sorry, Mom," I said. "Okay, yes, someone did take a shot at us out at Max's farm. Derek's right. It's too dangerous to have you asking questions around town. You could get hurt, and I would never forgive myself."

She popped one eye open. "What kinds of questions are you talking about?"

"Um, well, I was thinking we could ask if there's anyone in the area who reloads their own ammunition. I'll pretend I want to learn how."

"But that's a lie," Mom said, opening both eyes and reaching for her teacup.

"Of course it is."

"You're no good at lying, remember?"

"I'm working on it, Mom."

She thought for a moment. "Maybe we should all learn how to reload."

"Better if you don't," Derek said.

"Anyway," I continued, "if someone gives us a name or two, I thought I would then mention casually that I seem to recall that one of the teachers out at the Art Institute used to do his own reloading."

"Who's that?" Mom asked.

I hesitated. Did I really want to get my mother involved in this whole nasty situation?

"She might as well know what she's getting herself into," Derek said, taking the decision away from me. "His name is Solomon. He goes by the one name only. He's dangerous. Do not mention his name to anyone you speak with."

Mom frowned. "Is he the one who took a

183

shot at you?"

"Possibly."

She raised her fist in the air. "Then let's get him."

"Rebecca, I'm not sure —"

"Don't you worry about me, sweetie," Mom said, waving away Derek's fears. "I'll just be my friendly old self, nattering up my neighbors. You know, people in small towns do like to talk. And you wouldn't believe the things they know about their neighbors."

"I would believe anything at this point," he said. "I just wish you both would opt for more caution."

"But we need to move fast," I said.

"Yes, I agree. But I'm concerned for your safety. The fact is, someone with extremely evil intentions is behind this operation. Don't forget that they've already killed one person and tried to kill one of us."

"That's right," Mom said. "Your book-seller friend was killed."

Derek nodded. "Yes."

"Then we need to get on with it," she said with a determined nod.

I squeezed Derek's arm. "Besides, you'll be around to keep watch on things."

"But I won't be, darling," he murmured, touching my cheek. "I have to go back to the city."

"Oh. Right." I tried not to show my disappointment, but it was impossible. I hadn't forgotten, exactly, but I'd hoped . . . But of course he had to go back to the city. It was Monday, a workday. My sense of time had flown out the window with my phone's dead battery. I used the phone as both a clock and a calendar.

"I'm sorry, love. I'll be back as soon as I can get away."

"Maybe I should go back with you," I said without enthusiasm.

"No, you stay here with your family and Max. I'll drive back tonight and bring your phone charger with me."

"You'll drive all the way out here to do that?"

He chuckled but didn't say a word. He didn't have to. His look said he'd drive to the moon for me. At least, that was my interpretation.

"Thank you," I said. "And please don't worry. We'll be fine. I'll call Gabriel to let him know what we're doing."

"Yes, do call him," Derek said, then checked his wristwatch. "He's already left for Point Reyes, but he expected to be back by noon."

"I forgot he was driving out there." I sighed. I guess I'd forgotten all sorts of things. "Well, then it'll just be me and Mom."

"Take extra care while I'm gone, darling," Derek said, pushing away from the dining table. "You may be stirring up more trouble than you know."

I smiled and hugged him. "I'll be surrounded by my family and friends. This is my town. Nothing bad could ever happen to me here."

"Whoa, sweetie, don't push your luck." Mom's eyes were wide as she quickly rapped her knuckles on the tabletop. "Knock on wood."

CHAPTER 13

Derek and I held hands as we walked out to his car. It was still early so the sun hadn't cleared the hill. The sky was blue and cloudless, but the air was still nippy, though it promised to warm up later. It was so quiet out here, not like the city at all, and we both seemed to notice it at the same time.

The scene was tranquil, uncomplicated, sweet. Naturally anxiety began to dribble through me like an IV drip. Was it my fault that Derek was on the verge of becoming completely domesticated, as my friend Robin had recently observed?

We chatted about the weather and what he planned to accomplish at the office today. He intended to look deeply into Solomon's and Angelica's backgrounds to see if there were any red flags. Even though the local sheriff had considered Solomon a pillar of society a few years back, Derek wasn't convinced — especially in light of what Max had told us about Solomon's wild parties. Was it possible that the man had escaped arrest all this time?

As he spoke, I flashed back to the moment yesterday when he'd matter-of-factly pulled that serious-looking gun from his jacket on his way out to hunt down a killer.

So he wasn't completely domesticated yet. I breathed a sigh of relief at the realization, then wondered how one man could be so normal and yet so dangerous at the same time. I didn't know the answer, but I think it was that very dichotomy in Derek that most appealed to me. Was there something wrong with me that I loved his tough, dangerous side a lot? Was it wrong that I found it thrilling that this guy would go to any lengths, including carrying a gun and hunting down killers, to protect me and the people I loved?

But, hey, I also found it thrilling that he liked to make sandwiches and sit around watching TV, too.

"Your brain is working overtime again," Derek said as he reached out and pulled me closer, moving his hands up and down my arms and across my shoulders.

"Just thinking about how much I'll miss you," I said, and wrapped my arms around him.

"Such a bad liar," he murmured.

"I'm not lying about that," I said, laughing.

"No, you're simply withholding information."

"Never."

He chuckled and we stood holding each other for a while, until he leaned back and looked at me. "I know right now isn't a good time, darling, but once Max's problems are taken care of and things are back to normal, we have to talk."

I didn't like the sound of that. "Is everything okay?"

His eyes were focused on me, intense and indecipherable. "What do you think?"

Am I missing something? "I think everything's wonderful."

His knuckles grazed my jawline and moved down my neck, causing shivers and tingles to rise with his touch.

What does he want from me? I mean, besides the usual sexual favors and mindless devotion.

I was kidding, sort of.

"Are you feeling all right?" I asked, serious now.

"Yes." He kissed me then, touching my lips so tenderly that I went boneless, almost dissolving in his arms. My eyes fluttered open to see him smiling at me in a way that was almost . . . victorious? Had I just capitulated to something? Was there a contest I didn't know about?

"Be careful, please," he murmured, kissing me again. "I love you."

"And I love you," I said. It was getting easier to tell him how I felt, especially when he said it first. Was that so wrong? It wasn't like I needed permission to say it. But it was still nice to hear him say it first. Was I being neurotic? Hell, when it came to matters of the heart, when was I *not?*

He pulled open the car door and slid into the driver's seat. "I'll call you this afternoon when I'm on my way out of the city."

"Okay. Be safe."

He flashed me one of his sexy, twisted grins that made my whole body sit up and take notice. I smiled and waved as he started the engine and drove away.

Instead of racing back into the house, I stopped to pull some weeds growing among the flowers along Mom's walkway.

Derek and I had been together for almost six months now. The fact that we'd managed to maintain a strong relationship, given Derek's secret security assignments and my odd predilection for finding dead bodies, was a monumental achievement. If that wasn't love, what was it, right? So why rock the boat when it looked like smooth sailing ahead?

I mentally rolled my eyes. *Rock the boat? Smooth sailing?* So many clichés, so little time. It was never a good thing to hear myself thinking in clichés.

I had a great-aunt, Aunt Jessica, my dad's father's sister, who spoke only in clichés and the occasional mixed metaphor. Instead of ever giving advice or admonishing, Aunt Jessica would nod gravely and say, "Sleeping dogs." Or she would wink at one of us and murmur, "Bird in the hand."

So from an early age, my siblings and I recognized the true wisdom of her words. We would outdo one another trying to come up with some ridiculous comment to describe a given situation. Finally, my father outlawed all clichés and silly metaphors. He decreed that we were allowed to think only original thoughts. It was silent at the dinner table for a few nights until he relented. But we learned our lesson, and from then on we did try to avoid clichés like the plague. Ha!

My point was that when I caught myself thinking in metaphors, mixed or otherwise, I knew I was either extremely tired or in serious danger of losing my heart. Both of these circumstances could cause brain cells to diminish. It was a well-known fact.

I just hoped I wasn't getting stupid where Derek was concerned. He'd told me straight out that he worked in dangerous situations all the time, but maybe I'd missed the subtext. Maybe that meant he didn't want to face danger when he came home. Maybe that's what he wanted to talk to me about. Maybe he'd rather come home to someone more settled, someone less likely to stumble over dead bodies. Someone who didn't attract death like honey attracted flies. Or was it bees?

Didn't matter. Either way, it was another cliché. Good grief.

"Well, that's too damn bad, pal," I said stoutly, as I stood and brushed bits of grass and dirt off my pants. "You're stuck with me and I'm stuck with you."

And just like that, I felt better. Lighter. Happier. Weird, but I guessed I would have to pull weeds more often. No wonder Mom often looked and acted so Zen-like. Through her gardening, she had found a way to clear her mind. Good to know.

Walking around the side of the house, I tossed the handful of weeds into the green trash can to be dried and mulched.

Mom was waiting in the kitchen, putting away the last of the breakfast dishes. I smiled at her outfit: work boots and a faded denim jacket over a long-sleeved purple T-shirt and a calf-length crinkly skirt she'd tie-dyed several shades of sage green.

I felt so plain standing next to her in my blue jeans, a thick navy sweater, and loafers.

But her eyes lit up when I walked inside. "There's my beautiful girl."

"Mom, you look fabulous."

She whirled around like a little girl and we both laughed. Then she sobered. "I'm feeling a little antsy about our mission so I'm going to perform a success ritual before we leave."

Our *mission?* Ooh, boy. And rituals? God help me. I thought about stopping her, but how could I argue with a success ritual? After all, I'd never admit it to Mom, but I was a little antsy, too. I'd had a few bad dreams last night featuring Solomon and Angelica. And this morning, the same fearful thoughts had been recycling through my mind.

I could picture them both gloating over their malevolence, rubbing their hands in excitement at the power and control they wielded. I would really hate to run into them on the street in Dharma, knowing they'd be able to read the fear and loathing on my face.

As I waited for Mom to gather her herbs and tools, I recalled that summer I taught the bookbinding class at the Art Institute. I had loved my class, loved bookbinding, and enjoyed teaching in general. But any thoughts of pursuing a career as an art teacher had been effectively squelched, thanks to Solomon and Angie.

I suppose it was unfair to blame my decision not to teach solely on the two of them. Academia was a strange, provincial world and I simply didn't fit in. The insular attitudes of many of the professors and staff were suffocating at best. And Solomon, while fascinating in the classroom, ruled his department like a despot, handing out praise, assignments, and retribution as though he were Julius Caesar.

Angelica was worse. She was gorgeous, yes, but haughty and domineering. And possessive. Not just with Max, I realized now, but with the school itself and the students. This was Angie's territory and how dared I think I could ever be a part of it?

I shivered, and all of a sudden it struck me that I was still holding on to so much fear of her. I knew I would have to confront her one of these days.

"Assume the position," Mom said as she walked back into the room. She chuckled at her own joke while she assembled her ritual herbs and tools on the dining room table.

I gave her a look. "Very funny, Mom."

"Never gets old."

When my siblings and I were growing up, Mom and Dad used to regale us with tales from the sixties. One of their favorite stories was of the time they were arrested at China Lake for protesting nuclear weapons. (That's where my sister China was born, the day after Mom was released from jail. My parents were sentimental that way, naming us all after the places where we were born or conceived or, apparently, where they'd spent a night in jail.)

Mom had advised us that when the cops were arresting you, they would tell you to *assume the position.* That meant you should stand facing a wall with your feet apart and both hands on the wall. The better to be frisked, she explained.

Of course, Dad always maintained that the actual *position* you were meant to *assume* was the one where you bent over and kissed your ass good-bye.

So every once in a while, for no apparent reason, one of my parents would suddenly tell us to *assume the position.* Being obedient children, we would.

Some of us would go with Mom's position and stand facing the wall. But some — usually my two brothers — would go with Dad's choice. Mom and Dad would howl with laughter and we would all make faces and roll our eyes at them. My parents were a couple of cards. No wonder we didn't do drugs; things were zany enough around our house without the added buzz.

Mom placed three small dishes on the table, filled with rosemary, sage, and dried lotus petals to represent memory, concentration, and truth.

"Here, sweetie," she said, handing me one of the thick sticks of sage she used to cleanse, purify, and eliminate negativity. "You light the sage."

"Okay." I took a deep whiff of the sage before I flicked Mom's lighter on and held it to the top leaves. They began to smoke, then burn. I let the fire spread across the top of the stick before blowing it out. The strong aromatic smoke filled the room.

"I'm lighting the copal, too," she said, holding another, more bristly looking herbal smudge stick. Copal was a type of tree resin with a mild pine scent that was often used in incense. Mom used it sparingly with other herbs when she needed an extra boost to attract good spirits.

Seeing the copal made me realize she was

even more antsy than she was willing to admit. I guess I was, too.

I waved the sage bundle around, making sure the smoke wafted over us both, up and down and around our bodies and over our heads, while she did the same with the copal stick. We probably looked like idiots, and maybe we were, but I usually found Mom's rituals oddly comforting.

She rested the copal stick in a small pot she'd filled with sand. As she plucked up bits of herbs and petals and sprinkled them in two circles on a piece of white cloth, she chanted,

> Sage and rosemary,
> Clear our misty minds.
> Lotus, lead the way
> To the truth that we must find.
> Spirit, show yourself to me,
> Shine the light that we may see.
> Spirit, once this day is done,
> Your knowledge and mine will be one.

Mom waved the smoldering copal stick over the herb circles and tapped a tiny bit of ash onto each of them. Then she buried the burnt end of the stick in the bowl of sand and did the same with the sage bundle. With scissors, she carefully cut the cloth in half and gathered each of the corners together around the little piles of herbs and ash. After tying each of the bundles with a short raffia string to make two small sachets, she handed one to me.

"Hold this close and I'll do the same. It'll keep our minds open and our thoughts pure. That way, we'll recognize the truth when we hear it."

"Cool." I slipped my sachet into the pocket of my jeans.

Mom pressed her hands together, closed her eyes, and breathed slowly in and out. After a minute, she opened her eyes and blinked at me. "The spirits believe you will succeed, Brooklyn."

"They do?" I nodded, not quite sure of the proper response. "That's great. Thanks, spirits."

"The spirits say, 'No problemo.'" She grinned. "Let's boogie."

As we walked down the Lane toward Warped, my sister China's yarn and weaving shop, Mom leaned close. "Tell me more about the people we're looking to get intel on."

Intel? Seriously? But I relented and gave her some of the history of Solomon and Angelica, explained Max's desperation and his reasons for staging his own death. Mom had tears in her eyes and I wondered if I'd said too much. But I figured if Max ever needed help in the future, Mom would know why and would be there for him. She was easily the most empathetic person I knew.

Mom stopped me a half block up from Warped and stared right into my eyes. "Can you honestly see either of these odd people getting in a car and following all of you to Marin, then taking out a long-range rifle, aiming at you, and pulling the trigger?"

Now that she put it like that, all black and white and out in the open, I really had to think about it. Frankly, I had a hard time picturing anyone in the world doing something so horrible. I didn't see evil in the world like Derek or Gabriel saw it. It always caught me by surprise.

Finally I admitted, "Solomon was a creep, but I don't see him as a murderer."

"What about the woman?"

I sighed. "Maybe my memory of her is a little distorted because she was cruel to me, but she seems fully capable of pulling the trigger. On the other hand, around the campus she passed herself off as the artistic earth-goddess type in bare feet who loved all creatures and wouldn't be caught dead with a gun in her hand. I didn't buy her act for a minute, but a lot of people seemed to believe it."

"Okay, not very helpful," Mom said, nodding. "Let's see what we can find out around town." She wove her arm through mine and we continued walking. I gripped her arm, not sure why I was so nervous. We were just strolling along the lane, the same as we would do on any other day of the week. We were going to visit my sister China, then check in with my sister Savannah across the street at her new restaurant. It would be fun to see how well the restaurant was doing and find out how the critics had enjoyed their meals. After that we would stop at Anandalla, our friend Annie's kitchen shop. Along the way, we would talk to friends, greet other people on the sidewalk, and try to find a killer. The usual.

CHAPTER 14

"You should talk to Savannah if you want the scoop on Angelica," China said after we told her what we were looking for. "She would know a lot more about those people than I would."

"Why do you think so?" I asked.

China gazed at me as if I'd lost part of my brain. "You don't remember that Savannah took her first cooking classes at the institute before going off to study in Paris?"

"Um, I know she did, but . . . so what?"

China shook her head. "She used to party with that whole crowd. Don't you remember she called Angelica a bitch with attitude?"

"She should talk," I muttered. Savannah could be prickly when she wanted to be.

"I know, right?" China glanced quickly at Mom, who was on the other side of the shop, comparing skeins of neon purple yarn. Only God knew what she planned to knit with that.

"I heard that," Mom said mildly. "Be nice."

China and I exchanged glances. Had we really thought we could get away with saying anything negative about our siblings? Mom had the ears of a desert fox.

I frowned at China. "How do you remember all that stuff about Savannah and Angelica?"

"I was younger than you two so I hung on your every word." She held up her hand instantly. "And no, I don't do that anymore."

"Too bad," I said, grinning.

"Anyway, I remember everything Savannah used to say when she'd come home from the culinary school. I thought being a chef would be the most exciting thing ever. I mean, food everywhere, right? I was captivated by everything she told us about her training."

"Huh. I just tried my best to ignore her."

"Like we all do with London," China whispered.

I snorted and we both whipped around to see if Mom had heard. She didn't brook any disparaging words uttered about her youngest and most darling daughter, London. After all, our little sister led a charmed life in nearby Calistoga with her gorgeous, wealthy doctor-cum-oenologist husband and twin babies.

A bell tinkled prettily to alert China that the door to the shop had opened. We turned and saw Crystal and Melody Byers, two sisters who'd gone to high school with us.

"Yoo-hoo, China," Crystal said, as she rushed over to hug my sister, then me. "Brooklyn, it's so good to see you. We saw you coming in here and thought we'd stop in to say hello."

"Hey, Crystal," I said, smiling. "How are you?"

Mom walked over to greet the sisters, then said, "You girls look so cheery today. Melody, that color is perfect on you."

Melody preened in her golden yellow jumpsuit. It was a good color for her blond hair and lightly tanned skin, but lately when I saw a jumpsuit, it reminded me of a prison uniform. If hers were slightly more orange, she would fit right in at the county jail.

Crystal was my age and we'd been in the same classes all through grammar and high school. Melody was a year younger. Both were pretty, blue-eyed blondes, tall and big-boned, who were strong from years of working in their parents' orchards, where they grew olives, walnuts, and apples. Thanks to the two Byers sisters, our high school women's basketball and baseball teams had held the state championship for five years running. The sisters were popular with the girls at school, but most of the boys were afraid of them, probably because the two girls could beat them at almost any sport.

"What are you ladies up to today?" Mom asked with a smile. "Shopping?"

"We're always up for shopping," Melody said, and everybody laughed.

"We're in town on business," Crystal said, efficiently straightening the jacket of her perky blue seersucker suit. "Just stopped by the chamber of commerce to pick up our very own street-fair permit."

I knew they both worked in their parents' booth at all the different street fairs and farmers' markets in the county. They sold their apples and olives and walnuts, along with all sorts of oils and soaps they made on their farm.

"Are you setting up shop on your own?" I asked.

"Yes." Melody could barely contain her excitement. "We found this fabulous new line of fruit dehydrators we'll be demonstrating and selling."

"That's wonderful," Mom said. "Will you be selling the dried fruit, as well?"

"Oh, you mean to eat? That's a great idea,

Mrs. Wainwright," Crystal said. She looked at Melody with her mouth wide-open. "OMG, why didn't we think of that?"

"LOL, I don't know," Melody said, laughing at their silliness. She gazed back at us. "Crystal uses the dried fruit to make jewelry. She's a genius. Show them."

Crystal pulled back her hair and flicked her earring, a shiny, round red disk hanging from a silver post. "Don't you love it?"

Curious, I looked closer at the glittering red circle. China leaned in next to me. "What is that?"

"It's a strawberry slice," Crystal said gaily. "I dry them and shellac them and turn them into earrings."

China and I exchanged glances. "Wow."

"Aren't they chic?" Melody said as Crystal beamed. "Wait till you see her dried-apple necklaces. They're true art. If you're around tomorrow, stop by our booth."

China raised her hand. "I'll be there."

"We'll be selling our other products, too," Crystal added.

"I'll come by, too," I said. I wanted to pick up more of the olive oil–based cuticle cream they sold. The stuff was golden, especially for me and my propensity for paper cuts. Seriously, if they sold this cream at Bloomie's, the Byers sisters would be millionaires in a few months.

"Girls, I wonder if you could help me," Mom said, glancing from one Byers sister to the other.

"We'll try," Crystal said, and Melody nodded with enthusiasm.

"I'm looking for someone in the area who reloads their own ammunition cartridges." Mom leaned in to add confidentially, "I'd like to learn how to do it and maybe cut a little something off our annual hunting budget."

"I didn't know you hunted, Mrs. Wainwright," Melody said.

"Oh yes," Mom said, waving in an offhand way. "Well, not around here, of course. Jim and I take a trip up toward Yuba City every year and do a little dove hunting."

"Oh, I love dove," Crystal said, then blinked and turned to Melody. "Love. Dove. Get it?"

"You're a poet and didn't know it, LOL," Melody said, slapping Crystal's arm.

"LOL," Crystal agreed, giggling.

"Girls?" Mom said softly.

"Oh," Melody said, shaking her head to get back on track. "Sure, we know lots of people. Most of the men in our church have reloading presses. The Ogunites go through a lot of ammo every year. It just makes good sense to load your own."

I'd forgotten that Melody and Crystal were members of the Church of the True Blood of Ogun, a local church whose members believed in honoring the creative spirit of the earth. That was their story, anyway. Most of the members tended to be shameless proselytizers with borderline survivalist mentalities.

A few of Guru Bob's fellowship members referred to the Ogunite church as a cult because some of its teachings were downright bizarre, but I figured the Ogunites probably felt the same way about Guru Bob's followers. People tend to mistrust anything they don't understand.

Years ago, my mother had taken us to the small Ogunite church, a charming wood and adobe structure the followers had built themselves from material found in the canyons and valleys of Sonoma. It was part of their teaching that their place of worship reflected the earth on which it stood. They'd fashioned the stained-glass windows from smooth chunks of glass and minerals they'd found in the Russian River nearby. I was young enough at the time of our visit that I held up my hand, thinking I could catch the rainbow of colors streaming through the windows.

Melody and Crystal had never been blatant about trying to convert any of us, so my sisters and I had always been friendly with them.

"Doesn't Bennie have a new Lock-N-Load?" Melody asked her sister.

"He's got everything." Crystal turned to Mom. "He might be willing to teach you, Mrs. Wainwright."

"Bennie?" Mom said. "I'm not sure I know a Bennie."

"You know him, Mom," China said. "He went to school with London."

"Bennie." She thought about it. "Benjamin Styles?"

"Yes, that's him," Melody said. "He and his friend Stefan have a place halfway up Moon Valley Ridge Road."

"Stefan's cute," Crystal said, and winked at me.

"*Really* cute," Melody said, nodding emphatically.

"Moon Valley Ridge isn't too far," Mom said. "I could drive over to see him."

Moon Valley Ridge Road skirted a wide, rocky canyon that some of the locals referred to as the Hollow. A number of the Ogunites had built homes in the area. There was a fast-moving stream running through the canyon that provided plenty of fish and attracted a lot of wildlife, so many of the Hollow residents prided themselves on living off the land. Me, I liked my Frappuccinos.

Melody wrinkled her nose. "Wouldn't you rather have Mr. Wainwright load the ammo for you? It can get kind of dirty."

"Oh no," Mom said in a rush. "He's so busy working. And besides, I want to surprise him."

"You can load ammo yourself, Mrs. Wainwright," Crystal said, casting a look at her sister. "I do it all the time."

"She does," Melody conceded. "Crystal is a wiz at so many things."

Mom leaned closer to Crystal. "We ladies do it all, don't we, sweetie?"

Crystal laughed. "It's true. So I'll tell Bennie to call you. I see him every morning at church."

"You would do that for me?" Mom said.

"Oh, Mrs. Wainwright, you've always been so good to us." Crystal wrapped her arm around Mom's waist. "Of course we would."

"You're a sweet girl, Crystal." She reached over and patted Melody's arm. "You, too, Melody."

China grabbed a store business card and wrote Mom's phone number on the back, then handed it to Crystal.

She glanced at the card and smiled. "I'll

call you as soon as I've talked to him."

Mom squeezed Crystal's arm lightly. "Thank you, sweetie."

"We'd better get going," Melody said, and her voice rose with excitement. "We're driving over to Sonoma to pick up ten new dehydrators. OMG!"

"TTYL," Crystal said, waving as they left the store.

"Hasta la vista," China said.

"Whew," Mom said when the door closed. "Those girls always had more energy than ten of you two."

China's shoulders slumped. "I'm exhausted."

"Good thing they played for our team," I said, then grabbed Mom for a quick hug. "You were awesome, Mom. You lied like a real pro."

"Watch and learn, sweetie," she said, stepping back and patting her hair.

"OMG," I muttered.

We dropped by Savannah's and caught her racing around, preparing for the dinner crowd.

She stopped for a minute to answer my questions about her time at the Art Institute and about Angelica and Solomon.

"I hated her. What else did you want to know?"

"Did you know Solomon?" I asked.

"Well enough. I went to parties at his house."

"Did Solomon use guns?" Mom asked, going off script. Apparently she was running her own investigation. I guessed I would watch and learn.

"Oh, God, Mom," Savannah said, pressing her cheeks with her hands. "You just reminded me of this really creepy thing that happened one night."

She told us of a party she attended with the usual gang of institute partygoers at Solomon's place out in the woods somewhere. It must've been two or three o'clock in the morning when the host came out of his bedroom with a couple of guns and a box of ammunition. He announced that he wanted to play Russian roulette.

"I got up to leave right then," Savannah said, "and Angelica sneered at me. 'What? Are you scared?' And I said, 'Yeah. You people are sick,' and I walked out."

"That's my girl," Mom said, with a sharp nod of approval.

"They really were sick," I said, feeling chills skitter up my arms.

"Completely," Savannah said.

"Did they really play Russian roulette?" Mom asked, her face showing her shock and worry.

"I asked a girlfriend later," Savannah said. "She told me that somebody threatened to call the cops, so Solomon kicked everyone out. He said they all needed to lighten up because he was just kidding around. But I know they weren't kidding."

Savannah's cell phone beeped and she checked the text message. Her mouth dropped open. "It says the *Chronicle* will be publishing a three-star review of Arugula in tomorrow's paper."

"Oh, sweetie," Mom whispered in awe. "I'm so thrilled for you. You've worked so hard. You deserve every wonderful accolade you get."

I could see tears in Mom's eyes as we all hugged and laughed. Then we laughed harder as Savannah screamed and ran back into the kitchen to check the cabernet reduction sauce she'd left simmering.

"It's still alive," she cried out.

"Hallelujah," Mom said, and we left Savannah to her cooking.

Mom got in the car, but didn't start the engine. Instead she turned to face me. "I want to see Max."

"Yeah, I was afraid of that." I'd had an itchy feeling all morning that she'd bring it up at some point.

"I'll go by myself if you'd rather not come along."

"It's not that I don't want to. It's just that it could be dangerous."

"Do you honestly think these people are watching us right now?"

I sighed. How could I answer without giving her a heart attack? I decided to keep it light. "It's just that they're tricky, so we have to be trickier."

She pursed her lips, thought about it for a minute, then started the engine. "Okay, I'll take care of it."

She took off toward home but passed the turnoff that led up the hill to our house. A half mile later, she passed the street that would've taken us to Jackson's house, where Max was staying.

Meandering a few more miles out of town, she suddenly turned left into a gas station. Stopping at one of the tanks, Mom got out and bought two gallons of gas. I could see her watching every car that passed.

We drove off again, this time heading down the old two-lane road that ran parallel to the highway. She turned off again and took back roads, skirting Dharma's downtown district completely, until she finally came back to the road that led up to Jackson's house.

You know, my mother would've been a great spy. Just like my dad apparently was.

"Nice job, Mom."

She checked the rearview mirror for the hundredth time as she stepped on the gas and zoomed up the hill. "I don't think we were followed."

"I doubt it." I was still nervous, though. I had a sneaking suspicion that yesterday's bullet had been aimed at me. What if they took another shot? What if they hurt my mom? That thought made me so sick to my stomach, I immediately shoved it away.

I'd thought a lot lately about buying a gun and carrying it with me. The flaw in that plan was that I wouldn't use it, and if I did, I'd probably shoot myself in the foot. Guns freaked me out. But at times like these, when I felt threatened or intimidated, I thought it would be kind of nice to whip out a big-ass weapon, strictly to intimidate the bad guys.

Since I didn't have a weapon, I sort of wished Derek were here with us. I know, I know — a woman can take care of herself. Who needs a man? Well, I don't know about you, but I liked having a gorgeous, dangerous man around when I was scared. Call me a sellout to the feminist cause. Right then, I could live with it.

Mom parked in Jackson's driveway, and we ran to the front door. We knocked; then I used my key to open the door and we walked inside.

"It's Brooklyn," I called, as we headed into the living area.

"What the hell are you doing here?" Max shouted from above us.

I flinched, then looked up. He stood gazing down at us from the office loft above the living room. In his hands was the high-powered rifle he'd brought from home.

"You've got to stop aiming that thing at me," I said calmly, although my heart was thumping a thousand beats a minute. "Put it down. There's someone here to see you."

Mom moved out into the living room and looked up. "Hello, Max."

Max stared for a long beat; then his shoulders slumped. He lowered the rifle and disappeared from the railing. A few seconds later, I heard his footsteps on the stairs. Then he was in the room and hugging Mom as if he were her own long-lost child.

Mom had tears streaming down her cheeks when she stepped back. I could see Max's eyes glistening a little, too.

"Well, it's good to see you're alive and well," Mom said, sniffling between words.

"It's good to see you, too, Becky." He hugged her again, then found us all some tissues to dry our tears.

"Robson was here earlier," he said.

"I thought he might come by to see you," Mom said, smiling.

"Did anyone see you drive up here?" he asked.

Mom waved off his worry. "I drive up here several times a week to see Jackson."

"Well, Jackson isn't home," he said, pacing in front of the windows.

"Nobody knows that," Mom said. "And even when he's home, I come up to water his plants. Lord knows he won't remember to do it."

Max sighed. "I don't want to put you in danger."

"Oh, Max," Mom said softly. She walked up to the man, who towered over her, and patted his chest. "Don't you know there's nothing we wouldn't do for you? Everyone in Dharma feels the same way. I just wish you'd trusted us more with your problems all those years ago. We could've helped."

He glanced at me sideways. "I've heard that a few times now. Believe me, as soon as this nightmare is over, you're stuck with me.

216

I'm never leaving again."

"Good." Mom smiled. Then, without warning, she punched him in the stomach. "Make sure you don't."

"For God's sake," he said, doubling over. "What's with you Wainwright women?"

"You pissed us off," I said, grinning. "Don't do it again."

"Jeez, I won't," he muttered, rubbing his stomach. He looked at me and jerked his chin toward Mom. "She's got a stronger right hook than you."

"Don't I know it?" I said, smiling fondly at my mom.

CHAPTER 15

"Emily has to be kept safe," Max said. "That's the first priority." The four of us — Derek, Gabriel, Max, and I — had regrouped at Jackson's house that night. We'd driven in a roundabout route up the hill in one car, Gabriel's BMW, and now we were seated at the dining table, eating pizza and salad, drinking wine, and plotting our next moves.

Derek hadn't found anything criminal in Solomon's or Angelica's backgrounds. "Yet," he emphasized. He had two people in his office looking through their finances. They were also looking into any questionable activities involving the Art Institute over the past few years. I hadn't considered that connection, but Derek thought it was worth investigating because Solomon was such an important member of the faculty and the art community in general.

Once Derek finished talking, Max moved

on to the subject of Emily.

"Her safety was the only reason I disappeared all those years ago," he said. "I won't let her be hurt again."

"I agree with Max that we have to track her down," I said. Unfortunately, I hadn't heard back from Emily yet and I was more than a little concerned. Derek, my hero, had returned to Dharma an hour earlier with my battery charger. As soon as my phone began to charge, I checked my messages. There was still nothing from Emily.

There could be any number of reasons why she hadn't returned my call. Maybe I'd called the wrong Emily. Or maybe I'd called the right one and she just didn't want to talk to me. Or maybe she was out of town and forgot her charger like I had, or she hadn't checked her messages yet. Or, worst-case scenario, she had been kidnapped by those two homicidal art professors and was tied up with duct tape in some closet somewhere. I preferred not to go with that possibility. Whichever way you looked at it, it couldn't be a good sign that we hadn't heard from Emily.

"One of us needs to track her down," I said.

"Me," Max said. "I'll have to borrow a car. If I go tonight, I'll be able to —"

"Max . . ." I just looked at him. "You said you didn't want to risk her safety, but you want to be the one to go see her?"

"I can be careful," Max argued.

I felt for him. I knew he was dying to see Emily — the problem was, we didn't want Emily dying because she'd seen Max.

"I'll go," Gabriel said. "First thing in the morning."

Max scowled. "You'll scare her."

"No, I won't," Gabriel said easily. "I'm a very charming guy. But that doesn't matter, since she won't even know I was there."

"She won't," I assured Max. "He's kinda scary that way."

"And now you're scaring *me*," Max muttered, and chomped into another piece of pizza.

"I know it's hard," I said, reaching over to squeeze his arm. "But you need to sit tight for another day or so. Besides, you would completely freak her out if you just popped up out of nowhere. She thinks you're dead. Remember?"

"Why should I sit tight?" he demanded. "I'm asking seriously. Why? I'm tired of hiding. Let's push this thing wide-open."

"Not until we know who's running the show," Derek said. "You want Emily safe, so we must go slowly. Until we have answers, you cannot be seen outside this house."

"Nobody's going to see me if I walk outside. There aren't any neighbors for a thousand yards in any direction." Max flopped back in his chair, clutching his wineglass. "And I can see from upstairs if any cars come up or down the hill. I think I'm pretty safe up here."

"Maybe for a while," I said. "But Solomon and Angelica both know me. They know my sister Savannah. They know you were friends with my brothers. So there's a clear connection from my family to you. If they follow any of us, they'll eventually wind up here. And God only knows what they'll do to you when they find you."

"Now who's being paranoid?" Max said.

"It's not paranoid if they're really after you." I laughed without humor. "I don't want to be shot at again, and I don't want you to get hurt."

"All right, all right," he said, waving his hands in surrender.

"Thank you." I smiled briefly. "So Gabriel will go check on Emily tomorrow. And Mom and I made some progress with Crystal Byers and her sister today. We'll find out tomorrow if Bennie Styles can give us some answers on ammo loading."

"Sounds like a long shot," Max said.

"It's just a way of getting Bennie to talk about the people he knows in the gun community. The Ogunite church has some connections to the Art Institute. He might know someone who knows someone. You know how that works."

"Yeah, yeah." Max shook his head stubbornly. "I just have a hard time believing Solomon and Angie are still sitting around thinking about me. It's been three years. Maybe they've moved on."

"You know they haven't." I leaned forward with my elbows on the table and stared hard at Max. "Joe Taylor was killed four days ago. And yesterday someone took a shot at us. They haven't moved on."

He let out a slow, heavy breath. "I know. I just . . . Maybe I should've stayed at the farm and fought them on my own turf. Now that I'm here, I can't do a damn thing. I've got too much time on my hands. I'm just sitting around waiting for something to happen."

"Something will," Derek said ominously.

"Yeah. That's what I'm afraid of." Max pushed his wineglass back. "Okay, I'll hang tight. But be sure to check on Emily tomorrow. I'll feel better knowing she's safe."

"Got it covered," Gabriel said.

■ ■ ■ ■

In the morning, Derek took off for the city. We'd already decided the night before that he wouldn't drive back to Dharma tonight and I was sort of okay with that. But he wasn't.

"I'm coming back tonight," he said, changing his mind as he pulled the car door open.

I leaned in close to him. "It's not necessary."

"As long as Max is in hiding and we don't know who's after him, I need to be wherever you are."

I gazed up at him. "I won't argue or complain if you want to come back tonight."

"Good." He grabbed my sweater and yanked me up against him. "I like a docile woman."

I laughed. "Then you've come to the wrong place."

"Don't I know it?" He grinned, kissed me thoroughly, then jumped into his car and drove off.

The Dharma farmers' market was bustling by the time Mom and I arrived. After visiting Max the previous night, I'd decided to actively pursue the Crystal connection with some of the Ogunite members who loaded their own ammunition. I figured that connection would provide us with the fastest route to whoever gave Solomon those hand-loaded bullets — without having to confront the man face-to-face.

"I just hope we don't have to buy a dehydrator to get information from them," I whispered to Mom as we approached the Byers sisters' booth.

"I've been using two old window screens to dehydrate my apples," Mom said. "They still work like a champ after ten years."

"Yeah, but can they make jewelry?"

"Hey, Brooklyn!" Melody chirped when she saw us.

We greeted them with hugs and congratulations on their new enterprise.

"Your booth is the prettiest one," Mom gushed.

"I think so, too," Crystal said, and did a little happy dance in front of us. Then she jutted her chin toward the next booth over. "But don't say that too loudly. Mary Ellen Prescott over there thinks she's the cat's ass with her hair-product line."

Mary Ellen stood surrounded by hundreds of long swatches of hair that were hanging from the crossbars of the booth. She worked as a manicurist in the Dharma hair salon, which explained her expertise with fake hair.

Mary Ellen was a shameless recruiter for the Church of the True Blood of Ogun, but they kept her on at the salon because she was a dynamite manicurist.

Interesting to know there was dissension among the Ogunite women.

"Is she selling hair?" Mom asked.

"She calls them glamour tails," Crystal said, pursing her lips. "I just look away."

Personally, I thought they looked like scalps. Which kind of gave me the heebie-jeebies.

"Try some banana chips," Melody said, presenting me with a small bowl of dried brown discs.

I'd never been a big fan of dried fruit but I took a few chips and popped them into my mouth. "Mm. Yummy."

"And if you think they taste good, just look how exciting they are as jewelry!" She flung her hair back to reveal her earrings, tightly overlapping clusters of thin, lacquered banana chips that ruffled and fluttered around her earlobes.

"Unbelievable," Mom said.

"Stunning," I whispered. I wasn't kidding; I was stunned. They were . . . pretty. Light and flirty and feminine. Very clever. But, come on, they were bananas!

A customer came over and Melody turned to offer her banana treats and advice on fruit dehydration.

Crystal led me and Mom over to her jewelry display. "These rings are my latest creations," she said, pointing to a display of dried fruit slices affixed to simple silver bands. "They're made from plums and apples and sweet potatoes. Oh, and this little coral-colored one is made from apricots."

Some of the wafer-thin slices fluttered straight up like a fan. Others were flat and layered, with ruffled edges. The dried-plum ring looked like a rich, dark red rose with its petals rippling gently in the wind. Many of the rings had the vintage look of a plump fabric rose pinned to a forties-era cocktail dress.

I picked up the plum ring and slipped it carefully onto my finger. It wasn't my style, but I admired it against my skin. "It's beautiful, Crystal. Where did you learn to do this?"

"I've always made jewelry for me and my sisters," she admitted, suddenly shy. "My parents aren't ones for spending money on frivolous ornamentation, so I found ways around them. The dried-fruit designs are my latest experiment."

"Well, these are really unique. You should

make a bundle on them."

"Thanks," she said. "I hope so. Enough to pay for my classes, anyway."

Mom picked up on the conversation as she admired a green-speckled kiwi ring. "Where do you take classes?"

"Over at the Art Institute. I've been taking jewelry classes off and on for a few years."

The Art Institute? I wondered immediately if Crystal knew Solomon. Or Angelica. Before I could grill her, her sister, Melody, still in conversation with the customer, flashed Crystal an impatient look.

Crystal got the message and scurried over to the table where a few more customers were lined up to sample the edible dried fruit.

I leaned close to Mom. "This jewelry is amazing, but I'm not sure I'm capable of hanging dried fruit from my ears."

"I find it strangely compelling," Mom whispered, and slipped a rose-tinged chunk of desiccated fruit onto her finger.

After a few minutes Crystal turned back to me and Mom and held out a plate piled high with round and twisted dried stuff. "These are pineapple. They're my favorites. Try some."

I examined it first to make sure it wasn't

227

jewelry, then took a small bite of the overly sweet, chewy fruit. "Thanks. But that's it for me. I'm starting to get full."

"Dried fruit will fill you up, but in a good way," Crystal insisted. "Much better than potato chips."

I ignored that blasphemy as she forced several more types of fruits on me. Finally I grabbed my stomach and begged to take a break.

"She's always had a delicate system," Mom murmured to Crystal, who nodded sagely.

"It's all delicious," I lied, "but I think I'd rather wear your dried fruit than eat it."

Pleased, Crystal clapped her hands. "I love to hear that."

"OMG, we have our first dehydrator sale," Melody whispered, surreptitiously waving a check at her sister before shoving it into her pants pocket.

"OMG," Crystal whispered back, tittering with excitement. Then she somberly pressed her hands to her chest and gazed heavenward. "Thank you, great Ogun."

"Congratulations," I said.

"Dried fruit for everyone!" Melody cried, shoving plates out toward the people passing by.

After a few minutes of giggles and text

talk between the sisters, my mother was finally able to corner Crystal to ask if she'd talked to Bennie about teaching her how to load ammo.

"Oh, I meant to tell you first thing," she said. "Yes, we talked, and Bennie will be happy to show you how to do it. But he said he'd have to come over to your place."

"It's simple enough for me to drive out to his house," Mom said. "I hate to inconvenience him when he's doing me a favor."

Crystal made a face as she held up her hand. "Let him come to you, Mrs. Wainwright. His place is always a mess. I've been there, so I know it's true."

"Crystal, do you think Bennie's a good teacher?" Mom's tone was confidential. "I don't have a clue what I'm doing, so I don't want him to get too frustrated with me."

"You'll be fine." Crystal patted Mom's forearm. "I know for a fact that he recently taught one of our church deacons how to reload ammo."

"Well, if he's patient enough to teach your deacon, he should be perfect for me."

"Oh yes," she assured Mom. "Our deacon is very demanding. A wonderful man, but demanding."

"I'm not sure I know who that is," Mom said artlessly.

"He keeps to himself so you probably don't know him, Mrs. Wainwright." Crystal arranged more pineapple slices on a plate and began to munch on them herself. "His name is Solomon and he's a professor out at the institute. Have you heard of him?"

I just about fell over onto a plate of dried apricots, but I managed to keep my cool as I jumped into the conversation. "I taught a bookbinding class out there a long time ago and I met Solomon. He's really something, isn't he?"

"Oh yes." Her sigh was close to orgasmic. "So you know how virile he is. I shouldn't say such things about a church deacon, but I confess I'm half in love with him."

"I remember he was very handsome," I said, biting my tongue. "How did he and Bennie get to be friends?"

"Well, they're both Ogunites, of course," she said offhandedly. "But also Bennie and Stefan work in the stock-room of the Art Institute's museum store, so they see Solomon every day."

"That's convenient," I said lightly, but inside I was reeling from the revelation that Solomon was a member of the Church of the True Blood of Ogun. And he was a *deacon.* I knew the Ogunites weren't particularly religious — they were more wrapped up in the worship of nature and earthly arts — but this was ridiculous. If what I suspected of Solomon was true, the man was a cold-blooded killer.

"Yes," Crystal said, slipping another fruit slice into her mouth. "A number of our people work for the Art Institute and, of course, some of us take classes there."

"That must be nice for you," I said. "I remember there was a real sense of community at the institute."

"I love taking jewelry classes there and I've sold a lot of my fruit jewelry to the other students." Crystal smiled softly as her cheeks turned rosy. "And it doesn't hurt that I get to see Solomon every day."

I said with some surprise, "You really like him."

Her eyelashes fluttered. "Is it that obvious?"

"Only to us," Mom said with a wink. Sobering, she asked, "Is he a nice man, Crystal? Is he good enough for you?"

Crystal wiggled her finger at us. "Come over here and look at this."

Mom and I followed her like two puppies.

"This is the Monarch 5000." She ran her hand across the top of a boxy white plastic dehydrator. "It's the very same model that Solomon bought last week. The top of the line. Deluxe. It's got a timer and temperature gauge for all your food groups, and it comes in five- or nine-shelf models."

"Nine shelves," Mom said. "That's impressive."

"Isn't it? Solomon took the nine-shelf unit."

Mom nodded. "Of course he did."

"It works with meat and fish, and makes the best squirrel jerky you've ever tasted in less than six hours. Nobody can touch that time. Solomon knew it and grabbed it. He's smart, he's strong, and he has the best taste in everything."

Mom gave a thumbs-up. "He knows his dehydrators. That's for sure."

"He does indeed," Crystal said, then flashed a smug smile. "I also sold him the newest water-filtration pen that all the Ogunites are excited about. My point is, Solomon will survive wherever he goes. And what woman doesn't find that an attractive quality in a man?"

"The survivalist instinct," Mom said, pondering the words. "It certainly speaks to our most basic needs as women."

Cave*women,* I thought, but didn't say it aloud.

"I know!" Crystal beamed. "I'm so proud to be a small contributor to his evolution.

He's a budding naturalist and, oh, such a deep thinker."

"Well, he is a full professor," I said.

"Exactly." She sighed. "I can't tell you how happy I am that Solomon's taken Bennie and Stefan under his wing. I know he only befriended them to learn more survivalist skills, but that's a good sign, isn't it? Bennie's taught him how to shoot and reload, and last week, Stefan showed him how to skin a squirrel."

"How thrilling," Mom said.

"Isn't it?" Crystal nodded excitedly. "But, personally, I think the boys will learn so much more from having a man like Solomon around as a role model than he'll ever learn from them."

"Oh, I'm sure you're right," I said sincerely. I would warn her to stay away from Solomon later, but right now I wanted to keep her talking.

She leaned closer so she wouldn't be overheard. "It's sad, though, because Bennie and Stefan are so immature." She laughed. "Seriously, I could live off the land better than those two knuckleheads ever could. And I can say that because they're my brothers."

"They are?" I didn't remember them all being related.

233

"Oh, I mean they're my church brothers. I've known them forever and, you know, they're still boys." She laughed and waved her hands philosophically. "They can be so juvenile."

"I have brothers so I know what you mean," I said, chuckling in camaraderie.

"But Solomon is a *man.*" She closed her eyes and breathed deeply.

Mom stepped forward eagerly. "I simply must have another taste of that pineapple."

"You know, Crystal," I said, rushing to change the subject, "it's been a long time since I taught at the institute, but I distinctly remember one woman who taught there. What was her name?" I thought for a few seconds. "Angela? Angelina?"

"Angelica." Crystal nearly spat the word.

"That's her," I whispered triumphantly. "She was a piece of work."

"I know it's wrong, but I really hate her," Crystal said in an undertone. "She's horrible. Nasty. Brooklyn, I swear I never say things like this, but that woman is the *B* word."

Whoa. The *B* word. That was some kind of serious condemnation coming from Crystal.

Her shoulders tightened and she busied herself by grabbing her fruit knife and slicing up fresh peaches to demonstrate the miracle action of the Monarch 5000.

"I didn't like her, either," I confessed.

"I'm so glad to hear that, Brooklyn," she said. "I don't like to speak ill of anyone, but she's just a mean person. I don't know what Solomon sees in her."

"So they're still dating?"

"If you want to call it that. But I've seen her with other men," she whispered. "I call that cheating."

"Have you had some run-ins with her?"

"Multiple run-ins," she said, emphasizing every syllable. "I live in the Hollow, and my church members over there are my best customers. I'm always stopping by to drop off the latest updates on dehydrators and survivalist tools, plus I hand out free samples of my family's orchard products. Everybody loves those."

"I know I do," Mom piped up.

Crystal grinned as she continued slicing up fruit. "Since Solomon is such a good customer, I've stopped by his place a few times, too. He's been so nice to me, I like to bring him baked goods and things. The last few times I've come by, he's told me I can come anytime and I think he means it in a special way. But Angelica is so rude. She actually threatened me once. I know it's because she's jealous that Solomon shows an interest in me. She chased me all the way out to my car the other day and said horrible things. It made me so mad, I wanted . . . oh." She dropped the knife as blood spurted from her finger.

"Oh, goodness," Mom said, grabbing a napkin and wrapping it around Crystal's finger.

"Thanks, Mrs. Wainwright. I'm such a klutz sometimes."

"What are you whispering about over there?" Melody asked, staring pointedly at her sister. "Get over here. I've sold two more dehydrators."

"OMG, yay," Crystal said unsteadily, then tried to laugh, but it came out a nervous titter. "Gosh, Brooklyn, you really got me going about that woman."

"I'm so sorry." I touched Crystal's arm in sympathy. "Believe me, she used to drive me crazy, too."

"So it's not just me?" She loosened, then pressed the napkin tighter around the cut. "That's a relief. LOL."

CHAPTER 16

"I'm going to have to buy a new dehydrator just to assuage my guilt," I said as I absently swirled the wine in my glass.

Mom nodded. "As long as you're buying into the guilt, you can't go wrong with the Monarch 5000."

As the sun fell behind the ridge, Mom and I sat outside on the terrace, tasting the latest pinot noir Dad had brought home. He'd thought Mom would appreciate its lighter, elegant cherry and mocha tones, and he was right. I liked it, too.

Now that the sun was gone, the air cooled quickly and I wrapped my jacket a little tighter around me. I was waiting for Derek to arrive before Gabriel swung by to pick us up and drive us to Max's for our nightly meeting.

"I really don't need a dehydrator," I said. "But I hated pumping her for so much information. Maybe I should buy one to pay her back."

"It's all for a good cause, sweetie."

"I guess so. And she really wanted to talk. But it was awful to hear her talk about Angelica. It made me remember how nasty she was to me. I feel sorry for anyone who's ever had to deal with that woman."

"Yes, but you need to let it go. Crystal seemed to enjoy our visit."

Poor Crystal. I could relate to her having to put up with the mean and nasty Angelica, but it flipped me out that Crystal was so enamored of Solomon. Had the guy really changed that much in the years since I'd known him? I doubted it. He had always been a ladies' man, and now it looked like he was buttering up Crystal to make his move on her. I didn't believe for a minute that he was faithful to Angelica.

The thought of him hitting on Crystal made me cringe, but Crystal didn't seem to mind. She was so innocent, she didn't even seem to realize that he might be trying to lure her into his bed. She had no clue just how manipulative he could be.

I took another sip of the pinot and tasted the dark cherry tones Dad was talking about, along with a hint of raspberry. "So Solomon has only recently developed an interest in survivalist stuff. Coincidence?

Just when the *Beauty and the Beast* comes onto the market? And just when we find out about Max? It's all connected, isn't it?"

"Of course it is," Mom said. "I don't know the man, but if he's living in the Hollow, he's surrounded by Ogunites. And you know how they are. Not rough, exactly."

"No, just rugged individualists," I said dryly, finishing her thought. "Even the sheriff used to avoid going down there."

"Yes, but it's been cleaned up quite a bit since then."

"It can't be too awful if Crystal goes there every day to sell her products."

"She lives there, too, and she knows those people," Mom pointed out. "And she can take care of herself."

"I'll say." I chuckled. "She's a little naive, but physically she's tougher than most men I know."

"Now, Brooklyn, Crystal Byers is a lovely girl," Mom proclaimed, then added under her breath, "Big-boned, but lovely." She tasted her wine, then smoothed a wrinkle out of the tablecloth. "You know, she and Melody come by here every few weeks to buy apples, so I keep up-to-date with them."

"But they already grow apples out at their place," I said, confused. "Why do they come here?"

"Their orchards only produce Gravensteins so they come here to buy my varieties."

"Ah." Mom liked to experiment with all sorts of apple varieties — Gala, Fuji, two different types of Delicious, Granny Smith. She didn't sell her apples commercially or at the farmer's market, so she wasn't under the same constraints as the farmers whose apples were their main source of income. Apple-wise, Gravensteins were the biggest moneymakers in our area.

"Of course, I didn't realize I was subsidizing her jewelry business when I sold her my beautiful apples," she said, laughing.

"Maybe you can work out a deal," I said. "Dried-fruit earrings for every occasion."

"There are my girls," said a cheerful male voice.

We both turned as Dad and Derek walked across the terrace. They each carried wineglasses and looked happy to see us.

Mom sighed. "Have you ever seen such a handsome sight, Brooklyn? I'll take the cute, rangy one on the right."

I laughed. "Fine with me. I've got dibs on the dark-eyed, dangerous one."

"A fine choice."

"I think so," I murmured. Derek's eyes never left me as he approached, set his glass down, then sat down next to me. I snuggled up close and was instantly warm and cozy.

Dad leaned over and kissed Mom. "What've you two been plotting?"

"Sit and relax, and we'll tell you."

"I'm more interested in what you two have been plotting," I said. Ever since I found out that Dad had played a prominent role in Max's disappearance, I'd been grilling him for information. He'd filled in some of the blanks on Solomon, but I hadn't known until Crystal mentioned it that the man was a member of the Ogunite church. I had no idea what significance that held, if any. Dad didn't know, either.

Derek said he'd make a note to look into the group's background; then Mom gave an abbreviated rundown of our conversation with Crystal that morning. I added comments here and there.

"I don't know those boys, Stefan and Bennie," Dad said.

Mom reminded him that Benjamin Styles had been in London's high school class, and Dad nodded. "Now I remember him. He's been in some trouble before. Arrested for attempted burglary. Road racing. Idiot stuff."

"That goes along with what Crystal said about him, although she never mentioned he'd been arrested."

"So Solomon has Bennie teaching him to load ammunition," Derek mused. "Interesting choice of chums."

"Yes, isn't it?" I said, smiling at his use of the word *chum*. What a perfectly darling word. I was going to use it from now on.

I stared at my half-full wineglass and wondered if I'd had too much to drink. I didn't think so, but, then, I didn't often wax lyrically over a bit of British slang.

"Becky and I are friendly with several survivalist families who have moved in together down in the Hollow," Dad said. "But those people maintain sober, vegan homes and are relatively harmless."

"I doubt Solomon is one of that ilk," Derek said.

"He's far from harmless," Mom agreed.

"Well, I guess the term *harmless* is relative," Dad said. "After all, even the nicest families in the Hollow have arsenals in their basements that rival Fort Ord."

"Is that right?" Derek said, his eyes darkening. "I'll be sure to look into that."

Later that evening as we took a circuitous route up the mountain to Jackson's house, Gabriel was in a somber mood, so we avoided discussing anything too heavy. I tried to lighten things up by regaling Derek and Gabriel with a description of Mom's roundabout tour of the countryside in her attempt to avoid being followed the other day.

They were both chuckling as we walked to the door, then sobered up as I knocked twice and used my key. They both drew their weapons as I pushed open the door and walked inside. Max stood in the living room with the rifle pointed directly at me.

"All rightie, then," I said, and held up the shopping bag I was carrying. "I've brought dinner."

"Let's talk first," Max said.

"Let's eat first." I was no fool. Men were way calmer after they had some food in their stomachs. So was I.

Fifteen minutes later, we were gathered around the dining table with plates in front of us. Mom had insisted on supplying us with her famous taco casserole, thinking we'd been ordering pizza every night. I didn't have the heart to tell her that Max was a fantastic cook and we'd been eating well almost every night. I heated up her casserole and tossed the salad she'd made with the lettuce, tomatoes, and cucumbers she'd picked from her garden that morning.

The men ate heartily but silently for a few

minutes; then Max threw down his fork and glared at Gabriel. "So?"

Gabriel looked up, gave Max a long, steady stare as he slowly swallowed his last bite. "Emily wasn't home, man. There were no signs of foul play, but it looked like she hadn't been home in more than a week."

"She could be on a trip," I said lamely.

"Where could she have gone?" Max stood up and walked away from the table, then turned and muttered, "Forget it. I have no right to know."

"Don't make me hit you," I said mildly. The sad tone of his voice caused me to worry, and I hated worrying. "You have every right to worry about Emily's safety. Now finish your dinner."

"Yes, Mother," he said, but at least he was half smiling. I really did sound like my mother sometimes, which probably turned off most guys. I glanced at Derek to see his reaction and caught him grinning at me. Proving once again that he wasn't like most guys.

Max sat and took a few more bites, then threw down his fork again. "Okay, just tell me. Is someone else living there with her?"

So that was the bug that had been crawling up Max's butt. He'd been worried that Emily might have moved on and found a boyfriend — or, worse, a husband. I couldn't blame him for being concerned.

"She lives alone," Gabriel said.

Max's jaw clenched and he nodded briefly. "Okay." He took another bite, then frowned at Gabriel. "Just for my own information, tell me what you look for when you go through someone's house."

Gabriel shrugged, then sat back in his chair. "The first thing I want to determine is how long it's been since someone was in the house. There are clues to look for. Dates on milk cartons. Postmarks on a stack of mail. Dishes left out or washed and put away. Emily's place was neat and tidy. That indicates she didn't leave suddenly. The mail was postmarked over a week ago, but there was no mail stacked up in her mailbox, which means she arranged for someone to collect it. There was no indication that she left in a hurry or was abducted. She planned to go away."

Max looked impressed. I know I was. Gabriel was way too good at this sort of thing.

"So for all we know, she could be on a cruise ship somewhere," I said.

"Possibly," Gabriel said. "I looked for signs of that, too. Women packing for a vacation often leave clothes hanging out on a doorknob or thrown on the bed. They try on various outfits, then leave the rejects hanging there."

I stared at him. "You know far too much about women."

"That's my job," he said, grinning.

"What sort of job might that be, mate?" Derek muttered under his breath. Gabriel just smirked.

"So now what?" Max said.

I told them what I'd learned from Crystal about Solomon being taught ammo loading and other survivalist skills from Bennie and Stefan in the Hollow.

Max leaned forward. "Maybe it was one of these kids, Bennie or Stefan, who took the shot at us."

"But it couldn't be them," I argued, glancing from Derek to Gabriel. "How could they possibly have eluded you two?"

Gabriel shifted his shoulders philosophically. "It happens."

"No, it doesn't," I said.

"Brooklyn's right," Derek said flatly, and looked at Gabriel. "You and I were out there together. There's no way those two evaded us." Then he gave Max some background on the survivalists in the Hollow and how, according to my dad, they all kept arsenals in their basements.

"All those people stocking up for World

War Three?" Gabriel said. "Not sure we'll get inside anyone's house."

"I wouldn't be surprised to find out they've all got booby traps set up," I said. "Bennie and Stefan sound like the type who would do that. Crystal called them immature, but they've also got intimate knowledge of munitions."

"Immaturity and ammunition," Gabriel said, shaking his head. "Bad combination."

"Yes," Derek said, nodding slowly. "Which is undoubtedly why Solomon decided to use them. For all we know, he might've sent them to kill Joe."

"And flatten my tire with Max's knife?" The memory of seeing that knife still irritated me. "I just don't think they're smart enough to pull that off."

"It's just sticking a knife in a tire," Max said. "How smart do you have to be?"

"But their timing had to be perfect," I explained. "They had to know I was coming. They had to know my car. They had to plan exactly when to kill Joe and escape out the back door, then vanish into thin air. I know I'm sounding paranoid and persnickety, but I just don't believe those two could pull off that sort of precision maneuver."

"I believe you're right, darling," Derek said, typing something into his smart phone.

"Tomorrow I'll contact the feds to see if they've any information on this local band of survivalists. I'm also interested in that church you mentioned."

"The True Blood of Ogun?"

"Yes." He frowned. "Seems I've heard of that group before."

"You have." I smiled. "Do you remember Mary Ellen Prescott, your new best friend at Abraham Karastovsky's memorial service?"

He thought for a moment. "I haven't a clue what you're talking about."

I laughed and reminded him of how Mary Ellen had tried to convert him. It's what happened when you let your guard down around Dharma.

He shook his head. "That'll teach me to wander too far from you at those affairs." He glanced around the table. "Now, where were we?"

"According to Crystal," I said, "Angelica is still living with Solomon. But also according to Crystal, Angelica cheats on him. I'm wondering if she has her own place somewhere."

"I'll check it out," Gabriel said.

"Good," I said. "Maybe you'll find the rifle she used."

"If it was she who shot at us," Derek added.

Max sat forward, his hands clutching the arms of his chair. "There has to be a way to find out where Emily's gone. Can one of you go to her school? Or her parents' house? I can track down their address."

They all turned and looked at me. *Well, why not?*

"I'm on it," I said.

CHAPTER 17

The next day, while Derek looked into the survivalists' weapons arsenals and Gabriel went off to find out if Angelica had her own place somewhere, I drove north to Windy Bluff Elementary School on the outskirts of Santa Rosa.

I had no idea if Emily still worked there or what I was going to say to her if and when I found her. I mean, how did you just walk up to someone and announce, "Remember that guy you were engaged to, and he died? Well, not so much." Yeah, this was going to be tough no matter how I looked at it.

Luckily for me, I arrived between classes, so the hall was packed and nobody thought to stop me. Walking past the rows of miniature lockers that lined the walls of the long, artificially lit corridor, I wove my way through gaggles of kids who were dressed much more fashionably than I had ever been able to manage.

Through the reinforced glass in the door of a classroom, I spied a room filled with desks for little people and a wall of alphabet-strewn blackboards — and shuddered.

I wasn't one of those kids who loved school. I liked my friends and I liked spelling bees and I enjoyed a few of my teachers, but I wasn't what you'd call a whiz kid. No, I didn't turn into a super achiever until I reached high school and realized that if I excelled, I could actually go to a school that would allow me to obtain a degree in book arts. And then my bookbinding would be considered a real career. At that point, my desire to excel became insatiable.

But this long walk down the hall brought back some less-than-pleasant memories from the early years. And why was it, I wondered, that grammar schools all seemed to smell the same? Chalk dust, fruity-flavored gum — in my day it was Fruit Stripe Gum — and a hint of gym socks. Back in my time, the scent of the mimeograph machine permeated the air, but those days were gone.

I brushed those thoughts away as I finally came to the door of the administration office. Walking inside, I watched while three women behind a counter busily carried out the duties of running a school while teachers and students came and went. I didn't see any reason to interrupt them, since I still wasn't sure what I would ask them.

After a few minutes, the door to an inner office opened and an attractive, well-dressed woman walked out. She looked at least ten years older than me, but maybe it was the outfit that added a few extra years. She wore a plain black suit with chunky black heels, a crisp white blouse, and a gray-and-black-striped ribbon tie at the collar. The only word to describe it was *matronly.*

"Are you waiting to see me?" she asked.

"You're the school principal?"

She nodded. "I'm Mrs. Plumley."

"Nice to meet you," I said, smiling. "I'm looking for Emily Branigan."

She frowned slightly, and I knew right away this was a tough principal. I felt sorry for any kid who was sent to this office. Mrs. Plumley, despite her sweet name, was a no-nonsense kind of woman.

"Is there a problem?" she wondered.

"Oh no. I'm an old friend of hers." That much was true, anyway, but I didn't have a clue what to say next. I would have to make it up as I went along, and even I knew what a bad liar I was. "We were, um, supposed to meet for lunch yesterday, but she never showed up. I just thought I'd take a chance and come by the school to see if she was ill, or if something happened to her, or if —"

I stopped talking abruptly. All that sounded reasonable, but I had a tendency to blather incessantly when I lied, so the less said, the better.

Mrs. Plumley smiled gently. "I'm so sorry she missed your lunch, but no, she's not ill. Unfortunately, she's not working, either. She recently took a short leave of absence. Perhaps you could write down your name and number in case she calls in."

"That's a good idea." I pulled out a business card and wrote a quick note on the back. *Emily, call me. Important.*

I handed her the card and watched Mrs. Plumley slip it into one of the many message slots that covered one wall.

"There," she said. "She'll get the message when she calls in."

"Thank you. I appreciate your help. Can you tell me how long she'll be gone?"

She pulled on her lower lip for a moment, then said, "I'm not comfortable giving out that information. I'm sorry."

"I understand." And I did. I stood there for a few seconds, hoping inspiration would strike and I would think of another brilliant question to ask the helpful Mrs. Plumley.

Something along the lines of, Is Emily still in love with Max Adams? Does she ever talk about him? Or has she finally moved on? Is she happy?

But Mrs. Plumley probably wouldn't be comfortable giving out that information, either. No other questions came to my mind, and it was probably just as well. I needed to skedaddle, as my mother would say, before I said something stupid and blew my cover.

"Well, you all have a good day," I said cheerfully, and walked out.

The GPS in Mom's car directed me to a street a few blocks off the main square in Sonoma. I came to a stop in front of a pretty house perched behind a vine-strewn fence. I didn't know why, but Emily's parents' house was exactly as I imagined it would be. Touches of fairy-tale allure blended nicely with rustic, wine-country charm. A pretty porch circled the house with a Victorian-style spindle railing, painted white. There were no cars in the driveway and I wondered if anyone was home.

"Might as well go find out," I mumbled as I unfastened my seat belt and climbed out of the car. I walked over to the gate that was closed across the driveway and checked the latch. There was a lock on it. Damn. I looked around, wondering if there was some other way to get close to the house. Even if her parents weren't home, I could snoop around, look inside a window or two. What would Gabriel do in this situation?

"They're not home," someone shouted from behind me.

I turned around and saw a young woman standing on the front porch across the street. She was dressed in pajamas and held a tiny baby on her shoulder. It looked like she was trying to burp him.

"Have they been gone all day?" I asked.

"All week's more like it," she said. "Maybe longer. I guess they're on vacation, although I couldn't say for sure. I haven't been around much." She patted the baby's back. "I've been in the hospital on bed rest for the past month, but I came home with this little one, so it was worth it."

"Congratulations," I said.

"Thank you. He's a darling thing." She turned her head and buried her nose in his little blue blanket. "Yes, you are. Yes, you are."

From across the street, I heard a long, loud baby belch, and laughed. "He sounds healthy."

"He sure is," she said, grinning, then patted his little baby butt. "Yes, he is. Oh yes, he is."

Oh, dear God. She sounded like she was talking to the family dog. I guess it worked for babies, too.

"Thanks for your help," I said, waving. Then I got back in the car and headed for Dharma.

"My day was a bust," I griped, and slumped in my chair at the kitchen table.

"Good thing there's wine," Dad said, and grinned as he handed me a glass. "Try this. It's a new Fumé Blanc from Chateau St. Jean. Crisp and smooth with a hint of melon."

"Sounds yummy," Mom said, and took a petite sip. "Mm, it is."

"Thanks, Dad," I said, accepting the small glass of wine from him. I took a sip and checked the wall clock for the tenth time. Derek hadn't yet called to say he was on his way, and I was feeling edgy. I wasn't sure why. Maybe because I'd been driving around playing private eye all day. I got up from the table and moved around the kitchen, checking the refrigerator, checking the soup on the stove, glancing out the window.

I went into the living room and tried Emily's phone number again. Even though her principal had verified that she was on a leave of absence, she would still be checking her messages. Wouldn't she? So maybe my first message got lost in the telephone-answering void.

Listening to the sound of her voice on voice mail again brought back memories. The first time I called, I wasn't absolutely certain it was her, but now I knew for sure. I left another message with my home and work numbers. I told her I lived in the city and could drive out to meet her anytime she wanted. I just really needed to talk to her, I said, then realized I was starting to sound desperate, so I hung up the phone.

I was agitated about more than just Emily not contacting me and Derek being late. I was homesick for my apartment, for my work, for the city. I'd been away from home too long. I imagined my mail piling up and deadlines being missed, even though my neighbors were collecting my mail and my clients had all been alerted that their books would be ready in the next two weeks. I loved my parents, loved my hometown, but I still ached to get back to the city.

I came into the kitchen and idly tore a piece of paper from Mom's notepad. I began folding it, first forward, then back, turning and twisting and making tiny folds. This was what I did when I was nervous. Within two minutes, I'd made an origami stork.

"For you." I held it out to Dad.

He chuckled as he took it from me. It wasn't much bigger than his thumb, but he held it carefully in the palm of his hand and shook his head in amazement. "You're a genius."

"Hardly." It was my turn to laugh. "I do make an awesome paper bird, though."

"A work of art," Mom said lovingly.

The phone rang and Dad picked it up, listened, then handed it to me. "It's Derek."

I grabbed the phone. "Hi."

"Darling, I can't make it out there tonight. There's simply too much going on."

"You sound tired.

"Just aggravated."

"I'm sorry."

"Yes, I am, too. I want you to be extra careful. I don't like to leave you alone at night."

"I don't like it, either."

I asked him if he'd unearthed any information on the Ogunite church or the survivalists, but he confessed that he had been too busy to deal with any of that. We spoke for a few more minutes; then I hung up and called Gabriel to give him the news. He assured me he would stay at Jackson's tonight and we would all talk tomorrow.

I hung up the phone and immediately felt lonely. And that was ridiculous. I couldn't go one night without seeing Derek? What was wrong with me? I had a rich, full life and was perfectly capable of entertaining myself. I enjoyed my time alone. Besides, I wasn't actually alone. My parents were both watching me carefully.

"Derek can't make it tonight," I said. "He's still at work and it sounds like he'll be there for a while."

"In that case, we'll just have to play three-handed Bananagrams," Mom said.

The next day, I decided it was time to make a bold move. I asked Mom for the keys to her car, but when she found out where I intended to go, she refused to be left behind.

"All right," I said, "but this isn't a carefree stroll in the park. We'll take one quick walk around the campus, gather whatever empirical data we can glean, and then we're out of there."

"Aye, aye, captain," she said, saluting smartly.

"And don't wear anything too colorful," I warned. "We don't want to attract any attention."

"Don't worry, sweetie. I'll dress just like you," Mom said.

I looked down at my dark jeans and slim, black leather jacket, then back at her. "Ouch, Mom."

She waved me off. "Oh, you know what I mean. You always look beautiful." Then she ran down the hall to change clothes.

I wasn't so sure she meant that, but ten minutes later, she came out in blue jeans, a thin red sweater, and a cropped navy jacket.

"Mom, you look very chic."

"Just like you," she said, making me laugh.

We drove four miles to the Art Institute and found a parking place in a local shopping area a block from the school. As we strolled briskly along the wide, tree-lined walkway of the campus, I noticed colorful banners on every light pole touting the latest artist retrospective being held at the institute's well-respected art gallery. The banner's image was blurry and I paid little attention to it, figuring it was some local artist I'd never heard of.

"It's a pretty campus," Mom said. "Did you enjoy your time teaching here?"

"I did, most of the time." As I gazed around at the students hurrying to classes, I felt a rush of nostalgia for my college days.

We passed the student union, and I considered walking inside to indulge in a little vicarious taste of student life, when someone shoved a flyer into my hand. I was ready to toss it in the trash, but happened to notice the large headline: GENIUS ON PAPER.

I stared at the stippled face of the honoree, then glanced up at one of the banners flapping on the light pole. I could finally make out that blurred image. Gazing back at the flyer, I read all about the upcoming retrospective featuring the most important works of that late, great papermaker, Max Adams.

"Oh, my God," I whispered, and scanned the flyer as Mom read over my shoulder. The opening-night cocktail party for the monthlong Max Adams Retrospective was scheduled for two Saturdays from now. The party was to feature several prominent artists, a live jazz band, a cash bar, hors d'oeuvres, and one very special guest.

"Look who the show's curator is," Mom said, pointing to the name at the bottom of the flyer.

I read the name, then did a double take. "Angelica Johansen. You have got to be kidding."

What in the world is Angelica up to?

"Didn't you suspect she knew Max was alive?"

261

"Yes, and now I'm sure of it." I shook the piece of paper. "This could be why she set the whole thing in motion, starting with selling the book to Joe."

"Do you really think so?"

"Of course," I said. "She expects Max Adams to be her special guest."

Mom and I stepped inside the dark lecture hall and found ourselves on the top tier of an arena-style auditorium. In the front of the class, standing at a podium next to a large slide screen that showed a photograph of the Greek Acropolis, was Solomon.

With a slide-change clicker in one hand and a laser pointer in the other, Solomon was delivering a stirring account of his last visit to the famous ancient ruin.

He glanced up at the top row and I shivered involuntarily. The lights were dimmed and he was busy lecturing, but I felt as though he could see right through me from twenty rows away. He seemed taller, older, better-looking, and more solidly built than I remembered him.

"Do we have latecomers?" he asked acerbically, his deep, smooth voice resonating through the room.

"Sorry, wrong classroom," I said loudly, and pushed Mom toward the door.

Once in the hall, I had to take a few deep breaths to calm my stuttering heart. I hadn't seen Solomon in almost ten years, but all it took was a few short seconds in the same room to leave me certain that the man could be a cold-blooded killer.

"I had no idea he was so forceful," Mom said, breathless herself.

"I'd forgotten," I muttered, wondering if I'd simply been too young and naive to recognize Solomon's potent sexual energy, or if his unpredictable, domineering ways back then had blinded me to his magnetism.

"No wonder Crystal is so in love with him."

"I know. He's got some lethal pheromones at work."

Mom's eyes narrowed in disgust. "Which helps mask the fact that he's a psychopath."

I looked at her in amazement. "Well put, Mom."

"I have my moments."

Laughing, I grabbed her arm and said, "Let's get out of here."

We made one quick stop at the gallery store. I wanted to find a poster of the retrospective to show Max. Wouldn't he be surprised?

The store had all different retrospective items available, from postcards to wall posters. I chose a medium-sized poster on good-quality card stock. Mom wanted one and so did I, so I ended up buying three.

"Oh, Max Adams," the salesgirl said with excitement. "I love his work. Don't you?"

"I do," I said as I handed her my money.

"If you're a student, you can get discount tickets to the retrospective."

I frowned. "I'm not a student."

"Me, neither," Mom said.

"Oh," the girl said, looking disappointed. But she perked up again. "Well, you should buy them, anyway, because it's going to sell out. The buzz has been incredible."

"Really? What are you hearing about it?"

"It's all his most important work, plus a lot of photographs of him during his lectures and appearances. He was so hot, you know? And rumor has it that somebody really important will make an appearance. I hear he worked with celebrities a lot."

"Sounds exciting."

"Oh yeah. Everyone on campus is crazy about Max Adams. It was an absolute tragedy that he died so young, so we're all determined to keep his spirit alive."

"That's so beautiful," I said.

"Yeah. Max rocks." She turned to the cash register. "You can buy the retrospective tickets here if you want."

I looked at Mom, who nodded, so I asked how much they were, and the price was reasonable enough. Not that it mattered. I wouldn't miss this for the world. "Okay, I'll take six tickets."

"Who's invited to the opening-night party?" Mom asked.

"It's free and open to the public, so it's going to be insanely crowded and stupid," she said. "I'm totally going!"

As we were leaving the sales counter, two young guys in green shirts and matching baseball caps walked into the store, pushing a cart loaded with boxes. I grabbed hold of Mom to stop her, just as the skinnier guy called out to the salesgirl, "Where do you want these, Shelley?"

"Stack 'em over here behind the counter, Bennie," the salesgirl answered.

"Hey, Bennie," I said, stepping closer. "Do you remember me? I'm London Wainwright's sister Brooklyn."

He looked me up and down, and his mouth curved in a lopsided grin. "Sure, I remember you, Brooklyn. How you doin'?"

"Benjamin Styles?" Mom said. "Is that you? Hello."

Bennie Styles was at least six feet tall and as gangly as a chicken. He still had adolescent pimples on his face and neck. It was

265

hard to believe that this was the weapons expert who'd taught Solomon everything he knew about ammunition, guns, and survival.

Bennie blinked at Mom; then his eyes widened. "Mrs., uh, Wainwright. How you doin'?"

"I'm dandy, thanks," Mom said.

Bennie's coworker elbowed him and Bennie jolted. "Oh, uh, this is my friend Stefan. This is Brooklyn and her mom."

"Hey, nice to meet you," Stefan said, flashing us a grin. Melody was right. He was really cute. He winked and gave us both a thumbs-up before grabbing the cart and rolling it over to the counter to stack boxes.

"So, what're you guys doing here?" Bennie asked.

"We were just purchasing tickets to the Max Adams Retrospective," Mom said. "Are you going?"

Bennie slapped his forehead in disgust. "If I hear that guy's name one more time, I'm gonna punch somebody."

Mom took a half step back. "Why is that?"

"Everybody's gone crazy over him, that's why. Especially the girls around here. Hello, the guy made paper. You know how he did it? With *paper!*" He waved his hands crazily. "Hello, I already got paper! There's paper everywhere. Who needs more paper? Well, toilet paper, maybe. But what's the big effing deal about this guy? Pardon my French."

"I appreciate your opinion, Bennie," Mom said carefully.

He pointed his finger to make a point. "Oh, it's not just mine. One of the professors here is totally pissed off about all the publicity this Max Adams dude is getting. I swear, if the guy wasn't already dead, Professor Solomon would've . . . Well, anyway." He scratched his neck, unsure where to go from here.

"Professor Solomon?" Mom said, her tone guileless. "I'm not sure I know who that is."

"Doesn't matter." Bennie's lips twisted up in a grimace. "Sorry I was rude. I got a big mouth sometimes. I better get back to work."

"Wait, Bennie," Mom said, stopping him. "Crystal Byers said you might be willing to teach me how to reload my ammunition. Can you still do that for me?"

"Oh. Sure. Yeah. I mean, yes, ma'am. Crystal was sayin' you needed some help with that, and I'm your man." Belatedly he remembered his manners and whipped off his baseball cap. His hair was stick straight and flopped into his eyes. He brushed it back impatiently.

"Yes, she said you were the best man for

the job."

He puffed up his scrawny chest and grinned. "Yes, ma'am, I am."

"Good. Now, I should tell you, I'm only interested in reloading shotgun shells for dove hunting, so I went out and picked up the Lee Load-All Reloader with the primer feed attachment."

He nodded in approval. "That's a good little starter kit."

"That's what I was told." She pulled out a piece of paper from her purse and wrote something down, then handed it to Bennie.

"This is my phone number. I can start anytime next week, and I'll be glad to pay you for your time."

He stared at the paper for a few seconds, then looked at Mom. "Yes, ma'am. I'll call you."

"You do that, Benjamin," she said, patting his arm. "You're a good boy."

Back at Mom's, we had our customary glass of wine while we waited for Dad to come home. I hadn't heard from Derek yet. I was hoping he would make it to Dharma tonight, not only because I missed him, but also because it would mean that things had calmed down at his office. But most of all, we needed to get back to Jackson's house to see Max and find out what Gabriel had learned about Angelica. And I had some interesting news of my own, thanks to our field trip to the Art Institute earlier.

I was sitting at the kitchen table, watching Mom whip up a marinade for the steaks Dad would grill later for the two of them. As I sipped my wine, I remembered something I'd meant to ask her. "Mom, did you really buy an ammo reloader?"

"Of course not. You know I hate guns."

"But how did you know what to say to Bennie?"

She winked at me and said, "Now, *that's* how you tell a lie."

I just had to laugh.

A car door slammed outside and I went running out the front door to see if it was Derek. Sure enough, there was the Bentley. I didn't want to appear too anxious, so I waited patiently for him at the front door. After a few seconds, I blew off that idea and raced down the front walk. He opened his arms just in time to grab hold of me, and we stood like that for a minute or two.

Gazing down at me, he asked, "What's all this about?"

"I was worried," I confessed. "How was your day?"

"Busy, but I managed to accomplish a few

things and escape with my skin intact."

I smiled. "I'm so glad. So, any news on the survivalists?"

He stroked my hair, calming me as if I were a jumpy young pony. "Let's wait to meet with Gabriel and Max and I'll tell you all everything."

But forty minutes later, when we arrived at Max's door, we found a large wooden mallet leaning against the threshold. It was the type of mallet used by papermakers to pound pulp.

"Max wouldn't leave his tools around like this," I said, staring at it.

"No, I'm sure he wouldn't." Derek pushed me behind him, but I pushed right back out again. It was just a mallet. Still, it was eerie to see it there.

"So if he didn't leave it here . . ." I didn't have to say what I was thinking. Derek was having the same thought. This was a message. Sent by the same person who had left Max's paper knife stuck in my tire.

I reached for the mallet.

"Don't touch it."

"It's . . . it's for making paper," I murmured. "You use it to beat pulp." Crushing fear spiraled right down into my bones. I felt my muscles give way and I had to lean into Derek. "This is impossible."

"Easy, darling," Derek said, grabbing me around the waist to keep me from slithering to the ground. "Maybe Max left it out here."

But neither of us believed that.

"Let's get you inside," Derek said softly.

Was he kidding? Go inside the house, where something might be terribly wrong? "No."

But he wouldn't listen to me. Prying the house key from my useless fingers, he knocked twice on the door, then pushed it open.

"Be careful," I warned him, my voice shaking with dread as I saw him reach for his gun and take a step inside.

Yes, he was brave and strong and really hot. But no matter how good he was at his job, I worried for Derek when he walked right into possible danger.

"Watch out, please," I prayed, unsure if he heard.

But when we got inside, Max was waiting in the living room, holding his rifle pointed at the door.

Gabriel stood nearby, drinking a beer. "You can put the rifle down now, Quick Draw."

Max lowered the gun. I sucked in a long breath and let it go. So all was right and safe inside my brother's house for the moment.

But Max insisted he hadn't left the mallet outside. He hadn't even seen that particular tool in years.

His enemies had discovered his hiding place. He was no longer safe in Dharma.

CHAPTER 18

Late that night, Derek and I spirited Max back to San Francisco. I'd offered my loft as the most secure place to stay, at least for a short period of time. Since my home had been broken into a while back, the building security had been upgraded. The parking garage had a shiny new security gate now, and the front door required a more intricate digital code to enter. I had lots of living space and an extra bedroom and bathroom Max could use. Not to mention the fact that Derek, supersecurity guy, was living with me.

Gabriel decided to remain in Dharma and keep track of Angelica's and Solomon's movements during the day. The nights were a different plan altogether. I confess it made my stomach a little queasy to know that Gabriel intended to stay at Jackson's house during the nights, in hopes of luring the bad guys into a trap.

Of course, after seeing that papermaker's mallet on the doormat, I wasn't sure if my stomach would ever be right again.

"I want you to call one of us every four hours," I demanded before I would give Gabriel the key to Jackson's place. "I swear I'll get in the car and drive up here if I don't hear from you. Then you'll really be sorry, mister."

I was channeling my mother again.

"Babe, I'll be fine," Gabriel said. "But thanks for worrying about me. It's sweet." Then he kissed me solidly on the lips and grinned as I blinked in dazed surprise.

"Must be time to go," Derek said wryly.

"Definitely," I mumbled when I was able to speak again.

I was happy to be home.

Derek and I showed Max around the house; then I got him set up in the guest bedroom. Once we were all situated, we met at the dining room table, where Derek called Gabriel and put him on speakerphone so we could discuss what we'd all found out over the last two days.

I recounted everything Mrs. Plumley told me about Emily being on a leave of absence. I told them what her parents' neighbor had said. It wasn't much information, but it gave

Max some hope that Emily and her family were probably out of town and hadn't met with foul play, as we'd feared.

I also braved Derek's ire and confessed to everything I'd seen at the Art Institute. I showed Max the retrospective poster and watched the mix of emotions that crossed his face. He wasn't sure how he felt about it, ultimately. From one angle, it was a huge honor, but, unfortunately, with Angelica putting the whole show together, it was just plain inexplicable.

When I mentioned that Mom and I had gone to Solomon's classroom, Derek's eyes turned dark with fury.

"We were in the back," I said. "He couldn't see me. And we only stayed a few seconds." But I knew that was a lie, and gazing at Derek's face, I could tell he didn't quite believe me, either.

Derek reported he was looking into Bennie's criminal record and was also checking into the weapons-arsenal issue. Specifically, he was interested in the buying and selling of guns in the area. If there were more criminals among the Ogunites and other survivalists living in the Hollow, Derek would track them down.

I studied Derek as he spoke and realized he looked exhausted. "Are you all right?"

"You mean besides my irritation with you and your mother for taking chances with your lives?" I gulped as he shook his head and turned to Max. "I apologize for being distracted. We've been having a bit of trouble with a new client. Everyone in the office is in a foul mood, and there's no end in sight."

That was the problem with having extremely wealthy clients who were used to getting their own way. But this was the first I'd heard of a troublesome client. I guess we'd all been distracted lately.

"That's okay," Max said. "I appreciate everything you're doing."

Gabriel spoke up from the speakerphone. "I managed to track down Angelica's apartment. It was still listed under an old roommate's name from almost five years ago."

"Good work," Derek said.

"Did you get inside?" I asked. "Was she there?"

"Did you find a gun?" Max asked.

Gabriel chuckled. "Thanks. Yes. No. No."

"Sorry," I said, sitting back in the chair. "Tell us everything."

"Her apartment was spotless," he said. "There was no mail piled up or food in the sink. She doesn't use the place much."

"Makes sense if she's living with Solomon," Derek said.

"But did you get the sense that she uses the place to meet other men?" I asked.

"Hard to say for sure," Gabriel said. "But I'm leaning toward no."

"Why?"

"Just a vibe. I'll check back there in a few days, just to see if I get the same vibe."

I could almost see his self-deprecating smile. He was the least "vibey" guy I knew.

Later, in bed, I apologized to Derek for going to see Solomon.

"We've had this conversation before," he said, turning onto his back and staring at the ceiling. "I worry about you. I should simply get used to it, or . . ."

My stomach dropped. *What is he saying?* I sat up and forced myself to ask. "Or what, Derek?"

He stared at me for a long moment. "Or I should hire a bodyguard for you when I'm not around."

"Oh." I sighed with profound relief. For a minute there, I was afraid he would leave me. Maybe I shouldn't have been insecure after all these months of our living together, but sometimes I couldn't help it. I still occasionally wondered what he saw in me. I'd made so many mistakes in the past. Love made me neurotic, I guess, but I was ready to snap out of it.

He sat up and brushed my hair away from my face in a tender gesture. "Darling, I might have to do a bit of traveling over the next few months."

"Because of your new client?"

"Yes. One of the partners has reached the end of his rope and I might have to take over for him."

"Oh. Can you tell me anything about the case?"

He shifted in bed and pulled me closer. "Not yet. There are security risks right now, but I'll tell you everything as soon as I can."

"All right."

He kissed me then and we forgot all about annoying clients and everything else but each other.

Over the next few days, we settled into a routine. Gabriel called twice a day, not at the four-hour increments I'd insisted on, but often enough to keep me from freaking out too much. Derek would drive off to his office each morning, even on the weekend, and that's when Max and I would go to our separate spaces within the apartment and get started on whatever project we'd planned to work on that day.

One morning, I spent some time re-arranging chairs and turned a corner of my living room into a reading nook. I'd been wanting some new bookshelves and now I had a full wall crying out for them, so I ordered a set online. The company guaranteed they'd be delivered within a week.

Clyde and I had bonded nicely. I decided I loved cats and was almost convinced they loved me, too.

It was all so normal, so domestic, I began to wonder if we really had overreacted. Yes, Joe was dead, but maybe his death had been a fluke or a mistake or completely unrelated to Max. Maybe the killer had shown up at Joe's bookstore and something got out of hand. He hadn't really meant to kill Joe. It was just a horrible accident. Maybe.

And maybe I'd sprout wings and fly off to Fiji for the day.

It was good to get back to my workshop and start on one of the big jobs I had waiting for me. I'd received the reference for this commission from my neighbor, Suzie Stein. Her aunt Grace was a book lover (a book *hoarder,* according to Suzie's roommate, Vinnie, but she'd said it as if that were a *bad* thing!) and she'd boxed up her shabbily bound set of Wilkie Collins in the hope that

I would be able to bring them back to life.

Aunt Grace had insisted on meeting me before I did the work, so a few weeks earlier, I'd driven out to Lake Tahoe with Suzie and Vinnie to meet Grace and pick up the books.

"She is a lovely woman, Brooklyn," Vinnie had insisted at least six times on the drive east. "Don't be afraid of her."

Suzie had finally glanced in the rearview mirror and said, "Vinnie, you keep saying that, and it's making Brooklyn even more afraid than before."

"It's best that she be prepared," Vinnie said darkly.

But Grace and I had gotten along famously, maybe because we both loved books so much. Grace, unfortunately, loved books in the worst way. Her home was a huge, sprawling mansion on the lake, and every room was stacked with books. There had to be at least twenty thousand books in her house. She had every author and collection known to man. Not just finely bound works, but paperbacks from every era. She was particularly proud of her forties noir collection with their grisly, sensationalist covers.

It was difficult to reconcile everything I knew of Suzie and Vinnie, the chain saw–wielding, animal-loving lesbian wood artists, with Suzie's eccentric and brilliant aunt, who'd made her money by designing computer games.

We'd had high tea with Grace and her friend Ruth. Grace had assured me she'd Googled my name and been impressed with my professional Web site. She trusted me to do a good job for her kids. By *kids,* I assumed she meant her Wilkie Collins books. But it wasn't until we had finished tea and Suzie mentioned that we needed to get back to the city that Grace finally asked the housekeeper to bring out the box of books she'd set aside for me.

Grace wouldn't allow me to open the box; she simply said that she wanted them rebound and that they contained lots of surprises and I wouldn't be sorry. I assured her I was very excited to do the work.

Now as I opened Grace's box of books for the first time, the pungent aroma of musty, moldy pulp wafted up. I picked up the book on top and stared at it in dismay.

"Good heavens," I muttered, putting it back in the box. "Did she use them for rat bait?"

I hurried over to a side drawer, pulled out several white cloths, and draped them across the worktable's surface. Taking all the books out of the box, I laid them carefully across the table to study their condition.

Once upon a time, the leather covers had been navy blue. Each book's front cover featured a miniature painting behind a small glass plate. They must have been exquisite when they were new, but now they were sad and dreary. That was okay; I appreciated a challenge.

I picked up the first book and checked the spine. *The Woman in White.* Its tiny painting depicted a woman in a billowy white dress standing on the bank of a lake with rippling water in the background. The detail was wonderful. It was lucky that the miniature paintings were protected by glass, because they all appeared to be in perfect condition, unlike the books themselves.

I checked the copyright page and found it was printed in 1860. I quickly looked up the publication date online and realized that this book might be a first edition. I would have to check other sources, but I had no doubt that the book was extremely valuable. While online, I also discovered that Collins had written twenty-three novels. The box Grace had given me contained only six books. I had to wonder whether there were more hidden throughout her rambling home that were in need of rescue.

Closing the cover, I turned the book over

and carefully began to thumb through the gilded pages. That's when I discovered the fore-edge painting.

"Oh, my God," I whispered. Was the entire collection painted? If so, the books were beyond priceless. The set belonged in a museum. I wondered if Grace would consent to donating them to the Covington Library.

The technique of fore-edge painting came into popular practice in the 1800s, and it was done by fanning the pages and clamping the book tightly. Then an artist would paint a watercolor painting on the fanned edge. When dry, the book would be clamped at its normal angle and the fore edge would be gilded in the typical way.

So when the book was closed, it would appear to be a normal, gilt-edged book. The painting couldn't be seen unless the fore edge was fanned. It was a charming surprise for any antiquarian book lover.

Some of the antiquarian books sold these days contained edge paintings that had been added more recently. There were artists who specialized in edge painting, and I'd worked with one talented but eccentric fellow a few years ago. It wasn't the sort of art you could hang on a wall and he was a little bitter about that, but his art was his master, or so he claimed.

But the fore-edge painting on this copy of *The Woman in White* was as old as the book itself and, thankfully, in excellent condition. The cover, however, wasn't so lucky; it was fully separated from the spine. The back cover was in even worse shape. The leather had disintegrated, the hard board beneath was crumbling, and one edge had been nibbled badly. It hurt my heart.

"Sad little book," I murmured. Yet when I fanned the fore edge, a sweet bucolic scene emerged of a shepherd boy and a flock of sheep grazing in a vast green field. "Amazing."

I opened the book and turned the pages slowly. There were a number of beautiful steel-engraved illustrations throughout. Strangely enough, the paper was still in good condition, with only light foxing, as far as I could see. I would have to check the others, but with any luck, they would be in the same decent shape.

I poured myself another cup of coffee, took a quick sip, then left the cup on my desk as usual. I never drank any liquids when I was working. Spilled coffee and old books didn't play well together.

As I reached for the next Collins, *The Moonstone*, I was already planning my strategy for restoring the set of six. I had several sheets of beautiful morocco leather dyed a deep navy blue, enough to cover all six books easily. It would be a challenge to resew and rebind them with their original fore-edge paintings, but I looked forward to it. I tested my strongest book press and was confident that it would hold each book in place as I resewed the signatures.

I spent most of that day in my sweats, going through every page of every book in Grace's Wilkie Collins collection. As with the *The Woman in White,* most of the paper was in good condition. A good thing, because the less work I had to do on the pages themselves, the less I would upset the natural lay of the fore-edge paintings. A tear or a replaced page would present a real challenge, so I was happy not to have to face that possibility.

After three days of working on the Wilkie Collins collection, I'd finished only two books and I needed a break.

It seemed that all of us were stalled in finding further information about Angelica and Solomon. Derek's office was in turmoil, so his time spent investigating weapons sales to the survivalists had taken a backseat.

I was happy I had my own work to do, because I would have gone stir crazy otherwise. Max seemed a little closer to the brink, although he managed to keep busy, as well.

Despite Derek's distractions, he'd taken the time to arrange for one of his assistants to pick up my car from the police, run it through the car wash, and fill it with gas, then deliver it to my home. I was thrilled to have my car back, even though I wasn't about to leave the house while there was a killer on the loose.

Monday morning, after Derek left for a meeting with clients, I took a break from the Wilkie Collins books and turned my attention to *Beauty and the Beast.* I'd received permission from Max to restore the book, even though he and Emily had originally insisted they wanted it left in its shabby condition. I gave him all sorts of reasons why it should be cleaned and rebound, but the reason that swayed him most was that the book had spent three years in the hands of someone who had shown ill will toward Max and Emily. Those bad vibes needed to be exorcised, and I was just the bookbinder to wipe them clean.

I didn't bring up the fact that the book had once belonged to me and part of me felt that it was back where it belonged. I certainly planned to turn it over to Emily and Max if they got back together again, but if the book really was mine, I would want to give it a shiny new cover. So that's what I was going to do.

That had been Ian's wish, too. Even if Emily and Max did reunite, I was hoping I could convince them to donate the book to the Covington after all.

In one of my map drawers where I kept sheets of leather, I found a beautiful piece of soft morocco in a spectacular shade of vermilion. I'd been saving it for the perfect project, and this was it. The color reminded me of the crimson paper Max had created from the juice and pulp of his homegrown beets.

I shuffled through the bags from Max's house and found the red paper among the many sheets I'd collected from his basement.

When I held up the paper next to the piece of leather to compare the colors, I was thrilled. The two shades complemented each other perfectly. I decided at that moment that I would build a storage box for *Beauty* and use Max's thick crimson sheets of paper for the lining.

The style of box I had in mind was commonly known as a clamshell because of its construction. A hinge on one side allowed it to spread open completely and reveal its contents, somewhat like the action of a clamshell. Most jewelry boxes opened this way, and many rare books were housed in similar style.

Max, meanwhile, had discovered that one of the doors in my living room led upstairs to my small, private rooftop patio, and he had taken over the space. Moving the patio table and chairs around, he set up a makeshift papermaking studio in the southeast corner, where the walls blocked the worst of San Francisco's winds.

He laid out his tools and supplies, then went around my house, pruning the plants and small trees I had in pots inside and out on the patio. He gathered quite a selection of twigs and leaves and petals that he would use to work into the sheets of paper he would make. I loaned him a week's worth of newspapers for turning into pulp, as well as my hair dryer, to speed up the drying process, and he was good to go.

I spent the afternoon in my workroom, studying the endpapers of *Beauty and the Beast.* They were worth saving. There was a fanciful rendering of a magical forest in shades of green and brown and gold that would work beautifully against the vermilion leather. The details of the forest were charming. Cheerful flowers lined a winding path that led deeper into the woods. Small forest creatures flitted among the trees. The picture was faded but still engaging, so I was extra careful to make a clean, razor-sharp cut along the inner hinge. I would splice the two sides together later and the little work of art would look as good as new.

It always took me a while to get started when I was taking apart a faded, broken book. The first cut was the most difficult. I know it sounds silly, but I felt as though I was cutting open an old friend, and I wanted to make sure that initial slice of the knife was exact and effective. I was always relieved to get past that moment.

I picked up my scalpel and used it to pick at the blobs of glue along the front inside cover. It was a mess and so thick that I wondered if some child had poured glue over the edges and their parent had tried to wipe it up to little avail. Stranger things had happened to books.

My mind wandered to thoughts of Max working upstairs. I hoped he was as blissful at pulping and mashing newspapers up there as I was with ripping apart an old book down here. I pictured the two of us, happy as dancing toadstools, working away in our own private worlds all day long.

Toadstools? I shook my head in bemusement. I'd been staring at that magic forest way too long. I blinked to clear my vision and glanced over at the clock on my desk. It was almost five o'clock. I'd been working for four hours straight.

"And didn't make it past the endpapers." Oh, well. I covered my tools and the book with a soft white cloth, slid down off my high stool, and stretched for a minute. Then I flicked off the bright ceiling light over my worktable and headed for the kitchen.

Max came walking out of his bedroom minutes later.

I stared, stunned by the change in him. "You shaved your beard off."

"I did. I felt like I was shedding an old skin."

"I love it," I said, smiling up at him. "You look years younger and very handsome."

"Shucks. I bet you say that to all the guys."

I laughed. "Are you ready for a glass of wine?"

"Sure. I'll open the bottle."

I pulled three wineglasses down from the shelf just as the phone rang. I answered it, listened and talked for a moment, then hung up. "Derek will be home in fifteen minutes."

While we waited for Derek to show up, we sipped our wine, a rich, dry Rhône that

I'd found on sale at the market and bought a case of last month. And I took the opportunity to beg Max to help me hone my cooking skills.

"I only know a few dishes," he said.

"But you cook effortlessly. There's no anxiety or kerfuffles in your kitchen. That's the part I'd like to learn."

"*Kerfuffles?* I've never baked those before."

"Ha-ha. Are you going to give me some pointers or not?"

He grudgingly agreed. "It's not like I have anything better to do."

"You really are a beast," I said, teasing him.

"About time you recognized my true nature," he said, and opened up my refrigerator to stare at the contents.

"I recognized it years ago, Beast."

"Yeah, I guess you did," he said, and tweaked my cheek. "Let's see what you've got in the cupboard."

We made a quickie version of what he called his world-famous chicken Parmigiana recipe from the six ingredients I actually had on hand: frozen chicken breasts, a jar of pasta sauce, bread crumbs, one egg, Parmesan cheese, and linguini. It would've helped if I had mozzarella cheese, too, but we worked around that. Because, really, who kept moz-zarella on hand, just in case?

Max pointed out that normally, he would have made the sauce from scratch with fresh tomatoes, onions, and garlic grown in his garden. He would have added heavy cream, too, because that's how he rolled. The consensus was that our quick-and-dirty version might not have been world famous, but it was pretty darn delicious.

The *effortless* part of cooking was something I still needed to work on. But watching Max, I could see his cooking techniques and his movements around the kitchen had everything to do with enjoying the journey and little to do with the results. He didn't get hung up if every tiny detail wasn't perfection. He just had a good time. To my surprise, I realized that this was the same philosophy I used with my bookbinding, and vowed that tomorrow night I would prepare dinner effortlessly.

Later that night, Gabriel called and I put him on speakerphone. Clyde sat on my lap during the conversation.

"I swung by Angelica's place again," Gabriel said. "Everything was neat and clean, same as last time, except for one little change."

I jumped forward in my chair. "What?"

"Did you find a gun?" Max asked.

"No," he said. "I found every piece of clothing from her closet tossed on the bed."

"So she probably wasn't there to meet a guy," I said.

Derek's eyebrow jutted up. "Bit difficult to carry on an affair when you can't find the bed."

"Were the clothes tossed neatly?" I asked.

"No," Gabriel said. "It was a mess. Jumbled."

"Like she was packing in a hurry?" I suggested.

Gabriel paused, then said, "Maybe. At first I was thinking she might've stopped by to pick up something different to wear. Except —"

"Except it's a mess," I cut in. "So why would she leave everything out in a pile on the bed? Especially when the rest of the place is so tidy?"

"Good question," Gabriel said.

"You'll watch for her next move," Derek said.

Gabriel made a sound of disgust. "I would if I could find her. She's disappeared."

"Maybe she did pack for a trip," I said.

"Maybe," Gabriel said, but he sounded unconvinced. Changing the subject, he said,

"I tracked down Bennie and Stefan. Or maybe I should call them Beavis and Butt-head. Whoever said they weren't exactly geniuses was right on. Personally, I think they would sell their souls for a box of candy bars."

"So they should be easy to manipulate," Derek said.

I had already told them about the conversation with Bennie at the Art Institute store the other day, so now I agreed. "Bennie would be very easy to manipulate. Stefan seemed to be a little more on the ball. Still, Solomon is a master manipulator. He would have no problem with either of them."

"That was my impression, too," Gabriel said. "And I took your advice and snuck into one of his classes. Interesting guy."

"For a psychopath," Max muttered.

"Exactly," Gabriel said.

"What else?" Derek asked.

Gabriel paused, then said, "Well, now that I've been out to the Hollow a few times, I'll admit I misjudged the place. Maybe it was because of that name, *the Hollow,* but I assumed the houses would be shacks and hovels. They're not. A bunch of them are really nice and some of them are huge."

"The Ogunites believe in having lots of babies," I explained.

"That must be why," Gabriel said. "Anyway, back to Bennie and Stefan. Solomon might be getting those two knuckleheads to do some of his dirty work, but my professional opinion? Neither of them is clever or vicious enough to have killed Joe Taylor."

Derek leaned one elbow on the table. "So that brings us back to Angelica or Solomon."

"Right."

"I'm betting on Solomon," I said, and felt a chill as I recalled his piercing look that day I walked into his lecture hall. There was little doubt a man like that could manipulate a weaker person into committing murder.

CHAPTER 19

Tuesday morning, Derek left for his office as the sun was rising. I was awake, anyway, so I decided to get an early start on my work. I was popping chocolate kisses and measuring out boards to cut for the new cover of *Beauty and the Beast* when Ian called.

"I'm checking up on you and the book," he said. "How's my *Beauty* doing?"

"I'm putting a whole new cover on your *Beauty*," I said with a smile as I reached for another chocolate kiss. "It's going to look fantastic."

"So you're going ahead with the restoration? That's great news."

Yikes. I probably shouldn't have told him I was restoring the book. If he asked if I'd gotten permission from Emily, I would have to lie. I couldn't tell him about Max. Not yet, anyway. I hung my head in dismay at my big mouth. "Um, yeah. I decided it needed an overhaul, so I've made an executive decision to take care of it while I wait to hear from Emily."

"So you haven't talked to her yet?"

"Not yet." I scrambled for an excuse. "I left a message. She's, um, out of town right now, but I expect to hear from her soon."

"You're still going to ask her to donate it to the Covington?"

"Absolutely." I had to bite my tongue to keep from telling him I would ask Max about it. I was a terrible liar and almost as bad at withholding information. Of course, Ian was so focused on work at the Covington, I wondered if he'd even heard about Joe Taylor's murder yet. Oh, he had to have heard by now. The book world was so small and garrulous, the news would have spread like crazy. But I wasn't about to bring up the topic, and I certainly wasn't going to admit that I was the one who found Joe's body.

"Look," he said, "shouldn't there be a statute of limitations or something? You know, if you haven't heard from her in thirty days, the book is mine?"

I smiled. "I'll look into that."

"I'm just encouraged that you're restoring it. Maybe I'll drop by to see it."

I almost choked on my Hershey's Kiss.

"Um, I'm not sure I'll be home, so you'd better call first."

"I'll take my chances. See you later, Brooklyn."

The following day, Ian made good on his warning.

On a whim that morning, I'd made a batch of chocolate chip cookie dough and put the first two dozen cookies in the oven to bake.

While I waited for the cookies, I mixed up some polyvinyl acetate, or PVA, the archival glue I used for bookbinding and book repair. It had a low moisture content, dried quickly, and remained flexible.

I had my largest cutting board out on the worktable, ready to go. But first I began drawing a template. The vermilion morocco was too precious to cut without measuring it precisely first. After I made the final cut, I would be ready to glue it to the boards and the spine.

I was getting ahead of myself. I still needed to resew the signatures and clean the book thoroughly. But I couldn't wait. The leather cover made me giddy with excitement. And didn't I sound like the biggest book geek ever?

The timer went off and I ran back to the

kitchen to remove the two cookie sheets from the oven. The cookies were baked to perfection, golden brown with perfectly melted bits of chocolate and still soft to the touch. While transferring them to a rack to cool off, I almost stuffed one into my mouth, but I resisted, barely.

As I slid two more sheets into the oven, my telephone rang. It was two quick rings, then nothing, which meant that someone was at the front door of my building, buzzing to be let inside.

"Max," I called, but he didn't respond, so I knew he wasn't in the apartment. He had to be up on the roof.

I was expecting my new bookshelves to be delivered today or tomorrow, but just in case it wasn't the delivery man, I needed Max to stay hidden. Feeling a hint of desperation, I grabbed the phone to see who was downstairs.

"Hey, Brooklyn, it's me," Ian said.

"Ian, what do you want?" How rude was that? He was going to think I was off my rocker. "I'm sorry, Ian. I'm just a little stressed. What's going on?"

"I'm right outside," he said. "Let me in. I want to say hi and see the book."

"Um, sure. Great. Here you go." I pressed the code numbers to release the door lock, then raced upstairs to the roof.

"Max," I yelled, since the wind made it hard to hear. "Someone's coming to see me, so stay up here, okay? Don't come downstairs."

"Okay, no problem," he said, waving me off, as casual as could be. "Let me know when it's safe to come down."

"You got it." I went running back down the stairs and closed the door that led to the roof, wondering how the hell he could be so laid-back when I was running around like a crazy person.

Ian stayed for almost an hour. I showed him the leather I'd chosen for the cover, and we discussed the ideas I had for gilding the leather. He suggested an elaborately gilded, highly stylized cover with curlicues in each corner. Since the book was from the Victorian era, I went along with his idea for a fancy design.

While he was here, I pulled more cookies out of the oven. Ian grabbed two while they were still warm. Shortly after that, he took off, and by then I was ready to collapse. All this running around and worrying was taking its toll. The PVA had hardened, so I would have to make another batch. But not right away. Just now, I felt like taking a nap. Maybe I would take the rest of the day off, eat cookies, and read a good book.

I was starting up the stairs to let Max know the coast was clear when the phone rang twice and stopped again. *Someone else is at the front door? What the heck?* I ran to the kitchen phone to answer it.

"Hey, Brooklyn. It's me, Ian."

"Did you forget something?"

"Nope, just wanted to let you know a delivery guy is here with a huge box for you. I let him inside."

"Oh, my bookshelves. Thanks, Ian."

We hung up, and it was a full minute later before I heard our building's ancient industrial freight elevator chug into action.

I cleaned off my worktable and tossed the PVA in the trash can.

The elevator shuddered to a stop and a few seconds later there was a knock on my door. That was one speedy deliveryman.

Max was hidden away on the roof and everything was fine. I took a few deep breaths to steady my heart. I really wasn't cut out for a life of intrigue.

Oh, who was I kidding? I thrived on intrigue, but this day was driving me batty.

"Brooklyn, yoo-hoo!" A voice called through the door. "You are home?"

My neighbor Vinnie? I ran to open the door.

"Hello, my friend," she said, and stepped inside.

I wrapped her in a warm hug. "Where's Suzie? How are you? I haven't seen you all week."

"We are fine," she said in her chirpy voice. I held her at arm's length to take in her outfit of black bustier, denim cutoffs, and army boots. On her it all worked.

Then I realized there was someone standing behind her.

"Delivery for Wainwright?" he said, parking his furniture dolly while he wiped his forehead with his baseball cap. Towering over him was a large brown box, about six feet tall and almost three feet wide. No wonder he seemed out of breath.

"Right," I said, grinning. "My bookshelves. Come on in."

I led the way, and Vinnie followed me from my workshop studio, where my front door was, through the short hall that led to my living room. I pointed to the wall on the left that was bare. "You can leave the box right there."

"That is why I am here, Brooklyn," she explained in her lilting Indian accent. "I saw this man stepping off the elevator and I told him I would show him the way."

"Yo, Brooklyn?"

302

"There's Suzie," Vinnie said, then cried out, "We are in here, Suzie." Suzie and Vinnie were a loving couple as well as business partners in chain-saw artistry.

"I knew it, you sneaky bitch."

That wasn't Suzie's voice. A sharp pain in my neck made me gasp aloud.

Minka?

She pushed her way past the delivery guy, lumbered right up to me, and smacked my arm. "How dare you?"

"Hey," I said, rubbing my arm. "What are you doing here?"

"I followed Ian over here. I was sure he was up to no good." She wiped her nose with the back of her hand. *Ew. What a slob.* "When he left just now, he let this delivery guy in, so now I've caught you in a lie you can't slither out of."

"How'd you get into the building?"

"Your front door takes forever to close, so I got in after him."

"Well, get out."

Suzie moved in closer and Minka cringed. Good. Suzie looked a lot tougher than she was, but at times like this, flexing some muscle couldn't hurt.

"I'm not leaving until I get some of the books Ian delivered to you."

"What books?"

303

"Don't play dumb with me." She flicked her chin toward the delivery guy. "You've got that whole big box of books to restore. I want some."

"Oh, my God," I muttered. "You are deranged."

"Right here okay?" the deliveryman asked.

I whipped around and saw he was standing right where I'd showed him. "Perfect. Thanks."

"These are the bookshelves you ordered last week?" Vinnie asked. "Can we see them?"

"Yes," I said, shifting away from Minka. "They're a really nice oak and they're going to go on this wall. What do you think?"

"Perfect," Vinnie said.

"Cool," Suzie said. "I like books everywhere."

We watched the deliveryman maneuver the box off the dolly inch by inch; then he held one end and carefully laid it down on the floor. "There you go."

"Anybody home?" someone bellowed from my front door.

I jolted. Yet another person was at my door?

But Vinnie smiled and said, "It's Jeremy and Sergio."

More fun neighbors.

"Come in," I shouted in the general direction of the front door. "Close the door behind you, please."

"A party on a Wednesday afternoon — how delicious," Jeremy said as he hugged me. Then he gazed beyond me toward the kitchen. "Ooh, cookies."

"Bring the plate over," I said.

Jeremy went after the cookies, and his boyfriend, Sergio, grabbed me. "Hi, cutie."

"Hi, Sergio," I said, patting his back. "How are you?"

"Fabuloso, as always."

"Brooklyn, darling, are we having a party?"

"Derek?" I spotted him coming through the hall and into the living room. "You're home early."

"A good thing, apparently," he said, kissing me firmly, then wrapping his arm around my shoulder. "I do hate to miss a party."

Minka shoved me again. "I don't care if you're having a party. I want answers. And I want my share of the Covington work."

I turned on her. "They're not books, Minka. They're book*shelves*. I ordered them a week ago." I realized I was yelling but I couldn't help it. She was a delusional moron with a left jab that could land you in the hospital.

"Liar!" she cried.

"Oh, my God." I grabbed my own hair to keep from strangling her. "You're a lunatic and you're trespassing. Now leave before I call the police."

"Hello, Derek," Vinnie said brightly, ignoring the commotion.

"Vinnie," he said, giving her a hug as he observed my less-than-amusing tête-à-tête with Minka. "How are you?"

"Very well, thank you."

"Sign for this?" The deliveryman shoved a clipboard in front of me. A pen was taped to the steel clip.

"Sure." I signed my name and he tore off a receipt and handed it to me. Then he turned the dolly around and took off for the door.

"Thank you," I called after him. I heard my front door slam shut and felt momentarily relieved until I realized Minka was still there.

"Cookie?" Jeremy said, holding the plate out.

"Yes." I shoved half of the cookie into my mouth. "We have milk."

"Ooh, yummers," Jeremy said. "I'll get it."

"Darling, what's going on?" Derek leaned close and whispered in my ear, "Where is our houseguest?"

I stood on tiptoe and answered quietly, "On the roof." I turned and looked around at the confusion. Derek and I gazed at each other, then shrugged and laughed.

"I'll open some wine," he said, and I nodded my approval.

"Hey, Brooklyn, aren't you going to open the box?" Suzie asked as she munched on a cookie.

"Yeah," Minka snarled as she adjusted her hat. "I'm not leaving until I've seen exactly what's in there."

"Whoa." I must have been distracted before, because I was just now getting my first good look at her — and had to shield my eyes. *Pink* and *plastic* were her watchwords today. The shirt was a shiny, one-shoulder creation that stretched across her voluptuous bosom so tightly that if it came loose, I feared somebody would lose an eye. Her pink stretch pants were sliced vertically all the way up her thighs so her skin popped out appallingly. She wore a matching pink, glittery pillbox hat tilted jauntily to one side.

Words failed me.

Derek stepped forward and held up my heavy-duty Tough Tool box cutters he'd found in my workroom. "Shall we?"

"Yes," I said. "Would you do the honors,

please?"

He knelt down next to the big box and sliced the cardboard top open to reveal another box, this one made of wood.

"Are those the shelves?" Suzie asked. "They look unfinished."

A highly suspicious Minka stood over one end of the box with her arms folded across her chest, just waiting to point an accusing finger at me. Moronic twit.

"This is so exciting," Sergio said, fanning himself. "Ooh, Derek, you're so strong."

Jeremy licked his lips in agreement.

I giggled at Derek's momentary look of horror.

He moved around the edges of the wooden crate, using the heavy blade of the cutters to pry the top up. "Help me with this, will you?"

Suzie and I gripped one end while Derek took the other end. Together we lifted off the top and laid it along the side of the crate.

"Well?" I asked, turning around to look at my friends' reactions.

Jeremy screamed and slid to the floor.

"Holy crap," Suzie shouted and skittered backward.

Vinnie made some kind of wheezing sound and yanked Suzie back farther. She began chanting something in her native language, then cried out, "Dear goddess, what evil has come into our world?"

I turned and looked. And gasped. Derek grabbed me before I could join Jeremy on the floor, and pressed my head to his chest so tightly I could barely breathe.

"Oh, my God. Oh, my God," Suzie chanted.

"This isn't happening," I muttered, lifting my head to catch my breath.

Minka whipped around, pointed at me, and screamed, "You're a sick, twisted bitch!" Then she made a gagging sound and ran for the door. I could hear her screaming all the way down the hall.

I braced myself, then turned back to make double sure I wasn't hallucinating.

But no, it wasn't an illusion. Lying in the box was Angelica, almost as beautiful as she'd ever been, surrounded by faded, wilting flowers. Her hair was coiffed, her makeup was perfect, and she was very, very dead.

CHAPTER 20

Minka's screeching could be heard for blocks around. It brought Max racing down from the roof.

"What the hell's wrong?" he shouted from across the living room. "Sounds like a screaming hyena out there."

I whipped around. "Oh, Max," I cried, and ran to meet him.

"Are you okay, hon?" he asked, rubbing my back. "Was that you screaming?"

I shook my head but couldn't speak, couldn't tell him what was wrong, so I just stood there as he rocked me in his arms.

I could see Derek bent over the corpse, doing something. Knowing Derek, he was probably checking for a pulse and telltale signs of her cause of death. A minute later, he circled the room, surveying the people, appraising the situation, focusing on triage.

Finally, he approached Sergio and clutched his shoulder. "Take everyone to your place, would you? And tell them to stay there. I'll be over in a few minutes to ask some questions."

Sergio nodded, immediately accepting Derek as the top dog. Slipping his arm through Jeremy's, Sergio lifted his partner off the floor in one smooth movement. "Come on, sugar. Let's go get some air."

Suzie latched onto Jeremy's other side, then motioned for her partner. "Vinnie, baby, come on."

"Oh, Brooklyn, I am praying for you," Vinnie said, then grabbed hold of Suzie's hand and walked out with the others. I watched them go, wondering if my neighbors would ever speak to me again. And with that thought, my eyes filled with tears.

I know I was a terrible person, but I couldn't help thinking that even *dead,* Angelica was making trouble for me.

"It's okay, Brooklyn," Max murmured, then nudged me back and bent down to meet my gaze. "Now tell me what happened?"

I looked up at him and realized he had no clue what had just occurred. "Not sure you want to know," I said, but I grabbed his hand and turned and steered him slowly across the room.

Derek stopped him. "Be prepared for a

shock, mate."

"Over there," I said, pointing at the box.

"Yeah, okay." Max frowned, then straightened his shoulders and stalked over to the box. He took one look inside, then shouted an incoherent epithet and jumped back a foot. He began to swear like a sailor, then instantly found religion. "Holy Jesus! Mother of God!"

Finally, he whirled around and grabbed his head with both hands. "Christ! That's sick. Who would do that?"

That was pretty much the question of the hour.

"Put the cover back on the box, would you?" I asked.

"Yeah," Max agreed loudly. "Damn. Let's do that."

As he and Derek lifted the heavy wooden top, I brushed my hair back off my forehead and tried to catch my breath. I was still shaking, could still feel the residual terror of that first moment when I realized that a dead body had been delivered to my home.

What had I done? Why had someone sent me such a hateful, macabre message?

More important, what had Angelica done? Well, she'd been a bitch, treated a lot of people badly, but had she deserved to be used as an object of horror?

To someone, she obviously had. And I knew that someone was Solomon. That man had a lot to answer for.

Was this all about Max? Or me? Both of us? Who was the message intended for? My head was spinning with questions and no clear answers.

I watched as Derek and Max straightened the edges of the box; then they both stepped back. Max looked grim as he walked out of the room.

"How did she die?" I asked Derek.

He gritted his teeth. "I suspect asphyxiation."

"She was strangled?"

"Suffocated," he corrected.

"Like, with a pillow, you mean?"

"Perhaps," he said, his eyes narrowed in thought. "Something plastic is more likely."

I winced. "Oh."

After a moment of silence, he pulled out his cell phone. "I'll call Gabriel."

I nodded. "I'll call the police."

"Look who's moving up in the world," Inspector Lee said cheerfully as she walked into my workroom.

"What do you mean?" I said, lifting my head from the table. While she'd been observing the crime scene, I'd been resting

313

my eyes for a few minutes. But it hadn't helped to erase that vision of Angelica in the box. I feared it was permanently planted in my brain.

"I mean, you're not going out looking for dead bodies anymore," she explained with a smirk. "Now you're having them delivered."

I stared at her in amazement.

"What?" she said.

"That is just so mean."

She laughed. "Lighten up, Wainwright. We've got to keep a sense of humor about these things."

I made sure she saw me rolling my eyes before I walked away. I went into my bedroom, closed the door, and looked around. I loved this room, loved the colors I'd chosen. Pale greens in different shades from sage to apple. Crisp whites. Clean, soft lines. Nothing frilly, just all smooth and calm. I could relax in here, clear my thoughts, consider my options. I sat on the love seat and put up my feet. I didn't feel like relaxing. I wanted to kick something.

My life in the past week had been turned upside down. Two bodies discovered, one delivered in a box. A friend returning from the dead. Crazy survivalists. Someone taking potshots at me and my friends. I was sick of it.

" 'Got to keep a sense of humor about these things,' " I muttered sarcastically. Not fair! I had a sense of humor.

And I liked Inspector Lee — I really did. But, excuse me, I didn't think calling me a murder magnet was all that funny. She'd said stuff like this to me before, stuff about seeing me at every murder scene and how we had to stop meeting like that. She'd made it clear that she noticed I seemed to attract dead bodies.

Maybe *she* was the reason I'd developed this complex, the one I'd discussed with Guru Bob. But Guru Bob had seen it in a positive light. I wasn't sure I agreed with him. Could I ever consider my apparent proclivity for finding dead bodies a good thing? Did he really intend for me to take on the role of Nemesis, finding justice for the dead?

Did I even want to? Some of the dead were people I would never be friends with. Case in point? Angelica. She had treated me like a leper. Did I really care who murdered her?

I punched the pillow I was clutching. Yeah, I cared, damn it. Not because of her, certainly, but because the murderer had obviously targeted me. And Max. They'd shot a gun at us both, and at Derek and

Gabriel, as well. So we were all victims of a sort. Even Emily, wherever she was.

So I wasn't about to stop searching for reasons and clues and answers to my questions. And justice. I wanted justice. I wanted Max to have his life back. I wanted that damn box out of my living room. And along the way to finding answers, if I happened to find justice for Angelica also? Well, then, no harm, no foul.

But first I needed to swallow my annoyance and face Inspector Lee.

" 'Now you're having bodies delivered,' " I mimicked, shaking my head. Okay, now that the initial piss-off had passed, even I could admit that it was a little funny. Still mean and rude, but funny. And too damn true.

" 'Bodies delivered,' " I grumbled.

I punched my pillow one last time. "Okay, fine. It was funny." But you'd never catch me admitting it to her.

I was chuckling reluctantly by the time I left my bedroom. I mean, really, that damn woman's body had been delivered straight to my house. It was like the plot of a bad horror movie. Creepy. Diabolical. Stupid. Who had that kind of mind?

" 'Delivery for you, Ms. Wainwright,' " I muttered, shaking my head. "Bodies 'R'

Us." It really was too silly, if I looked at it objectively. A body delivered to my house. *Ridiculous!*

And all of a sudden, my eyes flew open. "Delivered. To my house. Oh, God."

I ran down the hall shouting, "Derek."

"Right here, darling," he called from the kitchen, where I found him drinking a beer. Inspector Jaglom sat on one of the bar stools, holding a Starbucks cup.

I averted my eyes from the scene in the corner of my living room, where the medical examiner and his assistants were hauling Angelica's body out of the box. I hoped they were taking the box with them.

"What is it, love?"

"The deliveryman!" I said gleefully. "He'll have information on whoever sent that thing."

"Brilliant, darling." Derek lifted his beer bottle in a toast to my genius. "Do you have the delivery slip, by chance? Inspector Jaglom can get started straight away with tracking him down."

My shoulders fell. "You already thought of that, didn't you?"

He gazed at me with fondness. "I believe you and I might've thought of it at precisely the same moment. Great minds and all that, you know."

"Right." I shot him a skeptical look. He smiled back at me and mouthed the words, *I love you.*

And just like that, I was smiling again.

Inspector Lee caught me coming out of the kitchen. "Listen, Wainwright. I mean, Brooklyn. You know I was just teasing you earlier, right?"

"Yeah, I know."

"Good." Inspector Lee grinned. "Because believe it or not, I actually like you a lot."

"You like me?"

"Hey, if I didn't like you, I'd kick you to the curb."

"Gee, thanks," I said. "I'm feeling the love."

"That's as warm and fuzzy as I get, Wainwright."

"But you mean it? You really, really like me?" I said, sniffling as I dramatically clutched my hands to my heart.

She held up both hands. "Okay, don't get carried away."

"Trust me, I'm not," I said sardonically.

She laughed and we walked out of the living room into my workroom. I needed a break from the crime scene and she seemed willing to hang out with me.

"You and me," she said, leaning one hip

against my desk. "We're sort of in the same boat."

I jumped up and sat in one of my work chairs. "How do you figure?"

She shrugged. "Well, first and most obviously, we're both foxy."

"Foxy?" I laughed and she grinned. Guess she was going for a laugh, so I played along. "That's so true. We do have that much in common."

"Yeah," she said, "and we both seem to find ourselves around dead bodies a lot."

"Also true." I observed her for a moment and realized she looked a little uncomfortable. *Interesting.* So I said, "You know, we have so much in common, we should probably try to get along. You know. Be friends, maybe."

She shrugged. "Only seems right."

"Okay." I held out my hand and she reached over and shook it. Her hand was cool and calloused. Friendly.

"Friends," she said with a satisfied nod.

I found the delivery invoice on my workroom desk and took it to Inspector Jaglom, who was still sitting in the kitchen. He stared at the slip, then dialed the number for Worldwide Shipping and Delivery Service. He read off the invoice number to the dispatcher, who had no record of the delivery.

After a few minutes of wrangling with the woman, Inspector Jaglom asked me to describe the driver. I gave him as precise a description as possible, and Derek added a few details. Jaglom repeated the information into the phone.

The dispatcher recognized the man in question and put the inspector on hold while she tracked the guy down.

It was at least ten minutes before the dispatcher came back on the line. I spent the time making more coffee for the cops and arranging another plate of a dozen cookies to put out. They were devoured within minutes.

"Yeah?" Jaglom said abruptly, then pulled out his notepad and began to write furiously. "I see."

Inspector Lee frowned as though she could read her partner's facial expressions.

"Yes, ma'am," Jaglom said. "We'll have a patrol unit there immediately. Right. Thanks for your assistance." He hung up the phone.

"They found the guy?" I asked.

"Yeah." His mouth was tight as he digested what he'd heard. Then he looked at me. "The good news is, they tracked him down. The bad news is, he's dead."

I was stunned into silence for a long moment. Finally I asked, "How did he die?"

Lee's reaction was a quick scowl; then she relaxed her features. I guess I was interfering with the investigation, but since she didn't smack me upside the head, I took it as a small victory.

"They found him with a plastic bag over his head," Jaglom said. "He suffocated to death."

I cringed. There was no good way to die, but that seemed like a particularly bad one.

While Jaglom called for a patrol car to go to the delivery company, Derek and I spoke quietly and reached a decision. As soon as Jaglom was off the phone, Derek revealed that Max was alive and completely innocent. He explained about the harassment Max had endured three years earlier and the circumstances behind his staged death. The detective trusted Derek completely, but that didn't mean he was about to pass on interrogating Max. So I led Jaglom to Max's room, where he spent almost an hour interviewing my friend. When Max and Jaglom walked out to the kitchen, the relief on Max's face brought tears to my eyes.

A few minutes later, I took Lee and Jaglom over to Sergio's place, where I hung out while the cops spent another forty-five minutes interviewing my neighbors. Given everything they'd been through today, I wondered if any of them would ever speak to me again. But they all hugged me and assured me they would, so at least I had that.

On our way across the hall to my place, I asked the inspectors if they'd made any headway on Joe's murder.

They exchanged glances; then Jaglom said, "Our lead suspect just showed up in a box."

I winced at that, then opened my front door in time to see the medical examiner leave. He and his assistant were steering a gurney that held the body of Angelica wrapped in a thick black plastic bag.

Another assistant followed, wheeling a dolly that supported the crate that had contained her body. I couldn't suppress a shudder as it passed by me.

Back in the kitchen, Lee looked around. "Have we talked to everyone now?"

I thought for a moment. "Everyone but Minka."

Lee gasped and her face turned into a mask of terror. "LaBoeuf? She was here?"

I bit back a laugh. "It's a long story, but yes. You might say she crashed the party."

Jaglom saw Lee's expression and laughed.

"I've interviewed her twice before during our last two investigations. It's your turn, Janice."

"No freaking way," Lee muttered darkly as they both packed up their notepads. I walked them out of my place and down to the freight elevator.

Jaglom was still laughing. "She's a nice girl once you get to know her."

Lee snorted. "She's a rabid dog."

Jaglom laughed and turned to me. "We'll be in touch."

"Thanks," I said. I thought I heard Inspector Lee growling as I walked back to my place.

Minutes after I got inside and locked the door, my telephone rang with two quick rings, then nothing. It was the doorbell. Again.

"I'm afraid to answer it," I said, flashing Derek an apprehensive look. But I picked up the phone anyway and said hello.

"Hey, babe."

Gabriel. My stomach relaxed and I buzzed him in. He bypassed the slow freight elevator and took the stairs and arrived at my door in a minute flat.

I couldn't bear to sit in the living room where Angelica's body had lain for the past three hours (memo to self: grab some of

Mom's cleansing white sage to purify and chase away the dead-body vibes in my living room), so we moved into my workroom and sat at the high table. I'd taught private classes in my home, so there were four comfortable high chairs. If someone else showed up, they would have to stand. I doubted that would be a problem.

I served hors d'oeuvres: more cookies, plus the last of some Brie I had in the fridge and half a bag of potato chips. Wine for me, beer for the guys. Nobody complained.

We amused Gabriel with the horrific story of the body in the box, plus the murdered delivery guy.

"Sorry I missed the fun," Gabriel said with black humor.

I gave him a dark look, but conceded, "This means that Solomon is a sure bet for Joe Taylor's murderer."

"Not necessarily," Derek said.

Max leaned his elbows on the table, looking puzzled. "Who else could've done it?"

"Angelica," Derek said cryptically as he swirled his wine.

"Meow." I glanced down and saw Clyde staring up at me. He'd spent the day hiding in Max's room and I couldn't blame him.

"Do you want to come up?" I asked.

"Meow."

I figured that meant yes, so I pushed my chair back from the table a few inches. He crouched, then jumped up onto my lap in one amazingly smooth move. He took his time getting comfy, staring up at me, rubbing his face against my chest. Then he circled around and wiggled a little until he found just the right spot, and plopped himself down.

"I love this cat."

"And he loves you," Max said easily.

I gazed down at my fuzzy friend and stroked his pretty orange fur. "You don't understand. Cats don't like me."

"Where'd you get that idea?" he said, and leaned over to scratch Clyde's neck.

From every other cat I've ever known, I thought grimly, but didn't say. Instead, I glanced across at Derek. "You still think Angelica could've killed Joe?"

"Yes."

"But why? And what do you think happened afterward? Did she and Solomon have a falling-out and he killed her?"

"Yes," Max said.

Derek nodded. "It's the most likely scenario."

"A lover's spat," Gabriel mused.

Max's face soured in disgust. "Those two would stop at nothing to destroy everyone else. Why not destroy each other?"

"Poetic justice?" I said.

"Works for me," Gabriel said, grabbing a handful of chips.

"But it could just as likely be Solomon who killed Joe," Derek conceded.

"We need to talk to him," I said.

"There's no *we* here," Derek said testily. "You're going to stay as far away from him as possible."

I rolled my eyes, looked around the table, and palmed another cookie. "So what do we do right now?"

"I'm going to get another beer," Max answered. "Anyone else?" There were no takers, so Max strolled out to the kitchen.

Someone knocked on my front door and I flinched, disturbing the cat enough that he turned and grunted at me and his claws came out. If I nudged him off, would he ever speak to me again? Could I live with that?

"I'll get the door, darling," Derek said, already halfway there. "Don't disturb your new friend."

"Clyde thanks you," I said, smiling gratefully. "It's probably one of the neighbors wanting to commiserate."

Derek glanced through the peephole and gave me a look. "It's a woman I don't recognize."

"As long as it's not Minka, go ahead and open it."

"I hate to disrupt the cat," he said, "but I'd rather you confirm that you know her first."

"Okay." I gently nudged Clyde off my lap and walked over to the door, where I squinted through the peephole at the woman waiting in the hall.

My jaw dropped to the ground and my heart stuttered in my chest. But I managed to recover enough to whisper, "Emily?"

CHAPTER 21

"One of your neighbors let me into the building," Emily explained, clutching her hands together nervously. "I hope that's okay."

"That's . . . wonderful." Taking Emily's arm, I led her into the apartment. "Come in, please. Wow. How are you? It's been a long time."

"Yeah, I know," she said, hesitating just inside the doorway. "Sorry to just drop in."

"It's no problem."

She took a moment to gaze around my workroom, and I could see her eyes focusing on the many shelves and rows and rows of threads and tools and papers and map drawers. "Nice space."

"Thanks. Oh, Emily." I grabbed her in a hug. "I'm so glad to see you."

Glad she was alive. Glad she hadn't been hurt, and just glad in general. Of course, this opened a whole new world of *uh-oh*s, too. Max was here. In the house. Emily thought he was dead. And I wouldn't have the chance to warn either one of them before they saw each other, so . . . uh-oh.

"Yeah, me, too," she said, hugging me tightly. "It's been too long." After a moment, she stepped back and ran a nervous hand through her long brown hair. She hadn't changed much, except that she'd grown her hair longer and had gotten even prettier than she'd been three years ago. More elegant somehow, and calmer.

"Look," she said, folding her hands as she spoke, "I'm sorry I didn't return your phone calls. I wanted to, but I was visiting my parents, who are staying in Cleveland for a few months. My dad's sick. He's at the Cleveland Clinic and . . . well, you don't need to know the details. Anyway, I just flew into SFO and didn't feel like driving straight home. So I thought that as long as I was in town, I'd take a chance and stop by. I hope you don't mind, but I Googled you and got your business address. Anyway, here I am — and, God, I'm talking too much."

"No, you're not," I said, laughing. "I'm sorry to hear about your dad. But I'm so happy to see you. I'm blown away that you came by."

I glanced over at Derek and saw the *What*

do we do about this? look on his face, and I answered with a shrug. One glance at Gabriel's smile told me he was enjoying the drama of the situation. I was willing to bet that Max wouldn't.

"What's going on, Brooklyn?" she asked. "Your messages made it sound urgent."

"Yeah, it is. But first, I hope everything's okay with your dad." I knew the Cleveland Clinic's reputation for working medical miracles — sometimes.

"Thanks," she said. "I do, too. I'm going back there next week, but I had to take care of some things at home."

"Well, we can go into the living room, I guess." No way to avoid the death cooties from Angelica's body now, and I couldn't keep Emily standing in the workroom. Now it was my turn to be nervous.

"Okay." But she stopped and smiled at Gabriel and Derek. "Hello."

"Hi there," Gabriel said with a grin.

Derek nodded. "Hello."

"Sorry. My manners went missing," I said. "These are friends of mine. This is Derek Stone and that's Gabriel."

"Hi," she said again, and went back to clutching her hands together. "Well. You look really good, Brooklyn."

"Oh, thanks. So do you." This was ridiculous. I had to give her some kind of hint about why I'd been calling. It wasn't fair to just spring Max on her. She was young, but a shock like that could bring on a sudden heart attack. God, why hadn't she called me first? "Look, Emily, I don't how to —"

"Found more chips," Max said as he walked back into the room, shaking the bag. He stopped abruptly and stared, gaping at the woman. "Emily?"

I heard a long gasp, then a moan. I was just in time to catch her on her way to the floor.

"Emily!" Max cried out, and ran over. I moved out of the way as he took her from me. He knelt down and laid her out on the floor, slipping his hand under her head and pressing his other hand to her cheek. "Oh, my God, Emily. Emily."

Shoot! This was awful! I should have found a way to warn her. But was there really any way to prepare her for seeing her dead boyfriend all hale and hearty? Watching the expression on Max's face, hearing the desperation in his voice, I had to blink to clear my tear-filled eyes. I'd been doing that a lot lately.

Derek closed the front door and, to be safe, knelt down to check her wrist for a pulse. "She's fine. Just a bit of a shock, I'm guessing."

"Just a bit," I said dryly. He stood and grinned and wrapped his arm around my waist.

"Max," I said softly. "You scared the hell out of her."

"She scared the hell out of me, too," he said, looking up and scowling mildly. "Probably took ten years off my life. Why didn't you warn me?"

"How could I warn you? She just showed up here! I didn't know she was coming. Besides, if I were going to warn anybody, it would've been her. *You* already knew you were alive."

He shook his head and looked back at Emily, moved his hand over her shoulder and her hair, barely touching her in case he might hurt her. All the while he whispered over and over, "So beautiful. Still so beautiful."

"She's waking up," I murmured. "Maybe you should get her off the floor."

I watched Emily blink a few times, then focus on Max's face. She groaned. "No. I'm dreaming."

"Oh, sweetheart, no. You're not dreaming."

She silently began to cry.

"Please," he said, burying his face in the

crook of his elbow. "Please don't cry."

"Max, pick her up," I whispered. But he seemed frozen in place, unable to take action. Derek squeezed my waist and I looked up at him. He tilted his head toward the living room, indicating we should leave them alone.

Is he kidding? I shook my head and he frowned at me. But come on. Seriously? Maybe it was nosy of me, but there was no way I was leaving the two of them alone. I wanted a front-row seat, wanted to savor every last second of their tearful reunion. I'm just a big sap that way.

As her tears began to dry, Emily hiccupped a few times, then swallowed awkwardly. Glancing around, she took a deep breath and let it out, then said, "Help me up, please?"

Max immediately slipped his arms under her and stood with her still in his clutches.

"You can put me down now," she said.

"No, I can't."

"Why not?"

"I'm never letting you go again."

"Like you did before? Let me go, I mean." Emily just stared at him, her expression unreadable.

"I didn't want to."

"But why, Max? You died. And now you're

here? What happened? Where did you go? Why did you leave me?" She sniffled and seemed to lose strength. Her eyes closed.

"Bring her into the living room, Max," Derek suggested. "She can lie down on the couch."

"And then you can try to explain what happened," I said to Max.

He gave me a foreboding look, then whisked his fair Emily off to the living room.

Gabriel's grin grew even wider. "Guess I'll have that beer, after all."

When Emily had revived, there were hugs and more tears and kisses. Her smile seemed permanently fixed to her face, and, frankly, I was sort of amazed at how well this reunion was going. If my boyfriend had disappeared on me, then popped up again seemingly from the grave three or six or eight years later, I'm pretty sure I would have been furious first and then maybe I'd think about being happy to see him again. Emily was clearly a much better person than I. Finally she sat up, asked for a glass of water, then went off to use the bathroom.

I went into the kitchen to get her water and carried it back to the living room. I set the glass on the coffee table and sat back down.

Max, meanwhile, had begun to pace the floor. "Is she all right? She's been gone too long."

"Chill out," I said. "She's been crying, so she's washing her face and fixing her hair. Give her a minute."

He started to pace again, then halted when Emily walked back into the room. Instantly, he was at her side, taking hold of her hand. "God, I'm thrilled to see you again. It's like we were never apart."

"But we *were* apart," she said flatly, her smile finally gone. "For three years, Max. You were dead, remember?"

"It was for a good reason. I promise."

"I'm sure it was. And so is this." She wound her arm back and slugged him right in the gut.

Now, that reaction I understood completely.

"Ow. Damn it!" He grabbed his stomach and inched back from her. "If one more woman takes a swing at me, I'll . . ."

"You'll what?" She stepped closer and pressed up against him, jabbing him in his chest with her finger. "What will you do?"

"Never mind," he muttered, glaring down at her. Even though he towered over her and outweighed her by a hundred pounds or so, she showed no fear.

"Never mind," she repeated, nodding her head in double time. "That's what I thought you'd say."

I choked on a laugh. Max was three for three in the gut-punching sweepstakes. I happened to glance at Gabriel, who was grimacing as he unconsciously patted his own stomach. That's when I lost it and laughed out loud.

"Stop that," Max said, pointing an accusing finger at me. "You're enjoying this too much." Then he turned on Emily. "And you. You've never been a violent person. What was that for?"

"What was tha— ? Are you kidding? You drove over a cliff and died! You left me alone for three years!" She pointed her own finger in his direction. "You're right. I never was violent before, but I'm feeling it now. I thought you were dead. But you weren't. You just left. I wasn't worth a call? A note? You couldn't text me?" She shook all over in anger. "You should be glad I only hit you in the stomach."

He looked uncomfortable at that, but then stubbornly insisted, "I couldn't tell you."

"You didn't trust me."

"I was protecting you," he said hotly. "And if you'd seen that body in the box that showed up here a few hours ago, you'd understand exactly what I was dealing with back then and why I was trying to protect you."

"Oh, please. What body in the box?" she asked, her voice tinged with sarcasm.

He whipped around and looked straight at me. "Tell her."

I stared at him for a second or two, then turned to Emily. "Would you like a glass of wine?"

"Yes," she said irately, and followed me into the kitchen. "A big one."

I grabbed a glass from the shelf, then turned to her. "Are you okay?"

She scraped her hair off her face, fell back against the refrigerator, and shut her eyes tightly. "Oh, God. I'm . . . I'm furious." She opened her eyes and watched as I poured the wine.

"I was furious, too," I confessed. "And the only reason I was laughing a minute ago was because when I first saw him, I punched him in the stomach, too. And so did my mother."

"Good," she said viciously. "God! I don't think I've ever been this down-to-the-bone angry."

"Well, maybe a few sips of wine will help."

"Thanks." She took a sip and placed the glass on the counter. She had to lean against the fridge for another moment. "Oh, God, I'm so mad at him."

I rubbed her shoulder. "I understand, sweetie."

"But, Brooklyn, I'm so . . . so . . ." She pressed her hand to her mouth and her eyes began to water again. She whispered, "I'm so happy."

"Oh, Emily." I wrapped my arms around her. "I'm happy, too."

An hour later, we all sat in the living room, talking. Max and Emily sat close together at one end of the couch, but I sensed plenty of nervousness from both of them. There were the occasional pats on the knees and shoulders rubbing together, but otherwise they barely made eye contact. When Max snuck a glance, Emily would look away. And vice versa. Essentially, they were strangers. I knew — well, I *hoped,* anyway — that they would work things out, but it was going to take some time. Unfortunately, there was a killer on the loose, and that could put a damper on any immediate plans of Max's to rush Emily back into his life.

I sat at the other end of the couch, close to Derek, who'd taken the big red chair. Gabriel had pulled over one of the leather Buster chairs and we all had our feet up on the coffee table and were thinking about ordering pizza.

Because Max had insisted, Derek and I had started the conversation by describing to Emily the gruesome details of what happened when we opened the box I'd thought would contain new bookshelves. I still shivered when I pictured Angelica inside that box, her lips blue, her skin devoid of color, her lifeless body arranged so demurely in a long velvet dress with dying flowers strewn all around her.

"How sick can you get?" Emily said, frowning deeply.

I briefly described how the Covington had obtained the stolen *Beauty and the Beast* and what happened when I got to Joe Taylor's bookstore.

Then Max told her everything he'd endured three years ago and why he'd concluded that his only option was to stage his own death.

"I wish you'd trusted me," she said, rubbing her face wearily. "I don't understand why you didn't say anything when little Jake was kidnapped or when my mother was hurt."

"I was scared to death, Emily," he said, clutching her hand. "I was on the edge and

339

not thinking straight. I have no other excuses."

"Well, I hate those people for destroying you that way," she said fiercely. "I hope I never run into this Solomon character, because he might not survive my wrath."

"I feel the same way," I said, fuming all over again after hearing Max repeat the story. "But I just realized that you may be more vulnerable to Solomon now than you ever were before."

"Why?" she asked.

"Because he's so much more desperate now," I said, looking at Derek for backup. "Three years ago, harassing Max might have been a lark for him, something he could well have done to impress Angelica. But now, whether he killed her or not, he's all alone, with only his twisted imagination to fuel his actions. I'll bet he's slowly losing whatever he has left of his rational mind."

"To do what he did to that woman," Emily said, shaking her head in disbelief as she considered everything we'd told her. "Not just killing her, but dressing her up and shipping her to you, Brooklyn? I would say he's completely lost his mind."

"And that scares me to death," Max said, glancing at the other two men. "We've got to go after this guy."

Emily gripped Max's hand tightly. "Maybe I'm lucky I didn't know all this before. I'm not sure how I would've dealt with the threats."

"I'm glad you understand why I did what I did," Max said, and laid his head on Emily's shoulder.

"Oh, I still haven't forgiven you," she said quickly. "But I might be willing to accept that I really was in danger all those years ago."

Later, over pizza and salad, we all came to the conclusion that since the body was delivered to my apartment, Solomon had obviously discovered that Max was staying here.

"I suggest we leave immediately after we finish dining," Derek said.

"But where will we go this time?" I asked.

He pushed his plate away and took hold of his wineglass. "Since it seems Solomon will find us wherever we go, we might as well return to Dharma, where we can keep an eye on the enemy."

"Yes, good idea," Max said decisively.

"But we can't go back to Jackson's house," I said.

"I know a place."

We all turned and stared at Gabriel.

"Nobody will find you there," he said, and

341

held up his hand in a pledge. "Guaranteed."

"Is it big enough for three or four of us?" I asked.

"Plenty big and fully stocked."

I had more questions, but he flashed me that raised-eyebrow look of his, so I let it go. For now, anyway.

"I'm coming with you," Emily insisted. "I still have my suitcase in the car."

"I won't go without you," Max said, taking her hand in his. "Never again."

CHAPTER 22

It took us a while to pack up our things. This time I knew how the days would go, so I brought some books to read and some pretty blue yarn from China's shop that I'd promised myself I would knit into a scarf. I included my travel set of bookbinding tools and supplies as well as *Beauty*. I would need some distractions to get me through the long days without Derek. Since he and Gabriel would be out there shadowing Solomon, I knew I would need plenty of work to fill up my time.

We planned our next moves carefully. If anyone had been watching my apartment building, all they would have seen was me in my nondescript Prius, leaving my garage somewhere around ten o'clock that night, ostensibly for a pizza-and–ice cream run.

Two hours earlier, they also might have seen Derek and Gabriel driving off in their own much-flashier cars, looking for all the world as though they were going off to their respective offices or homes.

In reality, Gabriel headed for Dharma to set things up at the house we'd be staying in. Derek, on the other hand, took a scenic drive around the city, in and out of different neighborhoods and up and down the steepest hills he could find. When he was certain he hadn't been followed, he doubled back toward my place, parked a few blocks away, and stealthily made his way into my building.

Emily's car remained in my security garage. Derek snuck back out to get his car while the rest of us exited my building out the back. A minute later, Derek pulled up for us and drove us to Dharma.

It might've seemed like a lot of trouble to go through just to get out of town. But after being tracked down and discovered three times now, I was willing to make the effort.

On the way to Dharma, I called Inspector Lee to let her know I would be staying at my parents' house for a few days. Lee had been to Dharma once before, after Abraham Karastovsky was killed, so she'd be able to find me if necessary.

The house Gabriel had arranged for us was hidden in a small canyon on the outskirts of town. It was situated at the dead end of a winding, narrow road, and I noticed that we passed very few houses on the way there.

This house wasn't as deluxe or as high up on the mountain as my brother's, but it was plenty big enough, clean, and well provided with food, supplies, and shelves of books. There was a wide-screen, high-definition television with every cable station known to man. The beds were freshly made, and clean towels hung in the bathrooms.

Gabriel showed us around; then Max and Emily wandered off to unpack their things. They had chosen — that is, Emily had insisted on — separate bedrooms, so that left the master bedroom for me and Derek, although Derek didn't intend to stay here much. The living room couch was a sofa bed, so Gabriel would sleep there tonight, if he slept at all.

We walked outside. Cloud cover hid the moon and stars, so the night was as dark as pitch. Gabriel carefully pointed out where the property ended abruptly at the canyon's sheer edge. At the bottom of the canyon was a stream and a dirt road, but there were no houses down there. He assured us we would be safe here for a few days.

I turned and studied him closely. "Tell the truth. Is this one of Guru Bob's safe houses?"

After a pause, he said, "I plead the fifth."

"Chicken."

Gabriel's lopsided grin was positively devilish, but he remained mum.

"Fine," I said, a little huffy. "Don't know why I bothered to ask you. I'll pin down Guru Bob next time I see him."

"Better him than me," he said, still grinning.

Once more, Max and I settled into a daily routine, this time with the addition of Emily.

I had asked myself more than once, Why do I keep insisting on staying with Max? Who had appointed me guardian over the man? The answer was easy, after I'd thought about it awhile. I was the one who had found Joe's body. I had found Max's knife in my tire. It was my book, *Beauty and the Beast,* that had set everything in motion from the day Ian first called me in to restore the book.

No, it went back further. Three years ago, *Beauty* had played a role. Angelica — or Solomon, or someone, but I still believed it was Angelica — had decided that the book symbolized some elusive prize that, though currently unattainable, might someday be hers. So perhaps she had stolen the book from Emily in hopes of one day using it to attain that prize. Namely, Max.

It was a bizarre theory but it was the only one that worked for me. Deep down inside, I couldn't fathom why Joe's killers and Max's tormentors had carried out such unspeakable acts, but their motivations didn't matter. All I knew was that I had to take some personal responsibility for seeing that the bad guys were brought to justice. If that made me Nemesis, as Guru Bob had insisted was my role, then so be it.

So here we were in our safe, comfortable house. The three of us made polite conversation when we had to, and otherwise we avoided one another except when necessary. It was easier when Derek showed up at night or Gabriel stopped by. Then it felt like we had company and could socialize pleasantly with each other. But during the day, Emily, Max, and I moved cautiously around one another, trying not to tip the balance of the fragile bubble we'd created to protect Max and Emily.

Max and Emily spent the first two days treating each other with kid gloves, their manners painfully impeccable. Max wouldn't leave the room without asking Emily if he could get her something or if she needed anything or if she was comfortable. She did the same to him.

The second evening, Max turned on the television, and their interaction became a major exercise in diplomacy.

"Do you like this show?"

"Oh, I don't care."

"No, we can watch whatever you want to watch."

"Oh no. I'll watch whatever you want to watch."

Finally, I grabbed the remote and found a *Law & Order* we'd all seen twelve times before.

I was ready to scream. Derek had remained in the city that night, so I had no one to be honest with, no one to talk me down if I was itching to step out of line. So, naturally, I did.

"Meeting in the kitchen," I bellowed the next morning after I'd gulped down my first cup of restorative coffee.

The sliding-glass door in the living room opened and Max walked in. "They probably heard you yelling all the way down in Glen Ellen. What's wrong?"

"You shouldn't be outside," I snapped back.

"Who died and anointed you the pope?" he said.

I ignored him. "Emily, kitchen. Now."

"I'm in the middle of something," Emily said, poking her head out of her bedroom door across the living room. "Can't it wait?"

I stared cockeyed at her. *In the middle of something?* Where did she think she was? There was *nothing* out here to be in the middle of. "No, it can't wait. Sorry."

She huffed and puffed her way across the living room and into the kitchen, then flashed me a scathing look. That's when I realized that the sweet, docile Emily of yesteryear was now a pleasantly vague memory. I mentally cheered her on and wished Max lotsa luck. Meanwhile . . .

"I'm sick of us tiptoeing around each other," I said. "It feels like we're at some yoga peace retreat where we're all expected to be enlightened and groovy and polite."

"What are you talking about?" she said.

"I'm talking about the fact that I'm scared to death and I imagine both of you are, too."

She took a breath and some of her features relaxed. I took that as a good sign.

"Max," I continued, "you're a guy, so you're putting up a manly front. I get that. But, Emily, you're acting like we're at a garden party, having tea. And me? I've turned into a raving bitch." I glanced around. "Okay, no argument there. So look.

I know we haven't seen each other in a few years, but we were friends, remember? I think we need to start working like a team. As *friends.* Not strangers. Not anymore. We need to stay close and be aware of things around us. We need to be our own best security system."

"I've got my rifle with me at all times," Max said.

I nodded. "I know, and I'm glad. But if someone is watching this place, if they try to attack us, they're going to do it while Gabriel and Derek are away. So we're basically on our own here. I think we should talk about contingencies."

"Sounds like you've got it all worked out," Emily said sarcastically. "May I go now?"

I was taken aback and answered her in kind. "You *may* kiss my butt." But I immediately regretted it because I knew something was wrong. "Are you feeling okay?"

"I'm fine," she said bluntly, before I could finish my sentence.

"You don't sound fine."

Her face wrinkled in a scowl and she said, "Bite me."

It was so incongruous that I laughed. "Okay, you're supposed to be the nice one. What's going on?"

She fumed silently and went through lots of lip tightening and teeth baring. Finally she blurted, "I'm going stir-crazy! And I'm frustrated! I'm . . . I'm . . . urgh!"

Urgh? It sounded like she was growling. I had a sneaking feeling what the subtext of her words meant. I turned and looked at Max, who appeared poleaxed. But after a minute, his eyes cleared, then turned dark as he flashed Emily a dangerous scowl.

"Come with me," he said, grabbing her hand and pulling her out of her chair.

"No, you come with me," she said, and dragged him off toward the bedroom. Before they were out of the room, she hopped up into his arms and straddled him.

Oo-kay. My work here was done.

Over the next few days, I didn't see much of them. Well, except when they would stumble out of their bedroom, rumpled and replete and hungry. One evening I baked enchiladas, then went to take a long bath. When I got back to the kitchen, there was one enchilada left, and it was the straggly, half-filled one on the end. I guess the young lovers needed to keep up their strength.

When they weren't in their bedroom they sat close together on the couch or cuddled on the rug near the fireplace, having long, private talks. At night they would venture onto the deck and huddle in a blanket. I couldn't hear the conversations, just the occasional giggle or sigh.

I was superfluous, except in my role as cook, dishwasher, and feeder of the cat. I couldn't complain, though. I still had Clyde's friendship. And it was lovely to watch Max and Emily reconnect.

It wasn't all hearts and flowers, of course. It was slow going and there were glitches at first. I knew both of them were frustrated. Emily was occasionally tentative and Max had a tendency to brood.

Who could blame either of them? Emily explained to me that she hadn't been with a man since Max's "death" three years ago. She'd made every effort to move on, built a good, if quiet, life for herself. She'd been content to live alone. Now, suddenly, the man she'd loved so deeply had returned. But he'd lied to her, shown he didn't trust her. Was it any wonder she sometimes questioned their present relationship?

And Max had lived the life of a solitary refugee for the past three years. He had survived in the shadows of society, afraid to be too friendly or gregarious in case he attracted too much attention. He'd always been a bit of a brooder, but now he was world-class.

It was so easy for me to see the big picture from the sidelines, but I tried to avoid offering advice or critiques and simply kept my mouth shut. There was a very good reason for that: namely, I was the last person on earth to give anyone relationship advice. Hello? Once engaged to a gay man? Not smart!

No, the two of them would have to stumble through this one on their own. But I was encouraged and held out hope that they would come through stronger and more in love than ever.

If we all survived the safe house, that was.

Even though I kept my mouth shut, I did keep my eyes open and focused on the "happy" couple. Not simply for safety reasons, but because they were just so fascinating and *normal.*

For some reason, observing the two of them interacting together reminded me of a BBC nature program I'd been hooked on years ago when I was living in London. It was called *The Return of the Tit-Willows.*

Out in the woods, a camera had been inserted inside a tree where the young tit-willow couple had set up residence. Viewers could observe everything the birds were doing. The original reality show, right? It was fascinating to watch, but the absolute best part of the show was the narrator. He would describe each bird's movements as though he were doing commentary at a golf tournament, his voice hushed and extremely serious. It was gripping.

The male tit-willow approaches the nest. The female senses his arrival and readies herself. Wings flutter, feathers fly. Then . . . What's this? It's off with the boys he goes! Six weeks later, there's the piper to pay.

LOL, as Melody Byers would say. I couldn't get enough of those BBC nature programs.

After another long day and night, Emily and Max left their room and became sociable. We all got along well and Emily and I had some good talks, usually in the kitchen while playing flunkies to Max, our esteemed chef, who really had honed his kitchen skills.

Over dinners, Max talked about his life on the farm and Emily was enthralled. She loved hearing about the fig trees and the goats and the honeybees and the radicchio he'd grown. Loved hearing how Max had found Bucky through a dog-rescue service and how Clyde had walked into Max's kitchen one day and adopted him.

She was amazed that Max woke up so early and worked so hard on his farm, and she was fascinated by the way he'd changed his world so drastically. She grilled him on the process he went through to become a different person. Max's experiences became romantic and exciting when seen through her eyes.

Clyde warmed up to Emily slowly, and Emily made it clear she loved the cat. While I was thrilled to know that Clyde would be cherished by his new mistress, it was a bittersweet shot of reality for me. The time had come to decide whether to find my own little cat to love. But would another cat love me like Clyde did? It was a big chance to take and I would need to think it through very carefully.

During the day, though we'd never discussed it, Max and I had begun taking turns distracting Emily. He and I had our work to keep us busy, but we needed to find things for Emily to do. Otherwise, she would become so totally bored, she might run screaming out of the house.

That afternoon, Max taught her how to make paper. I watched, too, because while I'd learned the process long ago, I'd never taken a class from Max. He was fabulous and worth every groupie he'd ever attracted.

"It's so disgusting," Emily said, smashing the pestle into the large bowl that had been filled with soaking-wet newspapers and old magazines, which were beginning to turn into a mushy paste from constant beating.

"That's the perfect consistency," he said, sticking his finger into the gloppy gray pulp.

Emily grinned. "It might be fun to teach my students to do this."

"They would love it," I said. "It's like playing with mud."

"That's where I learned to do it," Max said.

"In school?"

"Second grade. My mother still has the first piece of paper I ever made, hanging on her bedroom wall."

"Aw," Emily said.

But I was watching Max's expression as it fell at the mention of his mother. The poor woman still didn't know her son was alive. I knew his mother, and I hoped his stomach was up for the punching it would receive at the hands of that woman.

That night, Gabriel and Derek arrived as usual, and we gathered around the table to hear what news they had, what they'd discovered that day, who they were tracking, the latest information from the feds on the survivalists, how the police were building the case against Solomon.

We knew Gabriel was taking one for the team by trying to date one of the Ogunite women to gain information about its members. We couldn't wait to hear the details.

Instead Gabriel dropped a bomb.

"Solomon has disappeared," he said.

The following morning, Gabriel and Derek both left, heavily armed, to investigate Solomon's disappearance from his home in the Hollow. We'd come up with plenty of theories last night. Gabriel thought that Solomon might have gone into full survivalist mode and was living in some backwoods cabin in anticipation of capturing Max and dragging him there.

Max doubted Gabriel's scenario. Solomon enjoyed creature comforts too much. He would never willingly go without plenty of good food and fine wine and a comfortable bed. I barely knew the man, but I agreed with Max.

Wherever Solomon had disappeared to, I was hopeful that Derek and Gabriel would be able to hunt him down.

Once the men left, in order to keep both Emily and me from crawling the walls, I pulled out all my bookbinding tools and set them up on the dining room table.

"I want to show you how to make an accordion book," I said. "I think your kids will love this."

"Let's do it," she said determinedly, and we sat down and got creative. It took a half hour to make the little book and Emily was delighted.

I'd used this same pattern for teaching simple bookbinding to attendees of conferences and book fairs. People loved making these miniature books. They didn't have to know what they were doing, really, and they came away with a charming, colorful keepsake.

"That was so simple," she said, holding her finished book in her hand. For the cover cloth, she'd chosen a modern Japanese print with shots of lavender, black, and red. A matching purple grosgrain ribbon wrapped it closed. "Even my first graders could make this."

"Definitely." I picked up the scraps and tossed them in the trash can. "I've taught kids before. And whenever I teach this class, I always pre-fold the paper and cut the ribbon and covers in advance. Makes it easier for everyone."

"I would do that, too." She chuckled. "They can handle the glue sticks, but first graders and scissors don't go well together."

"Right." I opened another bag of supplies.

"Do you want to make some more?"

"I'd love to," she said, spreading out the pretty swatches of cloth and choosing her favorites. "I can use the practice."

Emily caught on quickly and within the next two hours she'd made six colorful little books.

I used that time to set up a work area in my bedroom. I wanted to work on the *Beauty and the Beast,* but didn't want Emily or Max to see it until after it was finished. Even though Max had given his permission, Emily had no idea I was restoring the book and I didn't want to have that argument just yet.

I knew I wouldn't be able to do the more intricate work of gilding the cover while I was away from my workroom and office, so I busied myself with separating the cover boards from the text block. Some threads had already frayed, and some of the signatures, or folded pages, had separated from the rest of the block. I would resew the entire text block, but first I wanted to get rid of all the loose and tattered threads.

Using my tweezers, I started at the top of the folded pages and took my time, being careful not to split the vellum. The paper wasn't fragile, but after a hundred years or so, the threads had worn grooves in the folds, so there was a chance of tearing if I wasn't meticulous.

After almost one hour, the threads were gone. I cautiously thumbed through the signatures to make sure I'd caught any errant strings that might have gotten loose within the pages themselves. I wasn't very efficient because the edges were deckled, or uneven, so I began to turn each page, one by one, to check more carefully.

Halfway through the book, I came to two pages that were stuck together. I'd noticed the sticking pages before and knew I'd get to them eventually. It was common in deckled-edged books to find pages that hadn't been completely separated after they left the bookbinder's. But this book was so old and had been read often by children and their parents. Someone should have separated the pages long before now.

I remembered reading the book myself when I first bought it years ago. I didn't remember missing part of the story, but maybe I hadn't been paying attention.

I found my X-Acto knife, slipped it in between the two pages, and began to make little sawing movements along the edges. But the knife slid right through. The pages *had* been separated, so why were they stuck together?

I pulled gently at the ends and realized the two pages had been glued together!

My first thought was that this book had been the victim of Victorian censorship. Now I was dying to know what part of the fairy tale had been deemed too salacious to be seen by children. What juicy bits were contained in those glued pages?

I took hold of the edge of the pages in my hand and slowly, nervously pulled them apart, telling myself that if I met any resistance, I would stop. But I didn't. With some horror, I realized after the first inch that the glue used was rubber cement. The pages were coming apart relatively easily now, but at what price?

Little by little, another inch came unglued, then another. And that was when I saw the edge of a thick piece of paper glued in between the vellum. I continued to pull, revealing more. Finally, I could see more than one piece of paper. There were three or four pages. It took another bit of pulling to slip the papers out.

It was a long, handwritten letter.

My hands were shaking. Sometime within the past three years, someone had planted this lengthy letter inside the book. It became clear who that person was as I began to read.

Dear Max.

CHAPTER 23

Shocked by what I'd just read, I sat, momentarily frozen, in my chair. Gazing blindly at the paper, I waited while my brain slowly began to figure out the true meaning behind the words.

Oh, great. Emily and Max were just starting to get things worked out. And now I was about to throw another stick in their spokes.

Seconds later, I jumped into gear and ran out of the room. "Max," I shouted as I ran down the hall. "Emily!"

I stopped abruptly in the middle of the living room and looked around. "Max?"

But there was no answer and it chilled me to the bone. I'd been working in my room for the past hour. Had Solomon somehow gotten into the house and grabbed him?

"Emily?" She wasn't at the dining room table, where I'd last seen her. I stopped in the middle of the living room and looked around. Where was she? I kept perfectly still as I considered my next move.

"Don't panic," I said under my breath.

I heard a brush of movement and whipped around. The sound had come from down the hall. I took a few steps in that direction, then stopped as it hit me in a flash. They were probably in the bedroom together.

"Okay." I gulped, then sucked in a big breath and let it go. *Way to freak out for nothing,* I thought, mentally smacking my forehead.

A moment later, Max's bedroom door opened and he walked out into the hall. His hair was mussed, and I knew I was right about what he'd been doing.

"Hey, what's going on?" he said when he saw me standing there.

"You have to see this." I thrust the letter at him.

"What is it?" He walked past me into the living room, ruffling the pages as he dropped down onto the couch and rested his socks-clad feet on the coffee table. He stared at the paper for another few seconds, then gave me a sharp look. "Where'd this come from? I've never seen it before."

"I know. I just found it inside the pages of the *Beauty and the Beast*. She glued it in between two pages."

"She what?" He shook his head as though my words were all jumbled up in the wrong order. "This was inside the book?"

"Yes?"

"For how long?"

I chewed my lower lip and thought of how easily the rubber cement had given. Plus there were certain timely references in the letter. "It can't be more than a few weeks old."

Grimacing, he asked, "And you think it's real?"

Hands on my hips, I stared at him. "Did you read it, Max?"

"The first few lines," he grumbled. He looked a little sick to his stomach and I couldn't blame him. The note had been written by a pathologically damaged woman.

"Read the whole thing," I said, waving my hand at the letter. "It's real and it explains a lot."

"Yeah. That's what I'm afraid of." He shifted his feet off the table and stood up, taking a few stiff breaths as though gearing up for some sort of battle. And I guess he was in a way. He wandered the room, holding the papers steady as he read the rambling letter that, as twisted as it was, explained everything.

Feeling a chill, I folded my arms tightly across my chest. I couldn't sit, couldn't relax. I was reminded of another fateful love letter I recently had discovered in a book that belonged to a friend of my mother. Maybe I would start warning people not to leave their love letters inside of books. They only led to misery and sometimes murder.

Restless and unsure what to do, I wandered around the room, waiting for Max to finish reading.

Dear Max,

I know this letter will be a surprise — okay, a shock! I have so much to tell you and I'll try to be brief, but you know me!

First, let me say I'm sorry. And second, I love you. I've always loved you and I always will.

I still blame myself for Solomon going crazy three years ago and trying to kill you. He wanted me to love him and only him, completely and forever. I tried. But he knew I was still in love with you and he wanted you dead. I still have nightmares knowing what you went through all those years ago. That is my curse.

But, Max, once you were thought dead, Solomon was much more stable.

We were actually happy for a few years. But as you know, Solomon never could be truly happy. He had to pick and pick, and we would fight, then make up, then fight again. But we got through the worst of it and were relatively happy for almost three years.

Recently, though, you have become so popular again that the Art Institute decided to hold a retrospective of your life's works. All the attention directed toward your art in the last few months has made Solomon angrier and more paranoid than ever. He keeps threatening to kill somebody, and I'm so afraid it'll be me.

Then last month, the strangest coincidence occurred. I found your copy of *Beauty and the Beast* in a used bookstore! I guess your darling Emily didn't want the book, so when I found it on the shelf, I bought it. Call me sentimental, but the book reminded me of you.

But when Solomon saw the inscription you'd written in the book, he thought you had written it to me. I was your Beauty and you were my Beast! If only that were true!

Solomon went crazy. He demanded to know why I'd kept the book all these years if I weren't still in love with you. I told him I had just found it recently, but he didn't believe me. He beat me, Max. I thought he was going to kill me. I tried to stop him, but it was like throwing myself in front of a runaway train. He was unstoppable and all I could do was get off the tracks.

So I confessed. After years of pretending, I finally admitted the truth to Solomon and to the world: I loved you, Max, and I always would.

But that's not the worst of it. I was so beaten down that in a moment of weakness, I revealed to Solomon that you were probably still alive.

I'm so sorry, Max!!

Solomon's jealousy has boiled over into madness. You know he's part of that crazy church group, but lately he's become more involved with their more fringe survivalist members, who collect guns and practice shooting all day. I'm worried that he's become even more dangerous and unbalanced than he was three years ago when he harassed you so badly that you had to fake your own death to escape him.

Now I wonder if I will have to do the same.

I've decided that the only way to warn you is to put this book back on the market in just the right way that it will get to the right person. I've done my homework, but the rest is up to the fates.

The book will end up at Covington Library. When the curator sees the damage I've deliberately done to the book, I am confident that he will call in a book restoration expert. My research points to your old friend Brooklyn as the most likely person to restore the book. I'm counting on her being as single-minded and obstinate as she was years ago. She will find this letter and track you down. Fitting, isn't it? Since she was the one who gave you the book in the first place. I love a circle!

So, if you are reading this letter, it means you're still alive — thank God! Please, Max, be careful. Solomon wants you dead. For real this time. Don't underestimate his reach. He will find you and kill you.

I'm frantic with worry. Things have spiraled out of control. You might still blame me for ruining your life, but I am innocent. Solomon ruined both our lives, Max. We have that much in common, at least.

If the world is fair, if the universe sees fit to reunite true lovers, you and I will be together someday. But if it isn't meant to be, my one last wish for you, Max, is to be happy.

I love you. I love you. I love you!!

Your Angelica

"The woman thought of everything," I muttered, kicking the bricks that lined the hearth. "Right down to the tattered, overly glued turn-ins."

"Incredible," he muttered.

"And you know she's lying about finding the book in a used bookstore. She was the one who broke into Emily's house and stole the book. She was a liar then and she still was when she wrote this letter."

"She wants me to be happy? After everything she pulled?" Max crumpled up the note and threw it against the wall. "What a lying load of crap." He spat out the words.

"She did her homework about me," I said, feeling a little sick that I had played such a key role in her maneuverings. I picked up the letter he'd tossed, knowing the police would want it as evidence in Angelica's death. Carrying it into the kitchen, I grabbed a Ziploc bag from the drawer and tucked the pages inside. "In order for you to get the letter, she had to have worked backward, starting with me."

"Right," he said. "If she could get the book to you, then you would be able to track me down."

"But how did she know I gave you the book in the first place?"

"Damn it." He slapped his forehead. "I made it easy for her."

"How'd you do that?"

He leaned back against the sliding-glass door and closed his eyes. "Angelica kept calling me, even after Emily and I were engaged."

"But why? You mentioned that before, but you said she'd gone back to Solomon. So what was her deal?"

"It was all a game," he said, pacing again. "Always a game with her. I'm sure she kept calling me just to make Solomon jealous."

"That's the way she operated."

"Yeah. She called after my engagement party to rant about Emily, saying Emily wasn't good enough for me." He shook his head. "If only she knew how wrong she was."

"Of course she was wrong, Max."

He went on. "I argued with Angelica, then mentioned that you'd given me that book as a gift because the story symbolized Emily's and my deep love for each other."

"Oh, nice going."

"I know, I know. I was feeding the flames," he said, shaking his head in disgust. "But I was so damn grateful to be out of Angie's sick web, I wanted to rub her nose in it. You know?"

"Well, that backfired," I said, stating the obvious. "Anyway, she knew I gave you the book, so she had that to work with. Evidently, she did some digging and found out I was friends with Ian and that he hired me for a lot of restoration projects. She also must've found out that Joe Taylor did a lot of selling to the Covington."

Busy, busy, I thought.

He nodded. "That's probably how it all went down."

"She planned this whole thing, Max." I shook my head at the amazing intricacies of Angelica's plot. "She warned you and warned you about Solomon, so when your car went over the cliff, she must have thought you took her advice and faked your own death."

He frowned. "But how did she know Solomon wasn't actually responsible for that? How did she know I was still alive?"

I threw my hands up in the air. "I don't know. Maybe she was following you all that time, wanting to know if any of Solomon's dirty tricks worked. Maybe she saw that you got your car fixed after the brake line was cut, so she knew you couldn't have lost your brakes in Big Sur. Or maybe she just *hoped* you were still alive. Who knows for sure?"

"Who knows for sure?" he muttered.

"So when the retrospective became a reality, she must have decided it was time to resurrect you." I paced the room as I went through the steps Angelica might have taken. "So she put the book out on the market through Joe, then fed him all the right suggestions. Then she went back and killed Joe so she couldn't be tracked down."

"We don't know that for sure," Max said. "There's another possibility. Maybe Solomon killed Joe as a warning to Angelica."

I considered this. "I don't doubt that he is crazy enough to do it, but why would he? The letter indicates that Angie's the one who set the whole thing into motion with *Beauty*."

He turned and faced me. "But what if Angie wrote this letter and put it in the book, and then Solomon took it before Angie could start the ball rolling? She says that he thought I wrote the dedication to Angelica."

"So he started the ball rolling to get the book to you, to kill you."

Max shook his head. "This is making me crazy."

"Right there with you," I muttered. "My head's exploding just trying to keep up with the two of them."

"So Solomon brings the book to Joe; then he has to go back and kill Joe and then, later, Angie."

"It's all way too complicated," I said, needing either aspirin or wine. I knew which one I preferred, but it was a little early in the day to start drinking.

"No, it's all speculative," Max corrected.

"But it's all possible, too."

Max stared at the ceiling for a full minute, then shouted out an epithet. "I'm so pissed off. My life was turned upside down and backward for three long years because these two idiotic *children* decided to play some kind of sick game with me."

"You're giving children a bad name," I muttered in disgust. "Let's call it what it was. They were control freaks. Psychopaths. That's why they were so close. They each recognized that same twisted mentality in the other."

"And I played right into their hands," he admitted quietly. "I was attracted to Angelica because she was a gorgeous, experienced woman, but she was never in love with me.

She didn't know the meaning of the word." He scratched his head in frustration. "I'm an idiot."

"Yeah, you were."

"Thanks." He shook his head in disgust. "Everything Angie ever did was calculated and manipulative."

"True." I sighed. "Look, I'm going to give Derek a call. He needs to see this note." I walked toward the hall.

"Wait," he said, following me. "Let me have the letter. I want to show it to Emily. She should know the truth about what happened."

"Okay, but be careful with it. We'll need to show it to Inspector Lee. I'll be in my room, on the phone with Derek."

"Where'd Emily go?" He looked around, confused. "She was sitting right there at the dining room table a few minutes ago."

I frowned. "I thought she was in your room with you."

"No."

"Maybe she's in the bathroom."

"Yeah, maybe." He headed down the hall, calling her name, but got no response. He came jogging back to the living room. "Is she in the kitchen?"

"No." We could both see the kitchen from the dining room. "Maybe she's outside."

"Okay, you check the garage. I'll check the yard."

I grabbed his arm. "Don't worry. She knows better than to walk too far away."

Fear was alive and glittering in his eyes. "I know, but earlier she was talking about hiking down to the stream." He opened the sliding-glass door.

A woman's piercing scream echoed through the canyon.

"That's her. Emily!" Max shouted, and dashed out the door. He crossed the small terrace in two strides and raced toward the top of the narrow footpath we'd found the other day. Within seconds, he disappeared down the steep hill.

I sprinted back into the house and down the hall to my room, where I grabbed my cell phone. Then I bolted outside and over to the edge of the canyon to watch Max's progress as he hurtled dangerously down the treacherous dirt path. I cringed as a miniature rock slide caused his feet to wobble and he had to stop a few times to regain his balance.

"Be careful," I shouted. Okay, that wasn't helpful advice at this point, so I did the only other useful thing I could think of. I wanted to call Derek, but Gabriel was closer, so I pressed his number on speed dial.

He answered on the first ring and I'd never been so happy to hear his voice.

"Emily's been kidnapped," I said in a breathless rush. I didn't know that for sure, but why else would she scream? Why else would she be gone? "Please come quickly. And can you call Derek and ask him to get up here? Hurry, Gabriel. I'm going into the canyon with Max to look for her."

"Damn it, Brook—"

"Can't wait, Gabriel. I have to go."

"Br—"

I ended the call before he could start shouting. And if I didn't want to hear Gabriel's shouts, I *really* didn't want to hear Derek's. I hated knowing he would worry for the next hour, all the way over from San Francisco. But I couldn't think about that right now. I shoved the phone into my pocket and followed Max down into the canyon.

I was halfway down the canyon when I skidded on a patch of loose rock. I fell on my ass, but managed to grab hold of a small, prickly bush. My hand was stinging and my butt ached, but I couldn't complain. The little bush had kept me from plummeting headfirst down the steep, rocky hill.

I pushed myself up off the ground, then

jolted at the sound of car tires screeching in the distance. A plume of dust and dirt rose into the air from the bottom of the canyon a few hundred yards away.

"Son of a bitch!" Max shouted, his voice echoing against the solid rock walls. And I knew without a doubt that Emily was gone.

I sat down in the dirt and called Gabriel back.

CHAPTER 24

"This ends right here and now," Max said, stalking the living room like a caged lion. "I'm not hiding anymore. They've managed to find out where we are within days, anyway, so why bother?"

"You're right," Derek said, his tone deadly serious. "There's no use being discreet now that they've taken Emily."

He'd broken world speed records getting back to Dharma by two o'clock and had quickly run back to our room to change from his expensive, navy pin-striped suit into dark jeans, a black T-shirt, and black leather jacket. When he walked back into the living room, I took one look at him and had to remember to breathe. The man looked damn good in black — that's all I can say.

"I got a glimpse of the car," Max said, pounding his fist against his palm as he circled the room. "I couldn't see the exact make or model and it was too muddy to read the license plate, but I could tell it was a dark burgundy van."

"Late model?"

"No. Sort of boxy, so it's got to be a few years old. I drew a picture of it and also sketched the tire tracks." He pulled a folded sheet of paper from his pocket and smoothed it out on the dining table.

"Are you sure these are the tracks of the same van?"

"Hell, yeah. I went running after it when they took off with Emily, so I know which tracks were theirs."

"Brilliant, Max," Derek said, patting him on the back. "The police should be able to match this drawing to one of the survivalists' vehicles. Smart of you to think of it."

Max shrugged. "I had nothing better to do once you talked me off the ledge."

Earlier, I could barely get Max to come up from the canyon floor. When he did finally hike back up to the house, he was enraged, out of his mind with fear, and frantic to go after Emily. He was threatening to take out his rifle and shoot someone — and I couldn't blame him. But I also couldn't let him go off half crazed, so I got Derek back on the phone and begged him to talk Max down.

Whatever Derek said to him had worked. Max wasn't exactly calm, but he was willing to wait for Derek and Gabriel to join him in the fight.

Gazing across the room at Derek, who'd been scowling ever since he arrived at the house, I said, "You'd think we all had tracking devices planted on us with the way they find us so fast."

"It does seem that way, love," Derek said. "But I've checked my car each time. It's clean."

It was a very good sign that he called me *love*, because I knew he had to be furious with me for going into the canyon. But I couldn't let Max go down there alone. Not that I had been much help to him. My hand still smarted from the stickers I'd collected from that prickly bush. I'd slathered it in antiseptic cream as soon as I got back to the house.

It was also good to know that Derek had actually been checking for tracking devices regularly. I never would have thought of that, but we'd already established beyond a doubt that his mind worked differently from mine.

"Hey, maybe they planted a device in the book," I said, then shook my head. "No, that's just stupid."

Derek raised an eyebrow. "At this point, nothing is out of the question. Bring me the book and I'll check it."

I had to bring it to him in pieces. He sat at the dining room table and went through every inch of every page, explaining that there were now tracking devices on the market that were as small and thin as a piece of tape.

"The book is clean," he said finally.

"So these guys are just good trackers," I said.

"Seems to be the case," Derek said, still scowling. It had to be irritating as hell to know he was being bested by a group of local yokels. I was right there with him, and couldn't wait to nail whoever had been dogging us all over northern California.

I gathered up the pieces of the book and carried them back to the desk in our bedroom. I took a minute to arrange them neatly on the desk, then pulled out my cell phone and took a photograph of the display. Under normal circumstances in my bookbinding studio at home, I would've been documenting every step of my work on *Beauty,* so it was time to play catch-up.

By the time I came back into the living room, Gabriel had arrived. He was dressed from head to toe in black, and I had to say, he looked almost as good as Derek did.

The four of us regrouped around the dining table as we had so many times before, regardless of whose house we were in. This gathering was different, though. Tonight we would finally take action. We made a plan.

The search would center around the Hollow. Gabriel had already copied a Google Earth map showing every home and outbuilding in the area. Then he and Derek divided the map into ten approximately equal-sized sections. Gabriel brought out his notebook computer and coordinated directions into the individual areas.

Derek called my father and put him on speakerphone, then asked him to round up ten or fifteen commune members who were good with guns and tracking. I knew Austin would be the first one on his list.

"I'll get on the phone and call some others," Dad said, and I could hear the excitement in his voice. He didn't talk about it much, but he'd apparently been involved in a few dangerous operations in his past.

"And, Jim," Derek continued, "can you recommend a discreet meeting place for all of us, around seven o'clock this evening?"

There was a pause; then Dad said, "Savannah's restaurant has a private dining room. It's Monday, so the place is closed. There's a parking lot and entrance in the back. Nobody will be seen from the street."

"Excellent suggestion," Derek said, then noticed my eyes widen, and thought fast. "Would you mind approaching Savannah with that request, Jim?"

I grinned. Derek was getting to know my family so well. As bristly as Savannah could get, we both knew she would never say no to our father.

After we hung up from talking to Dad, it was time for me to bring up a thorny subject.

Dharma didn't have its own police force, but a number of the commune members were proficient at tracking and shooting. Guru Bob handled most smaller skirmishes within the confines of the commune, but if things got out of hand, the Sonoma County Sheriff's Department could be called in. We'd rarely had a need to call them in before, but this was a whole different ballgame.

"We should call Jaglom and Lee," I said, "and probably the Sonoma Sheriff's Department."

"No cops," Max said immediately.

"But we'll need them to arrest the bad guys when we find Emily." I touched Max's shoulder and felt him tense up, but I went ahead and said, "Look, she might need an ambulance, Max. I'm sorry, but we'll need the authorities on hand at some point."

"Emily will be fine," he said through clenched teeth. "Solomon's just using her to get to me."

I prayed he was right.

Derek squeezed my hand. "I'm afraid I agree with Max, darling. I'm hesitant to bring in law enforcement too early."

"Me, too," Gabriel said. "Sorry, babe, but they could try to pull the plug on the whole operation. Let's just say my confidence level in them finding Emily is low to zero."

I understood their feelings. We'd done all the groundwork and knew the players. We'd been the ones keeping Max safe, scoping out the survivalists, running searches on them, tracing recent weapon sales they'd made, along with keeping tabs on Solomon. None of us wanted to be told at the eleventh hour that it was time to step aside and let law enforcement take over. We wanted to be the ones to close the deal on Solomon.

I understood all that. And I felt for Max, too. The police had never helped him before. Why would they start now?

And how strange was it that I, not Derek, was the one who was insisting on a police presence? Times had certainly changed. Or maybe I'd just grown tired of running on pure adrenaline and terror every day. I wanted this nightmare to end. Tonight.

"I can see you're struggling with this, love, so I propose a compromise. We'll call the police *after* we begin the search."

I thought about it for half a second. "Okay. I'll make the calls."

The others agreed. The key would be in the timing of the phone calls. Our San Francisco detectives would need at least an hour to get up here, so I would alert them sooner. The sheriff was close enough to get here quickly, so I would make the call to him later.

With any luck, they would all descend on Dharma at precisely the right time to arrest and drag off to jail the vicious creeps who'd snatched Emily.

"Are you ready?" Derek asked as the sun set over the canyon ridge. He pulled his gun from the holster beneath his arm, slid the magazine back to double-check that it was fully loaded, then slipped the gun back into its holster.

Abject fear began to dance a jig on my nerve endings as I watched him. But I was just going to have to get over that.

"I'm ready," I said, breathing deeply as I

zipped up my Windbreaker.

"Hell, yeah." Max nodded brusquely and raised his rifle to prove he was all set.

I grabbed a few handfuls of Hershey's Kisses and shoved them into both of my pockets.

Gabriel grinned. "Ready to roll."

"Let's go."

It was dusk as we drove into the parking lot behind Savannah's restaurant. The place was closed, but she was in there, as always, working in the kitchen, preparing stocks and sauces for the week.

After a brief but emotional reunion between Max and my brother Austin, who, thank goodness, didn't slug his old friend in the stomach, we all got down to business. There were twenty of us gathered in Savannah's private dining room. It was odd to be sitting at this table, discussing what was essentially a covert operation, with my father and brother in the same room. I figured it had to be even stranger for them than it was for me.

This space also served as the wine cellar for the restaurant, so I was pleased to see that we were surrounded by thousands of dollars' worth of excellent wines. Somehow that comforted me.

As a few of the men talked quietly, Derek pulled me close and said under his breath, "You'll call Inspector Jaglom once the meeting starts."

"Yes."

"And the Sheriff's Department once we've finished."

"We went over this," I said gently. "I know what to do." Funny how he seemed more nervous about my making two measly phone calls than he was about a group of armed men traipsing in the woods, out to trap a killer.

Gabriel passed around the maps he'd copied to each two-person team in the room. Most of the locals knew their way around the Hollow, but it was still good to have Gabriel's directions so they could all stay out of one another's way.

Derek took his place at the head of the table and outlined the mission. He emphasized that no weapons were to be fired unless one of the teams found Emily and was met with resistance. The survivalists had trained themselves to attack first and ask questions later. Vigilance was essential.

The most likely place they would find Emily was somewhere near or inside Bennie and Stefan's dwelling. Derek and Gabriel were the point men there. Max would be with them.

Solomon had disappeared but we knew he was the power behind it all. Wherever he was hiding, we intended to smoke him out.

My heart was pounding like a bass drum on speed. My muscles were stiff from clenching the sides of my chair. I was both scared spitless and so damn energized, I didn't know whether to crawl in a hole or go bowling. My brain was spinning as I took it all in.

We were going to war.

After listening to Max describe the burgundy van he'd seen in the canyon that morning, Austin shook his head. "Sorry to be the wet blanket, but half the survivalists in the Hollow drive vans like that. Dark paint, nondescript. Some are camper conversions."

Ray, another commune member, piped up. "That's been the car of choice for the Ogunites for the past fifteen years or so. Most of them still drive 'em around. They're used for everything from hauling lumber to clearing trees to taking their kids on vacations."

"That's good to know," Derek said. "Narrows the search down to a few hundred suspects."

There was general chuckling around the table from everyone but Max, whose patience appeared to be holding by one frayed thread. Derek noticed it, too. So after advising everyone in the room to turn their cell phones on vibrate, he gave me the heads-up to call the sheriff, signaling that the meeting was almost over.

Earlier, I'd called Inspector Lee, who, after grousing at me about staying out of police business, promised to get on the road with Jaglom immediately. I was hoping my call to the Sonoma sheriff would go better.

I got up and left the room, closing the door behind me. I walked down the short, dark hall toward the back of the restaurant to use the bathroom and make the phone call.

It was a warm night so the back door leading to the parking lot was open, but the screen door was locked. I'd checked it myself earlier.

As I neared the bathroom, a woman came up and peeked through the screen door, trying to see inside. She was outlined in silhouette by the light over the parking lot.

"Can I help you?" I said, and yeah, I was a little freaked-out.

She ducked back quickly out of the doorway.

"Hello?" I said, but nobody answered. Well, that was weird. Was she just checking to see if the restaurant was open or did she have something more sinister in mind? Was I being paranoid?

Probably. But I snuck over to the screen door to see if she was still out there.

"Help!" a woman cried, then let out an ear-piercing scream that filled the night air. A high-pitched shrieking sound that could have come from only one person.

"Minka?"

Oh, dear God. How? Why? What was she doing here?

I whipped open the door in time to see someone fifty yards away dragging a squirming, leopard-leggings-clad woman by the neck. That was Minka, all right.

"Hey!" I yelled. "Stop that." I tore off running down the blacktop, shouting for the guy to stop.

Her hooded assailant continued lugging her toward a waiting car at the far end of the parking lot. Minka was not going quietly. She squirmed and screeched the whole way. But her captor was too big and strong and mean for Minka to fight off.

"Drop her," I shouted, but I was too far away to do anything except watch as Minka's attacker physically overpowered her, punching her in the stomach and tossing her into the car trunk.

The thug jumped into the driver's seat and peeled rubber out of the parking lot.

I dashed back to the restaurant door just as Derek and Gabriel and some of the men came running out.

Derek grabbed me. "Was that you screaming? What happened?"

"He's taken Minka," I cried.

"Minka?" Derek looked as stunned as I felt.

"This can't be a coincidence," I insisted. "It has to be connected to Emily's disappearance. That guy was following us and Minka got in the way."

"But what is Minka doing here?"

I shook my head, still flabbergasted. "I don't know. She probably thinks I'm up here working on some special bookbinding project that should've been hers."

"What about her assailant?" Gabriel asked. "Was it Solomon?"

"I couldn't tell. He was tall and wore a ski mask or some kind of hood."

Gabriel took off sprinting all the way to the far end of the lot, then ran back. "I know where they're going," he said, then darted over to his black BMW and started the engine. He backed out of the space and shouted, "Get in."

I hopped into the passenger's side. Derek opened the back door but stopped when someone called out his name.

Austin came running over "What's the story, man?"

"We're going after this goon," Derek said, deadly serious as he morphed into full commander mode. "You lead the rest of the men to the Hollow. Follow the original plan, but I want you and your father to go after Bennie and Stefan. Solomon, too, if you can find him. Take Max with you. Be careful."

Austin took his new role seriously, giving one grim nod. "Got it."

"My phone's on," Derek said. "Keep me posted."

"Likewise," Austin said, and ran back to give instructions to the others.

Derek jumped into Gabriel's car and we went racing after Minka's kidnapper.

CHAPTER 25

"How do you know where they're going?" I asked.

Gabriel whipped around another curve and I had to grip the grab handle above my door to keep from toppling over.

"Sorry, babe," he said, grinning tightly. "I saw them turn up Isis Way."

"So they're headed for Charity Mountain," I guessed.

"Bingo," he said, then flashed a quick look at Derek in the rearview mirror. "I've driven up there. The road winds around for an hour, and once you're on the other side of the hill, you're overlooking the Hollow."

"Interesting." Derek leaned forward from the backseat. "Are there more survivalist types up in those hills?"

"Yes," I said, looking over my shoulder. "They're scattered all over that area, even though most of them live down in the canyon. The real estate is cheaper there."

"Ah," he said, then glanced at our driver. "Can you still see their car?"

"Yeah," Gabriel said. "Every so often when they go around a curve. He's got one taillight missing."

Turning in my seat, I said, "I heard glass break while they were struggling. Maybe Minka kicked it out."

"Good girl," Gabriel said.

"It would be the one smart thing she's ever done," I admitted. "And she probably didn't do it on purpose."

"No, but she might've saved her own life," Derek said. After a few seconds, he asked, "What's on Charity Mountain?"

"There used to be a Catholic convent up there. The Sisters of Charity. Now it's been turned into a winery, naturally."

"Anything else up there?"

"Some homes," I said. "It's very isolated. Lots of nooks and crannies, dead ends. It's where some of the local kids used to go to make out."

"Make out? You mean snogging?" Derek sounded amused. "Do you know the area, darling?"

I slanted a look at him. "Well enough."

Gabriel chuckled, then stepped on the gas as we rounded another curve.

Every minute or so, as we drove higher

and deeper into the wooded hills, I could catch a glimpse of the car with the broken taillight. It had to be at least a half mile ahead of us. I marveled at the fact that, accidentally or not, Minka had managed to do the one thing that might save her life. The only unfortunate part was that I would be a member of the Minka LaBoeuf rescue party. Again. It wasn't as if she would thank me for it.

A full minute passed as we climbed higher. Tree branches hung heavily over the road and the number of houses grew even more sparse. Around one turn, a dirt road led off to nowhere that I could see.

"Are they going to the winery?" Derek asked. He was leaning forward far enough that he could have been sitting next to me. "I've lost track of the single taillight."

"I haven't seen it for a few minutes," Gabriel conceded. "It's disappeared."

"It's got to be up ahead somewhere," I said, staring into the woods in hopes of catching a glimpse of red brake light. "There's only one road up to the winery and we're on it."

"What about the turnoff we passed?" Derek asked.

"It doesn't go anywhere as far as I know," Gabriel said, and glanced at me.

"Yeah. I think it's another dead end."

"Then they must be up ahead somewhere," Derek said.

Gabriel slowed down and turned off the headlights. "I'll wait for a minute until our vision acclimates to the dark."

Derek sat back and opened the left-side window.

The air in the car instantly chilled and I shivered, but it was more in fear than anything else. With the headlights off, we seemed more isolated up here in the dark. But I reminded myself that I was with two fierce warriors, so I shook off my nervousness and concentrated instead on the passing landscape, looking for any kind of inlet or turnoff or light somewhere in that deep, rugged woodland. But it was difficult to see anything beyond the line of trees growing so thickly along the road.

Gabriel slowed down even more to allow us to better scrutinize the interior of the woods.

"There's a dirt road," Derek said. "Looks like a house light a few hundred yards in."

"I thought I saw a light flicker," I said, "but I didn't see a road."

"They're too damn well hidden," Gabriel muttered.

"We'll find them," Derek vowed.

And from the determined tone of his voice, I wouldn't want to be the person standing in the way of his goal.

Another minute later, Gabriel said, "We're getting close to the winery."

"I'm not sure they'll go onto the winery grounds," I said, taking an educated guess. "The whole area is well lit, and there's a family who lives on the property. I think they'll pull off into the woods."

"Yes, I agree," Derek said. "This is survivalist territory. They've got to have a place up here. They wouldn't come up this way otherwise."

"We're all agreed," Gabriel said, peering into the woods as he took another curve. "And we're clearly at a disadvantage, because they probably know every inch of this hill and these woods."

"Doesn't matter," Derek said grimly. "Nothing's changed. If they're out there, we'll track them down."

He kept repeating that vow, as if he would make it so by simply saying it. And, frankly, knowing Derek, I wouldn't have been the least surprised to find out he had that kind of power.

So I wasn't about to speak aloud my real worry, that we might find and rescue only Minka and not Emily. I knew the Sisters of

Charity wouldn't be pleased with me thinking that way. It wasn't my most charitable
moment, but I couldn't help it. So I kept
my mouth shut and continued searching the
woods.

Gabriel brought the car to an abrupt stop.

We all stared at the heavy chain that
barred the entrance to the long, winding
tarmac drive leading up to Charity Mountain Winery.

"That settles that possibility," Gabriel
muttered.

I sighed. Derek squeezed my shoulder in
an attempt to comfort me. Bitterly, I looked
at either side of the chain barrier. There was
no room for a car to have gone up and
around it and onto the property. So we
really were at a standstill.

But not for long. In silence, Gabriel made
a three-point turn around the dead end,
then, keeping the headlights off, drove
slowly back down the road.

With all the lights near the winery's
entrance, it took a minute for my eyes to
readjust to the darkness. Gabriel stopped
anywhere there was a break in the heavy
growth of trees that might be wide enough
to fit a car through.

Long minutes later, we rounded the curve
and drove past the point where I'd seen the

light flickering.

"Stop," Derek said.

"Did you see something?" Gabriel asked.

"That light is still on in there," Derek said. "And there's just enough of an opening to squeeze through."

Gabriel turned in his seat. "I'll drop you off and find another inlet farther down the hill to hide the car, then double back on foot."

The sound of Derek sliding the magazine into his gun made me jump. Then he murmured, "Turn off the interior light."

"Got it." Gabriel flicked a switch. "You're good to go."

"I'm going with you," I said.

There was a pause. "You'll do everything I tell you. No discussion."

"Of course."

I thought I heard him snort, but I could have been mistaken.

We both got out of the car and closed the doors as quietly as we could. Then Gabriel drove off. The moon and stars were blocked by clouds and the darkness was almost absolute.

I grabbed for Derek's hand, then flinched when he whispered in my ear, "Stay behind me. Let's go."

We snuck through the line of trees and

were instantly enveloped in woods. Leaves slapped at my face as we made our way toward the meager light a few hundred yards away.

Finally we reached the edge of a clearing and saw a small, rustic A-frame log house situated at the foot of a steep incline. The car with the broken taillight was nowhere in sight.

"Shall we?" Derek whispered, tugging at my hand.

"Shall we what?" I said in a hiss. What did he have in mind?

He didn't hang back to chat about it, but edged closer to the house. Somehow, he barely made a sound, while my feet were like jackhammers as I trod over fallen leaves, twigs, and dried-out flower beds someone had once cared enough to plant.

Is he going to knock on the door? Well, why the hell not? We'd done stranger things, and maybe the A-frame owners had seen or heard something.

But Derek skirted the steps up to the front door and crept around the side, where he peered into a window, then walked on toward the back of the house. I was making too much noise so I waited for him on the side of the house, pressing myself against the wall to avoid being seen.

"Hhrrmmmmrup!"

I jolted nearly a foot! Then I stumbled back against the rough log exterior, scraping my back. It hurt, but I tried not to moan out loud since someone else out here was in worse shape than I was.

Derek dashed around and found me. "Was that you?"

"No. It sounded like someone trying to call for help."

I scanned the woods before grasping the fact that the cry had come from inside the house. "Someone's in there."

Derek took the front steps in one hurtle and grabbed hold of the doorknob. I scurried after him.

"Locked," he muttered.

"Now what?"

My question was answered as Derek stepped back a few feet, then kicked the door in. I grinned. I couldn't help it. Even in this crazy, dangerous situation, I had to admit that Derek Stone was really something.

The door swung back and forth futilely and Derek pushed it out of the way; then we stepped cautiously inside the dimly lit front room. I looked around but didn't see anyone. The furniture — a sofa and two chairs, various tables — was all neat and matching. The house was clean. I peeked into the kitchen. It was tidy, with a few dishes drying next to the sink. So someone had to be living here; they just didn't appear to be around at the moment. Probably a good thing.

Derek crept toward a doorway leading to a short hall. I followed inches behind him. Peering down the shadowy hallway, I could make out four closed doors.

The first opened to a small bedroom. It was empty. So was the bathroom next to it. The third door was a closet so dark, I couldn't see a thing inside it.

We made our way to the last door and opened it. The light on the nightstand was turned on, illuminating the room enough that I could see what I never expected to see.

In complete shock now, I could barely breathe. I clutched Derek's arm and tried to swallow, but my throat was too dry. I could feel Derek's arm muscles tense up, as well.

A man wearing only a pair of knit boxer shorts was lying in the middle of the bed. Splayed in four directions, his hands and feet were tied to the four bedposts of the fancy, queen-sized bed. He twisted and struggled to free himself, but to no avail.

He could only grunt and moan because of the wide strip of duct tape covering his mouth. His eyes were wild with fear and desperation.

It was Solomon.

CHAPTER 26

Solomon?

"Good lord," Derek murmured, and rushed over to the bedpost to free the pitiful man's hands.

"Wait," I said. Tossing my shoulder bag on the small chair by the window, I walked up to Solomon and stared into his eyes. It wasn't fear I saw there. It was . . . defiance? He stared right back and I tried not to flinch. Even bound and gagged, the man had the ability to scare the heck out of me. I turned away.

"Derek, we need to talk in the other room."

"Let's get him untied first."

"No. Talk first, please." I walked out, down the hall, and into the front room.

He followed me and said quietly, "Brooklyn, that man needs to be released."

"That man could be a monster," I whispered so I wouldn't be overheard. By whom?

I had no idea, but I wasn't taking chances. "This could be a trap."

"Yes, it could be." He glanced around and I could tell he'd already considered that possibility. "But we still can't leave him here."

I folded my arms tightly across my chest, not yet willing to agree. "Both he and Angelica have calculated every move from the very beginning."

"That's true, but he's right where we want him now." He took hold of my arms. "We'll take every precaution. I'll loosen his wrists from the bedposts, then bind his hands behind his back to transport him down the mountain."

"Okay." Maybe I was making too much of Solomon's power, but I dreaded going back into that bedroom. I hated being in the same vicinity as the man. But more than that, I trusted Derek to take care of Solomon.

"Would you rather wait in the car?" Derek asked, squeezing my shoulder with concern.

"God, no. Well, maybe." But the thought of traipsing back through the dark woods alone wasn't appealing. And I knew that waiting by myself in the car would give me the creeps. "No. Let's get this over with."

We went back into the bedroom. I grabbed

the end of the rope holding Solomon's right foot to the lower post. The knots were intricate and it was slow going getting them loosened. Somebody knew their Boy Scout knots, for sure.

I glanced up, met Solomon's cold gaze, and quickly looked away. I stared at the taut rope and got angry. How dared he intimidate me when he was laid out in this ridiculous position? I looked back at him, refusing to show alarm or acknowledge the shivers I got from merely looking at him.

Solomon made muffled sounds through the duct tape and I figured he wanted us to remove it so he could speak. But I didn't want to hear his voice.

"The duct tape stays," I said gruffly, trying to ignore his muted grumbling. We still hadn't found Emily, and I wanted to blame Minka and Solomon for leading us off track. First, stupid Minka had stuck her big nose where it didn't belong, and now we had to deal with rescuing Solomon, of all people. It wasn't nice of me and I wasn't proud of myself, but there it was.

I concentrated on undoing the intricate set of knots trapping the man's ankles to the bedpost and wondered if this night would ever end.

Solomon continued to moan through the

duct tape and I realized it was cruel to leave it on. What if he couldn't breathe?

"Fine," I said reluctantly. When Derek glanced up, I asked, "Will you take the duct tape off?"

I didn't want to get too close to the man on the bed. And I didn't want to hear what he had to say — unless, of course, he knew where Emily was. But since he was hog-tied, I was guessing he wouldn't have any worthwhile information. This whole scene was all too grisly and weird.

Derek leaned over and grabbed hold of the tape, then warned Solomon, "This is going to hurt."

Solomon nodded vigorously and Derek ripped it off.

Solomon screamed liked a banshee, although, to tell the truth, I'd never heard a banshee scream.

"Thank God you came for me," he cried. "Oh, thank God. It was a nightmare. I couldn't get away. I thought I was going to die. I —" He took a breath and held it. Silence.

Neither of us bothered to clue him in that we hadn't come here for his sake.

I was thankful for the silence. Solomon in this grateful mood was jarring to me. I continued working with the rope. Someone had dampened it before tying, so it was even more difficult to get a grip on it. It was slow work and I was getting more and more anxious to leave before whoever tied up Solomon decided to return.

Solomon watched us both work to free him. I looked up and noticed he was frowning at me.

"What?" I said.

"I know you."

I shook my head. "No, you don't."

"Yes, I do." He peered at me; then one side of his mouth curved up. "I never forget a pretty face."

I tried to mask my shock but I failed. "Seriously? You're flirting with me? While you're tied up like a turkey waiting to be roasted? You're an idiot." I started to walk out of the room.

"Wait! Come back!" he cried.

"Keep it down, old man," Derek said sternly. "One more remark like that and I'll gladly leave you here for your captor to deal with."

"Oh, God, don't!" he said, his voice raspy, his eyes wide and wheeling. "Don't let her get me!"

Her? I met Derek's gaze.

"Who's going to get you?" I asked warily. He had to take a few deep breaths to brace himself before he could whisper, "Nobody."

"Too late," I said, moving back to the bed-post and the ropes. "You've just admitted a woman did this to you."

He clamped his lips together and his jaw worked rapidly.

"A woman tied you up and left you to rot," I taunted. "Isn't that interesting."

"She'll be back. It was just a little game we were playing."

"Some game," I said. "You were scared to death when we walked in."

"Shut up and undo the damn ropes before I —"

In that moment, he lost his ability to frighten me. Sort of. "Are you actually threatening me, Solomon?"

"I knew it," he said in triumph. "You know who I am. We have met, haven't we?"

I shook my head. "No, we haven't."

"But you look so familiar. Did we ever —"

I recoiled at his suggestive tone, but before I could speak, Derek said in a low, menacing voice, "Enough."

I blinked at the force of Derek's anger, and a rush of emotion flooded through me. Gratitude, love, excitement, fear. Derek was rarely moved to anger, but when it happened, look out.

He glared down at Solomon. "Tell us what happened here and who did this to you. Start talking, or we'll walk out and leave you here to rot."

Solomon stared up at Derek. He seemed to measure the man's words and intentions, then swallowed heavily. "A woman I know lured me up here, promising a night of pure fantasy. I was foolish enough to believe her. We had a glass of wine, and she was cooking something in a frying pan. It smelled fantastic and everything was going well. But then I turned away for a minute, and she knocked me out. I guess she used the frying pan. I don't know, but I have a massive headache. Anyway, when I woke up, I was tied to the bed. She told me that if she couldn't have me, no woman could."

"Why would she say that?" I asked. "What did you do to her?"

"I didn't do anything." He speared me with a look of pure loathing, but I didn't care. I just watched him, more curious than anything else. Finally, gritting his teeth, he continued. "She said I wasn't grateful enough. She had done me a . . . a big favor, but I guess I didn't show her enough appreciation."

"What was the big favor?"

He bared his teeth, obviously resenting

my questions. "Look, none of that matters. Just untie the ropes and get me the hell out of here."

"Oh, because you're so innocent?" I said. "Whatever she did to you, I know you deserve it all and then some."

"I didn't do anything," he said irately. "She's in love with me and completely obsessed. She's a raving — I didn't ask her to — Look, just let it go."

I was starting to get a really bad feeling about this whole scene. "We're not letting anything go, especially not you. The police are waiting down the mountain and you're going straight to jail."

"Me?" he said, outraged. "I'm the victim here."

"You have never been a victim, Solomon." I shook my head and looked away. I had feared the man and hated him for what he did to Max, but now I couldn't be bothered to expend that much energy. Now I felt nothing but contempt for him.

But that reminded me of something. "Why did you hate Max Adams so much?"

The immediate change in Solomon was startling. He scowled bitterly. "Max Adams was nothing but a two-bit hack. I have more talent in my little toe than he had in his entire body. But Max had the Midas touch.

He got everything he wanted delivered on a golden platter. Women by the dozens, acclaim, money. The institute got him a book contract. They sent him on lecture tours. When Angelica left me for him, I was furious."

"You were obsessed."

"So what?" he said on a snarl, then shook his fist. "Max Adams was a pissant. He was supposed to die."

"He didn't."

"I know that now, damn it, but at least he was gone. I no longer had to compete with him for every little crumb the institute threw our way. I didn't have to look at him."

"But he's still lingering. I've seen all those banners around the Art Institute campus."

He shook his head in disgust. "He's been gone three years and still they flock to see him and his work. It makes me sick."

"And Angelica was spearheading it," I added. "How did that make you feel?"

"I wanted to kill her, too," he muttered, then looked at me. "But I didn't."

"And we're supposed to believe that?"

"Believe whatever you want. I didn't kill her."

"Who killed her?" Derek asked.

Solomon turned and studied him for a moment. "Someone to whom I should've shown more gratitude."

I stepped closer. "So you're saying the woman who tied you to the bed also killed Angelica."

He whipped around to look at me. "I'm not saying another word."

"Fine. You can talk to the police." I pulled the last of the knots loose and threw the rope on the floor. "Max Adams is alive, Solomon, and he's going to have you charged with kidnapping and criminal harassment and attempted murder. You're going to prison."

He glared at me and muttered an expletive, then said, "Don't hold your breath."

Derek grabbed hold of Solomon's arm and yanked him off the bed. "Stand up."

Solomon wobbled but eventually gained his footing. Derek tossed his clothes at him and Solomon dressed hurriedly. Then Derek took hold of his wrist and spun him around. Using one of the ropes, he tied Solomon's hands behind his back.

Solomon struggled, but was no match for Derek. "Is that really necessary?"

"Yeah, it really is," I said.

"Let's go," Derek said.

I found my shoulder bag and stayed close to Derek as he led Solomon out of the bedroom. In the front room, Derek leaned over and whispered in my ear, "Gabriel should've been here by now."

"Do you think something happened to him?" He knew how I worried about Gabriel, and given the strange things that had been happening lately, I was scared to death he might become the latest victim.

Derek pulled out his phone and checked it for text messages. "I don't know. Let's go find him."

An hour later, we were back inside Savannah's restaurant. The Sonoma sheriff's deputy had come and gone after the San Francisco detectives claimed first dibs on questioning Solomon in connection to Joe Taylor's murder.

I just about fainted in relief when, within ten minutes of the cops taking Solomon away, Gabriel showed up. He'd been investigating another mountain cabin farther down the road, but had turned up nothing.

Gabriel, Derek, and I met quickly in Savannah's back room to figure out our next move. The other men were still out hunting for Minka and Emily. Derek thought we ought to return to the area around the secluded cabin where we had found Solomon, but Gabriel had somewhere else in mind. While they debated, I ran to the ladies' room. Walking out of the bathroom, I noticed someone in the parking lot and had a momentary rush of déjà vu. But it wasn't Minka.

"Brooklyn? Is that you?"

I peered through the screen door. "Melody?"

"Yeah, it's me." She shoved her hands in the pockets of her jacket. "I saw them take Solomon away."

"Melody," I said sympathetically, "I know Crystal likes Solomon, but I think he's done some bad things."

She smiled sadly. "He's better than you think, Brooklyn. He's done so much good for our church."

I didn't have the energy to argue with her. "I hope you're right."

"The Ogunites are setting up a defense fund for him, and Crystal and I will testify or do whatever it takes to exonerate him. He's been so important to our church and it's our honor and duty to serve him."

I felt sorry for her so I pushed open the door and went outside. "Do you really believe that?"

"Well, yes, and I really like him, too. My sister loves him. She can't help it."

I couldn't take any more about Crystal's love for Solomon, and that really bad feeling I'd felt up in the cabin was sinking in again. But I had to be wrong. "I hope things work out, Melody. I've got to get back inside."

"Brooklyn, thanks for listening." All of a sudden she smiled. "Hey — we made some more fruit jewelry using your mother's Fuji apples. They're really pretty. You should come to the farmers' market tomorrow."

"I'll try to come by. See you, Melody." I turned to leave, but something sharp and painful slammed against my head and I went flying forward. And that's the last thing I remembered.

I woke up in darkness, completely disoriented and with a blinding headache. I was covered up and lying on something cold and bumpy and moving so much that I kept sliding. After another few seconds, I realized I was on the floor of a truck or a van and someone was driving it around curves and up a hill.

Because of the tarp covering me, I couldn't see who was driving. But I knew it had to be Melody.

So now what? I hadn't even screamed to alert Derek and Gabriel, so I was on my own. Or was I? Maybe they had heard the screen door slam shut when I walked outside to talk to Melody. Maybe they were following us. I had to cling to that small possibility if I was going to survive with my wits intact.

Melody would arrive at her destination eventually, so I had to come up with a plan, fast. I maneuvered myself around under the tarp until I was facing the back doors of the van. Then I got up on my hands and knees. And waited.

I replayed my conversation with Crystal at the farmers' market the other day. She had been gushing over Solomon, to the point where I was slightly revolted. But I never thought it meant she loved him in the worst way, which was what that scene in the cabin bedroom clearly suggested.

Crystal must have been the woman who lured Solomon to the cabin with promises of sex and God knows what else. Solomon had confessed that he hadn't been grateful enough for some big favor she had done for him. Had Crystal killed Angelica as a favor to Solomon? As the van lumbered around another curve and I skidded across the cold steel flooring, I had my answer. It had to have been Crystal. With help from her sister, Melody?

Five minutes later, the van pulled to a stop and I heard the driver's door open and slam shut. Seconds later, the back doors were flung open and I sprang forward. Directly into Crystal.

Crystal screamed and threw her hands up. I tackled her and we both fell hard onto the ground. I scrambled to my feet and took off running. But it was pitch-black and there were trees everywhere. We were in the thick woods near the top of a hill and the moon was behind a heavy cloud. I couldn't see a thing, but I kept running, anyway, my hands out in front of me for protection. I bumped into a tree and careened around another one, but kept going. I wasn't quick enough, though, and after another thirty feet or so, Crystal grabbed my jacket and yanked me backward and down to the ground.

"I'm really sorry, Brooklyn," she said. "I hate to hurt you, but you need to stop running away."

Strangely enough, she sounded sincere.

I had to shake my head to clear it. With one hand Crystal pulled me to my feet, and it took me a few steps to get my equilibrium back. That's when I noticed the deadly-looking gun she held pointed at me.

"Crystal, why are you doing this?"

"I heard you through the window of the cabin and saw you take Solomon away. I followed your car down to the restaurant to see if I could help him, but the police were already there. So I sent Melody over to distract you." The gun shook as she spoke and I knew she was nervous. I didn't know if that was good or bad, but I knew Crystal wasn't really a bad person. Not like Solomon or Angelica.

"Crystal, let's talk about this. I can contact the police for you. Don't get yourself in trouble by kidnapping me."

"I have to think. Walk that way and let me think." She nudged the gun in the direction she wanted me to go and I turned and started walking. I stumbled over a tree root but managed to right myself. Feeling achy now, I clutched my jacket closer to me — and remembered my pockets were full of Hershey's Kisses. I pulled one out and dropped it on the ground, then repeated the same thing every fifty steps or so.

Crystal put the gun in her pocket and pulled me along as though she knew exactly where she was going, probably because she did. I couldn't see a thing in this deep part of the woods, but Crystal seemed to know her way without the aid of moonlight. She was as good a survivalist as anyone in the Hollow.

I prayed Derek wasn't too far behind. If he couldn't follow the chocolate-kisses trail, he wasn't the man I knew him to be. That thought kept me going as I tried to assimilate everything. "Did you kidnap Emily?"

"I didn't really kidnap her," she said. "I'm just doing Solomon a favor. It's for the greater good. I prayed over it, and I shared my blood with the earth."

"You shared your blood? How does that work?"

"A bloodletting is considered a sweet sacrifice by the Great Ogun."

After a pause, I said, "So you cut yourself? Is that what you do in your church?"

"Only in times of uncertainty, when you find yourself at a crossroads."

"So you cut yourself to find answers?"

She shrugged. "Sometimes Father Ogun requires blood sacrifice in exchange."

"In exchange for what?"

"Knowledge. Grace. Power. Whatever you're seeking."

A sense of dread overwhelmed me. "What did you mean when you said you're doing a favor for Solomon? Did he tell you to hurt Emily?"

"No, of course not," she said in surprise. "Solomon wouldn't hurt anyone."

She was so wrong, but I said nothing.

"It was my decision to take Emily," she

explained. "I'm using her to lure Max Adams out into the open. And then we'll see what happens."

So Emily was still alive. Thank God. But what did she have in mind for Max?

"Why do you want to lure Max into the open?"

"Because Solomon detests Max. Max stole Angelica from Solomon and it made Solomon crazy. I couldn't figure out why he cared so much about her because we both know she's a . . . well, a you-know-what. But after talking to Solomon some more, I realized that his pain wasn't about losing Angelica. It was because of Max Adams. He really hates that guy."

"Yeah, I get that."

"Exactly," she said with enthusiasm. "Solomon was so unhappy, I began to pray for him. And that's when Father Ogun revealed my true calling to me."

"True calling?"

"Yes, I was meant to bring order and calm back to the church. And to accomplish that, I first had to clear the path."

"Clear what path?"

"The path leading to peace. I had to take care of the obstacle in the path."

"And that obstacle was . . ."

"Angelica."

"You had to kill Angelica?" I said slowly.

"I had to," she said. "I'm sorry, but Solomon was losing sleep; he was beside himself with anguish. He couldn't concentrate on his church duties and it was beginning to affect the morale of the congregation, so I took the responsibility upon myself to help him." She faltered, but then straightened up and kept walking. "It was my honor. He's my deacon."

"So you owe him your honor and duty."

"Yes," she said, sounding pleased that I'd caught on. "It's all in the bible, Brooklyn. We can look there for all the answers."

"Which answer are you referring to?"

"An eye for an eye," she said.

I dropped another chocolate kiss and hoped for rescue. "What do you mean?"

She stopped to explain. "Max Adams took what Solomon wanted: Angelica. Now I will take what Max wants: Emily. This will cause Max to suffer, which will make Solomon happy. And it all provides blood for Ogun."

Blood? So she intended to kill Emily? "But Emily is an innocent bystander. She doesn't deserve to be hurt."

"Ogun decrees. I obey, honor, and serve." Crystal refused to talk to me after that, just continued walking me briskly through the darkness. Leaves slapped at my face and thick bushes pulled at my clothes.

I knew Crystal wasn't crazy; deep down, she was a good person. But between the zealous advocacy for her church and her obsession with Solomon, she had lost her way.

I thought about what she'd said. *An eye for an eye.* Emily for Angelica. Was she serious about the blood sacrifice? Max had stolen Angelica's heart from Solomon, so Crystal would . . . what? Cut Emily's heart out and give it to Solomon? No, of course not. She wouldn't really do that. My stomach turned at the very thought.

Still, the name of their church was the True Blood of Ogun. Was that what it meant — human sacrifice? True blood?

I almost laughed at the path my thoughts were taking. I didn't believe it for a minute. No way was there a band of wacked-out churchgoers sacrificing humans in Dharma.

My imagination was running overtime. I took a deep breath and let it out, then did it again a few more times. I needed to focus my energies, clear my thoughts, and channel my mother. What would Mom do to keep from flipping out? I found my answer.

"If Solomon gets out of jail, do you think he'll marry you?" I asked, determined to keep talking no matter what. That's what

Mom would do. Mom could talk so much and for so long, she could completely confuse the most clever kidnapper of all time — which Crystal wasn't. "He might be afraid of you after you bonked him on the head with that frying pan."

"He's a man," Crystal said calmly. "I'll get him back."

So she wasn't denying the frying pan incident. And she was probably right about Solomon coming back to her, but not because he was a man. No, it was because Solomon was an idiot.

"He is weak," she said, causing me to question whether she could read my thoughts. But we were talking about Solomon, after all. I guess even Crystal needed to keep it real.

"Yes, he's weak," I said in agreement.

"He'll need a strong woman to survive the coming apocalypse," she said matter-of-factly, then laughed softly. "Does a man really think a fragile flower of a woman can be anything more than a cipher, a worthless drag on his power? He'll need that power when we all meet in the Battle to End All Days."

I supposed I could see her point, although I wasn't familiar with the battle she was talking about. It had to be some Ogunite battle.

I'd known Crystal Byers for years and I continued to hold on to the belief that she wasn't insane. I was sure her actions sprang from a sincere desire to please her church. But I was beginning to see that what went on in Crystal's head was far more complicated than any of us had ever guessed.

I'd seen how men had treated her — or, rather, how they *didn't* treat her. I don't think she'd ever had a real boyfriend. She had always been too big and bold for most men. Too strong, and maybe too shrewd. She had never had someone who treated her like she was precious and special. Was she carrying a grudge? Did she have something to prove to all the men who'd ignored her or treated her badly or betrayed her? Maybe she did. Maybe she was determined to prove to them all that she was a survivor.

Good for her. But that didn't mean I was going to let Emily go down with her.

After another ten minutes and five Hershey's Kisses, the woods opened up. Clouds moved on the breeze, revealing the moon and stars for the first time.

Crystal pushed me out into the small clearing and I staggered to a stop. In the moonlight I could see from her expression that Crystal was deadly serious.

A massive fallen tree split the clearing in half. Both Minka and Emily were lying on top of the trunk, strapped to it with duct tape and rope. Another strip of duct tape covered each of their mouths. They were stripped down to their underwear. Minka was twisting and grunting and doing everything to escape her bonds, but Emily didn't stir at all.

"Father Ogun will feast tonight," Crystal declared with joy in her voice.

I whipped around. "You've got to be kidding."

She smiled coyly. "Figuratively speaking, of course." Taking the gun from her pocket, she pointed it at me. "Now it's your turn, Brooklyn. Take off your clothes."

I glanced around, stalling for time, feeling myself shaking right down to my bones. And wondering, *Just how hungry is Big Daddy Ogun, anyway?*

CHAPTER 27

There was no way on this green earth I was going to strip in front of this obsessed woman. I didn't believe in denigrating other religions, but as far as I was concerned, this Ogun dude was a pervert and a creep. And as for his faithful follower Crystal, at this point I was willing to accept that she might be a few sandwiches short of a picnic.

But I was also convinced that Solomon had manipulated Crystal into killing Angelica and taking Emily. He might not have said the words, but he would have made it clear that doing so would make him happy. And Crystal lived to make Solomon happy.

The only thing I could do right now was keep on blathering until Derek found us. I prayed it would be soon. I couldn't tell if Emily was conscious, but if she was, she had to be scared to death. I was getting there, too. *So start talking,* I told myself.

"So you killed Angelica," I said.

"OMG, Brooklyn," she said, smiling as she shook her head at me. "We already talked about that. Yes, I did it. I admit it. Out of duty to my deacon and my church."

"And because you're in love with Solomon and wanted him for yourself."

She sighed, mildly irritated with me. "I do love Solomon but it was more than that. Angelica's presence was harming our church. Anyway, you already know all this. Just take off your clothes and let's get on with it."

I held up both hands to delay the inevitable. "I just need to know: did you kill Joe Taylor, the bookstore owner?"

She frowned. "Who?"

"Joseph Taylor, the bookseller on Clement Street."

"In San Francisco?"

"Yes."

She tilted her head in confusion. "Why would I kill him? I didn't even know him. It was probably Angelica."

Yeah, I figured it was Angelica, too. But how would Crystal know? "Why do you think Angelica —"

"What day was this man killed?" she asked suddenly, as her frown deepened.

I was taken aback by the question but went ahead and figured out the day. "It was two weeks ago last Friday."

She thought for another moment. "Yes. That's right. After I realized that Angelica was meant to die, I followed her around for a few days, trying to learn her routines. On that Friday you're talking about, I followed her all the way to the Golden Gate Bridge. She crossed over into the city. I turned around and drove home."

"Why didn't you follow her into the city?"

Her lip curled in distaste. "Everybody knows San Francisco has been embraced by Satan."

"Ah. Good point."

What sounded like a dog or a wolf howling in the distance made me flinch. Great. All this and wild animals, too.

"Now, we've talked enough," Crystal said, waving the gun at me. "I'm afraid the Great Ogun is growing impatient. You've got to strip."

"One more thing. Why did you send Angelica's body to my house?"

She smiled. "That was for Max. A gift and a warning."

I opened my mouth, but no words came out.

"I can see you were shocked," she said. "But she looked pretty, I thought. I didn't want her to suffer, so I suffocated her in her sleep. And I embalmed her myself, so she should've been well preserved."

"You . . . embalmed her."

She shrugged. "It's a skill we all need to learn if we're going to survive the coming wars."

"Right."

"I didn't want you to be too grossed out, but I did need Max Adams to realize she was dead."

"Oh, he got the message. He saw her."

"Good. Angelica had been keeping tabs on Max Adams, and I had been keeping tabs on Angelica, so I was able to tell Solomon where Max was hiding every time you moved him."

Crystal had been watching us? She knew where we were each time? So her instincts had worked better than any GPS bugging device. I had completely underestimated the woman. Big mistake.

"At first," she continued, "Solomon was really surprised to hear Max was alive. Surprised and very, very hurt. He couldn't get over it. It started affecting his work, and I knew I had to take care of this for him. Poor man."

I had a hard time believing Solomon was "hurt." But Crystal had bought his act completely. So she had killed Angelica and sent her body in a box to my home through a delivery service. Oh yes, I had most certainly underestimated Crystal Byers.

"What about that delivery guy?" I asked. "You killed him, too?"

"Oh, I hated to do that, but he was a loose end," she explained. "Melody helped me. I didn't want to drive into the Pit of Satan all by myself."

I assumed the Pit of Satan was the city of San Francisco. "Your sister helped you kill that man?"

She bit her lip. "I probably shouldn't have involved her, but she insisted on helping."

I gaped at her. "Melody insisted?"

"She distracted him while I came from behind and slipped the plastic bag over his head." She smiled again. "We're very close, Melody and me."

The sisters are going to be even closer, I thought. Maybe they could share a jail cell. "You're right. You really shouldn't have dragged Melody into this."

"Please don't judge me, Brooklyn," she said. "Only Ogun can judge me. And he has judged me worthy." She held the gun with both hands and pointed it right at me. "Now stop trying to distract me. Just do what I asked you to do."

"Fine, but I think you're going about this

all wrong."

She sighed. "I'm not listening to you."

"Well, you should." I unzipped my jacket slowly, but instead of pulling it off my shoulders, I shoved my hands into the pockets, grabbed the candy kisses and flung them all at Crystal.

"What?" She cringed and held one hand in front of her face to fend off whatever she thought was attacking her.

Taking advantage of the moment, I rushed forward and knocked the gun out of her hand, but not before a deafening gunshot blast rattled the quiet air of the forest.

I had the advantage of surprise, but Crystal was even stronger than I'd always thought she was. She punched me in the face and I saw stars.

But I got a handful of her hair and yanked. She screamed and shoved me into the dirt, and we rolled around. She was slapping my face so hard, I could barely see. She got up and straddled me and started pounding. I held up my hands to protect my face from her flying fists, but they were fast and beefy.

In a surge of energy, I bucked her off me and we rolled in the dirt again. I was not strong enough to do any real damage to a crazed Ogunite built like Crystal, but I did my best. I had to hold on until Derek followed those Hershey's Kisses.

I tried to wrap my arms around her, if only to trap those dangerous hands of hers, but her chest and back were too broad. So I settled for scraping my fingernails down her face until she howled in outrage. Really, as a fighter I was pretty pitiful.

I was losing this fight by a mile, losing steam and consciousness. My head was spiraling from too many hard smacks. I made one last swipe at her face and raked my nails deeper across her cheek, drawing blood.

"There's your true blood, bitch," I snapped.

She grunted and slapped me again, and I knew I was close to finished. That's when I heard what sounded like a wolf pack stomping through the trees and into the clearing. There was snapping and growling, and Crystal was suddenly yanked off me.

Through blurry eyes I thought I saw the head wolf. *Derek?*

With one tremendous, incoherent roar, he flung Crystal away from me and pulled me close.

"My God, Brooklyn," Derek said, burying his face in my hair. "Are you all right?"

"Jus' fine," I muttered. "I coulda taken her."

"Of course you could've," he crooned, and swept me up into his arms.

From the corner of my rapidly puffing eye, I saw Gabriel catch Crystal. She tried to tangle with him, but he subdued her with one hand, yanking her arm and whipping her around. He clutched both of her hands behind her back, then dragged her over to the fallen tree where he found the duct tape and managed to wrap it around her wrists. Then he shoved her down to the ground.

Okay, Gabriel was back in action. Hooray!

I smiled at Derek. Everything was right in my world again. *Except for a little head spinning and vision fading,* I thought. Then everything went black.

When I woke up from my little nap, a female EMT was cleaning blood off my face.

"It's not my blood," I murmured, wincing when she touched a tender spot on my jaw.

"Yeah, it is," she said, chuckling as she continued daubing antiseptic on my chin and neck. "She nailed you good."

"Hey, I got a few jabs in."

I tried to sit up, but she stopped me. "Easy, Sugar Ray. You barfed the last time you tried that."

"I did?" I winced. "How pleasant for you."

"I love my job."

I felt dizzy again and decided to take her advice and stay right where I was. Looking around, I saw that I was lying flat out on some kind of tarp in the clearing where Crystal had almost killed three of us in the name of her beloved Ogun. Or maybe it was for her beloved Solomon. Who cared, as long as she rotted in prison for a few hundred years?

I assumed Emily and Minka were being treated by medical techs somewhere nearby. I couldn't see them, but I did see Crystal being led away in handcuffs by two Sonoma sheriff's deputies. She was screaming to Ogun to smite the nonbelievers. But apparently Ogun wasn't taking her calls.

I felt better already.

"Emily!"

I recognized Max's bellow and turned to see him rush into the clearing, glance around, and dash over to Emily. Aw, that was nice.

"Back off," someone groused. It was Minka, of course, bitching at whoever was trying to help her. Always the charmer. "Just get me the hell out of here."

I tried to ignore her migraine-inducing snarls and sputterings as I closed my eyes to conduct a mental checkup of my physical condition. Every muscle in my body groaned in pain. My neck ached and my head was pounding like I'd gone ten rounds with the champ. I guess I had, sort of.

Apparently my face was also bloody and bruised. Saving Emily made it all worth it, but why did the events of this horrific night also involve my saving two people who didn't deserve it — Minka and Solomon?

That whole Nemesis thing Guru Bob had talked about was highly overrated. Right now, all I wanted to be was the mild-mannered bookbinder I'd always been.

"Darling Brooklyn." Derek knelt on the tarp and took hold of my hand.

I told him what had happened in the parking lot with Melody, then blurted out, "I should have stayed inside the restaurant."

"Yes, you should have." He ran his knuckles gently along my hairline. "But by going outside and talking to her, you helped lead us straight to Emily. You saved her."

"What took you so long to get here?"

He paused, then said, "Gabriel ran into Melody."

"He ran into her?"

His mouth twisted in a sardonic grin. "To be accurate, Melody ran into him. She tried to run him down with her burgundy van."

"Is he all right?" I whispered. "Those

women are formidable. And crazy to boot."

"He's fit as a fiddle. He shot out her tire and she ran the van into a tree."

"Good," I said darkly. "I thought I saw him wrestle Crystal to the ground."

"You did indeed. You've no need to worry about Gabriel any longer."

"I'm glad," I muttered. But I was going to hold a grudge against both sisters for a long time to come.

Derek stretched out on his side next to me and wrapped his arm over me. My anger faded and I was warm and safe for the first time in a few hours.

"Darling," he murmured. "It was brave and ingenious of you to leave a chocolate trail. How did you ever think of it?"

I smiled, then moaned from the stinging pain around my eye. I figured I must look like a black-and-blue hag, but Derek didn't seem to mind.

"Chocolate saves lives," I whispered.

He laughed. "*You* saved lives. You did a fantastic job of keeping Crystal from killing all of you, even if you had to put your pretty face in harm's way to do so. I'm very proud of you." He leaned over and barely touched his lips to my cheek.

"I love you," I said.

His smile was radiant. "You said it first,"

he whispered, playing with my hair.

"I did." I laughed softly. "Well, then, it must be true."

"I hope so. I love you, too, my darling."

I smiled and closed my eyes. For a guy like Derek, I might even be willing to play Nemesis one more time.

There was the little matter of traipsing back to civilization through the dark woods. We were a merry band of cops, EMTs, heroes, and walking wounded. Derek offered to carry me, but while I was proud of my relatively low body-mass index, I wasn't about to test our relationship by letting him stagger through the forest with me in his arms.

Emily, however, was in no condition to walk a half mile through the dark, rough woods in the middle of the night, so Max carried her. Emily was sunburned and bruised and a bit traumatized, but she insisted that she would be fine as long as she was with Max.

Despite my aches and bumps and bruises, the walk might have been tolerable if it weren't for Minka. She bitched and ranted and shrieked at every brush of a tree branch against her, every root she lurched over, every bush she bumped against. All I could hear was her angry voice as she seethed and fumed, mainly about me. She refused to take responsibility for her own paranoid actions that led to her being kidnapped by Crystal Byers. No, it was all my fault. I was the Death Zone. Disaster loomed all around me. Beware to anyone who stepped within my Circle of Doom.

Derek hugged me close as Minka vowed loudly and repeatedly never to come within a thousand yards of me again.

Oh, if only she meant it. Honestly, what had I done to deserve being stalked by bloodletting survivalists and Minka La-Boeuf?

CHAPTER 28

Two weeks later, my living room was cleansed and purified of all lingering dead-body vibes and their associated cooties. My bookshelves arrived and we assembled them during a party that I'd actually planned. We all had much more fun than at the previous impromptu gathering, the one ruined by that party-crashing zombie Angelica.

Mom reported that the dust had finally settled in Dharma and the survivalists had crawled back into their Hollow. Of course, the whole town would be dining on the gossip stirred up by Solomon and the Byers sisters for the next two years.

Emily had recovered fully from her kidnapping ordeal. She and Max had traveled back and forth to the Cleveland Clinic, where her father was responding positively to the latest round of drug therapy. Emily was hopeful that he would be able to come home in the next month or so, in time for the wedding.

Crystal and Melody Byers were in jail. And if there was a God in heaven, the sisters would be wearing matching orange jumpsuits for a long, long time.

At the farmers' market in Dharma, all the local Ogunites were out in force, collecting money for the Byers Sisters Defense Fund. All of them, that was, except Mary Ellen Prescott, the manicurist who was only now proclaiming loudly that she always suspected that the sisters had murderous intentions.

Solomon had been held for questioning in Joe Taylor's murder, but a clue emerged that proved Angelica had been there on the day Joe was killed. Two of her long, curly hairs were found, one trapped in the screen door leading to the alley behind the store, and one on the back of the blue chair in the antiquarian room.

Solomon and his lawyer did everything they could to blame Angelica in the harassment and attempted-murder charges Max had pressed. The he said/she said strategy appeared to be working, and Solomon was eventually released.

I was no longer certain that Solomon was a psychopath, but he was a ruthless bully and a manipulator. The one bright light was that Inspector Lee had taken such an instant dislike to Solomon that she was determined to work like a bloodhound tracking down enough evidence to send him to prison. Several weeks later, Lee's efforts came to fruition when she found an eyewitness who had seen Solomon rigging Max's staircase a few hours before Emily's mother arrived and was hurt so badly. With any luck, more witnesses would be found and Solomon would end up spending a few years behind bars after all.

It was a sunny Saturday afternoon when Derek and I traveled back to Dharma for the official reengagement party for Max and Emily.

I'd invited everyone who had anything to do with the odd adventure we'd been through recently. Gabriel, Ian, all my neighbors. Even Mary Ellen Prescott, but only because she'd seen right through the Byers sisters' perky-blond facade.

The party was held on my parents' terrace and even Guru Bob was in attendance. We'd had a little talk beforehand that had left me with more questions than answers. But I would think about that later. Now it was time to party. The champagne was flowing and Savannah had catered the affair, so the food was spectacular.

I left Derek talking with Dad and Austin, and went to find Emily. She looked adorable in a pink dress with striped white and green piping around the waist, neck, and cuffs.

After we greeted each other with a tight hug, I said, "Emily, you look so beautiful."

"Thanks." She blushed and moved closer to whisper, "Your mother suggested a quick trip to the Laughing Goat sweat lodge and I think it worked wonders."

I tried not to roll my eyes as I backed away to scrutinize her more intently. "Mom swears by their fifteen-point detoxification program, and I have to admit it's definitely working for you."

I didn't care how refreshed Emily appeared; I wasn't about to slather myself in curried ghee and huddle inside a sweat lodge for a week. Mom swore by a lot of things I wouldn't dream of taking her up on, including cosmic bilocation, espresso enemas, and gandoosha. Don't ask.

I was all for a healthy complexion, but I was just as happy to leave the purging and gargling to Mom.

Emily told me she'd already found a new job teaching second graders in Marin County. She would start after the winter break, when she would move into Max's farmhouse in the hills above Point Reyes Station.

"I'm there every weekend now," she said.

"So you and Clyde?"

"We're like this," she said, holding up her crossed fingers. We both laughed.

"And how do you like the goats?"

"I love them," she gushed. "And Max has created a new goat-cheese blend in my honor."

"Ooh, what's in it?"

"It's a blend of sweet goat cheese, chocolate, and raspberries. It sold out the first day he took it into town."

"Mm. I hope I can taste it someday soon."

"You will." She gave me a bashful look and added, "He calls the concoction Beauty and the Beast."

"Aww," we said in unison, then laughed together.

I hugged her once more, promised that Derek and I would come to Point Reyes for a weekend soon, and left her to mingle.

There were so many people I wanted to talk to, but none more than my best pal, Robin, who was currently negotiating to sell her Noe Valley flat in the city in anticipation of moving back to Dharma to live with my brother Austin.

We hugged, then stood yakking excitedly with our arms around each other. I'd known her since the first day my family arrived in Dharma, and we were still inseparable whenever possible.

She let me know how happy she was with Austin, and I gave her the quickie version of the Max Adams scandal. Then she laughed when I told her that Guru Bob had suggested I was destined to remain a Nemesis, seeking vengeance and justice for the dead.

"Why are you laughing?" I whined. "It isn't funny."

"I'm laughing *with* you," she assured me, and squeezed my arm. "Look, I never would have survived the murder in my apartment if not for you and Derek. And then I found Austin, and my life is so full now. I'm happy, Brooklyn, and it's all your fault."

"Okay, I'll gladly take responsibility for you being happy." Robin had been in love with Austin since we were in third grade.

"Good," she said with an affectionate bump of her head against mine. "And now that you've worked your magic for Max and Emily, you can't quit now."

"That's what I was afraid of."

Robin chuckled again, and I let it go. I was fine with the happily-ever-after part of the equation. It was just the part about tripping over dead bodies — or having them delivered to my door — that tended to get me down.

We both used up another tissue as we watched Austin and Max in close conversation. They had reunited briefly the night Emily was kidnapped, but this was the first chance they'd had to talk. The two had been best friends growing up and Austin had mourned Max's death as deeply as any of us. I held my breath when it looked like Austin might punch Max in the stomach, but instead he punched his arm, then grabbed him in a tight bear hug that had everyone sniffling a little.

I mingled some more, then spied Derek prowling the perimeter of the terrace. I smiled, reminded of the first time I ever saw him at the Covington Library. He'd been prowling and stalking then, too. Little did I realize at the time that it was me he'd been watching so intently.

That thought brought back something Derek had said to me a few weeks back, so I circled and met him halfway. He wrapped his arm around my shoulder and held me close.

I looked up at him. "Do you remember, before all the craziness happened with Max, you said we needed to talk? What was that about?"

He nodded, then glanced around at the crowd. "It's nothing that can't wait until we're alone."

"Now you've got me curious. Can you give me a hint?"

He touched his forehead to mine. "I think it's time we discussed our current living arrangement."

Concerned, I stared into his eyes, trying to gauge his feelings. "Are you unhappy with it?"

His eyes narrowed, causing mine to widen anxiously. Then he laughed. "Not at all. But I do think we need more room."

"You want to move?"

"And leave Vinnie and Suzie?" he said, his tone teasing. "Never. No, I simply thought I might buy the unit next door to yours and open up the wall between the two. If you're amenable, that is."

"If I'm amenable?" I blinked, then swallowed. "Yes, I believe I am."

He grinned, then kissed me. "Good. We can talk about the details later."

"Okay." I breathed deeply, relieved and scared and still a little shocked all at the same time. This was so unexpected. I mean, we were living together, but we weren't *liv-*

ing together. And of course I was crazy about him, but I still wasn't sure what to think. I decided to try to relax and enjoy the party. I'd be doing a lot of thinking about things later.

Derek gazed across the terrace. "This might be the perfect moment to give the guests of honor their gift."

I turned and saw Emily and Max talking quietly by themselves. "Yes, let's go."

Emily had insisted that none of the party-goers bring gifts, but mine was an exception to the rule. Derek and I walked up to them, followed by some of the friends and family who knew about the surprise.

I handed them the newly restored *Beauty and the Beast.* Emily started to protest, until she saw what it was.

"Oh, Brooklyn," Emily said, holding her breath as she opened the crimson outer case and saw the book inside. "Oh, it's stunning."

I rushed to explain, "I know you originally wanted to keep the book all scruffy and tattered like my friend Max here."

Emily giggled and Max smiled indulgently.

"But I just couldn't deal with all the negative energy inside the pages. Those were some nasty hooves holding on to this book for too many years."

There were a few chuckles, and I took advantage of the moment to breathe. Then I continued to talk, trying to justify my decision and rationalize why I hadn't consulted with them on the final design. "Anyway, I went ahead and restored its timeless beauty. I hope you love the new version and find it beautiful. As new and beautiful and timeless as your love for each other."

Emily burst into happy tears. A very satisfactory reaction, except that nobody cried alone when I was around. Derek handed me his handkerchief and I sniffled along with Emily.

"Thanks, honey," Max said, and bent down to kiss my cheek.

"Thank you, Brooklyn," Emily whispered, as the crowd around us applauded.

Beside me, Derek wrapped an arm around my shoulder. I gazed up at him and smiled. Was everyone as happy as I was at that very moment?

Emily cleared her throat and gripped Max's arm firmly. "Brooklyn, I want you to know that my Beast and I will cherish and enjoy this book forever."

I felt someone nudge my elbow and turned around to find Ian waggling his eyebrows at me. I winced as I realized I'd forgotten to ask Emily about donating the book to the

Covington. I shook my head at Ian, but he just smiled.

Max took the book from Emily and said, "And since we want everyone to cherish and enjoy the book as much as we do, we're donating it to the children's wing of the Covington Library, where it'll bring happiness to children of every age."

My eyes widened and I whipped around. "You didn't."

Ian laughed. "I did. I'm pushy that way."

The crowd burst into applause again, and Ian cheered the loudest. "Champagne for everyone!"

"A toast!" Dad cried, holding up his champagne glass as Savannah's waiters sifted through the crowd, pouring the bubbly for everyone.

Emily and Max exchanged glances, then looked at me. Emily was blushing as Max said, "We'll be toasting with ginger ale. We're having a baby."

I gasped and Derek laughed as I fumbled for his handkerchief again. I couldn't help it. I just loved a happy ending.

The employees of Thorndike Press hope you have enjoyed this Large Print book. All our Thorndike, Wheeler, and Kennebec Large Print titles are designed for easy reading, and all our books are made to last. Other Thorndike Press Large Print books are available at your library, through selected bookstores, or directly from us.

For information about titles, please call:
(800) 223-1244

or visit our Web site at:
http://gale.cengage.com/thorndike

To share your comments, please write:
Publisher
Thorndike Press
10 Water St., Suite 310
Waterville, ME 04901